THE
POISONED
LEGACY

Other books by Su Adams:

Footsteps in the Sea
Nobody's Killer
The Dragon In Paradise

For all your kindness

THE
POISONED
LEGACY

To dear Jean

from

Su Adams

(Shirley)

xx
x

with love + best
wishes

ISBN: 978-0-244-44150-0

PublishNation
www.publishnation.co.uk

CHAPTER ONE

Alex woke up with a thundering headache, he was blindfolded and lying on his back with both wrists shackled to something above his head, in a small enclosed space. The crunch of approaching footsteps and banging of a metallic door made him realise he was in a vehicle of some kind then he heard the roar of an engine, not a car, something throatier, probably a truck. It started up, moving forward, slowly at first, then picking up speed, it lurched over a rough uneven track, swerving wildly round each bend. His arms were jerked painfully from side to side until he thought they were going to break. The erratic driving seemed to last for hours but at last, it stopped with a screeching of brakes as the truck slowly edged its way forward, ending his torturous journey.

A sudden rush of warm air filled his lungs as doors were thrown open. He gagged at the noxious smell, a foul mixture of rotting carcasses and rancid grease. Next, footsteps scuffling across a hard floor, then scraping and grinding noises as his caged prison was first lowered then dragged along the ground. His mind was clearing a little, he realised he must have been drugged. It was all beginning to make sense, this whole grisly business had to be connected to that last meeting in Marbella; he'd been warned to steer clear of it but thought it was perhaps a chance to recover his family heirlooms. It had taken him months of research plus that futile journey to the Ukraine to find the exact spot where they'd been buried. The recent email threats had made him more determined than ever to reclaim what was rightfully his, whatever the cost.

It was obvious now that he had enemies with other ideas. He was sure James, Roslyn's father, wasn't involved, he was a man of personal integrity, too well respected in the community to be part of anything remotely illegal. On the other hand, Roslyn's brother, Markus, was a possibility. According to her, he was usually in financial trouble because of his wild partying and gambling debts, so he was a likely candidate. But how had he found out that there was a possibility of money tied up in his inheritance? Then there was Krystyna, their so-called Polish friend; he'd had doubts about her from the start, the list seemed to be growing. Alex could think of only five other people who knew about his legacy and he was certain not one of them would think of kidnapping him, it was ludicrous. It just didn't happen in civilised society, they weren't living in Sicily or downtown Chicago. Perhaps, the drug they'd used on him was making him paranoid.

Interrupting his morose thoughts, he felt rough hands unlocking his chained wrists. A hood was rammed over his head, it smelled of stale urine and made him retch. He was being dragged along, stumbling and helpless. He could see nothing, only blackness, not even a glimmer of light, as he was put on a rickety seat, then both hands were re-tied behind his back. No voices, only the clicking of a switch and the glare of a blinding light in his eyes as his hood was removed. He tried to turn his head to one side to see beyond the dazzling glare, but his chair was kicked sideways as he crashed to the floor, his head hitting the concrete floor. He passed out again and only awoke when water was being thrown over him, he tried to shake himself free, but it was useless. He was completely at this man's mercy. He felt a needle pierce his upper arm and immediately succumbed to the euphoric power of another paralysing drug.

Later he woke up and opened his eyes, he was lying on some sort of a hard bed, in a dim room. He couldn't remember much. He vaguely felt his left arm aching, he tried to lift it, but his wrist was too painful as if it was in a vice. He looked around the small room with a torn venetian blind covering the dirty window, the sunlight barely filtered through on to the uneven floorboards. The plain walls were whitewashed; a single light bulb dangled from the low ceiling and a heavy wooden door stood like a sentinel in the far corner. There was absolutely nothing to tell him where he was. The sounds outside were unfamiliar; a dog barking in the distance, then the door opened, the outline of a big man filled the doorway. Alex couldn't see his face hidden in the gloom, but he thought there weren't that many people who could have staged such a bizarre and complex operation. Even then it didn't make any sense. Who could have been so desperate for money to want to kidnap him for such uncertain pickings? The man, towering over him, handed him a phone and grunted.

"You speak to Roslyn now, tell her no tricks, no police. Or else...."

He sliced his finger across his throat to show him what would happen if she did. Oh, my God, it was Bohdan. He was the man he'd suspected all along, ever since that fateful trip. How stupid he'd been to be taken in by his pretence of being Krystyna's cousin and a mere chauffeur who couldn't speak a word of English. He'd been a witness to everything; he'd seen Alex looking at both family properties and been a party to their search for the hidden fortune. Perhaps the thought of so much possible wealth had been too a great a temptation to resist and he'd engineered the meeting, the drugging and the kidnapping. It was all coming together now but could he have done it all by himself? Alex doubted that and felt sure that someone else was the brains behind the hostage taking. But who? Bohdan held out the phone to him and he only hoped she'd be there to answer.

Roslyn, still asleep in her bedroom at her father's villa, was completely unaware of what had been happening to Alex. She woke up and wondered if it was morning already, the heavy blinds kept the sun out of the room. Stretching out in the comfort of her luxurious bed like a cat and thinking of the day ahead, she'd slept like a baby. Maybe they would drive down to Puerto Banus for lunch and watch the playboys on their yachts with their exotic girlfriends, before coming back for a peaceful siesta. But, where was he? He should be lying by her side. Now that her father had gone fishing with his golfing pals for a few days, they could happily share the same bedroom; no sneaking back to his own room in the middle of the night. Even though she wasn't a child any more, she still felt uncomfortable making love when her dear old dad was sleeping close by.

She got up, showered and dressed. Alex had probably woken up early and gone for a run on the beach, not wanting to disturb her, but it was strange he hadn't taken his mobile phone or his watch, both still on the bedside table. She went downstairs and called his name but no reply. If he was out and had stopped off for a drink somewhere, he might have started talking to someone and forgotten the time. The trouble was she had no idea exactly how long he'd been gone. She popped her head round the door that opened into the kitchen and saw Maria preparing the vegetables for lunch, happily singing a Spanish song.

"Maria, have you seen Senor Alex?"

"No, senora, I no see him. He no in bed?"

"No, I think he may have gone out for a walk. Promenade."

Any more questions were hopeless, Maria's English was limited, Roslyn had had to mime 'walking' with her fingers so that the girl understood what she meant.

"You like coffee?"

"Si, gracias, Maria."

She took her mug out onto the terrace, she'd wait a little longer. No good worrying too much, there was probably some perfectly good explanation for his absence. If she had known the truth, she wouldn't have drunk her coffee quite so calmly. She picked up a magazine and leafed through it as another half hour passed slowly, then she got up and took a quick look in every room but no sign of him. Last of all, she went back into her own room. Why hadn't he taken his mobile, he always carried it with him, unlike her father, what good would it be anyway in her bedroom? She picked it up and saw a flashing icon on the screen telling her he'd got a voicemail. Maybe it was just an old message, she clicked on it anyway, getting the biggest shock of her life. She didn't recognise his voice immediately, it didn't sound like Alex.

"Is that you, Roslyn? Don't worry, darling, I'll be back soon, so please, don't do anything rash and don't contact the police."

Then the phone went dead, nothing else. She didn't understand. Why would he leave her a cryptic message like that? It didn't make sense, no explanation, nothing to say where he was or what had happened. He must have known she'd now be worried sick about him, his voice sounded strained, not like him at all. Something was terribly wrong but what?

She desperately needed her father to be here but apart from 'gone fishing', she had absolutely no idea where he was. Her brain was in overdrive. There was no one in Spain who could help her or tell her what to do. She could only think of Ben, her dad's business partner, but he was in London. She knew she could rely him to advise her; he was like a second father to her. She picked up her own mobile and put in a call to their head offices in London. No reply, she'd forgotten it was Saturday. Who could she call now? Then she remembered she had his secretary's home phone number, in case of emergencies. She looked it up in her contacts, then keyed in the numbers, a sleepy voice answered. Without any preamble, Roslyn said.

"Hi, Emma, this is Roslyn. Sorry if I woke you so early but it's a bit of an emergency and I was just wondering if you could put me in touch with Ben. I haven't got any of his mobile details on hand and I really need to speak to him urgently."

"I'm sorry, Roslyn, he's not in England right now. Something very pressing cropped up and he had to fly to Vienna yesterday for a couple of days to sort out a problem for one of our major clients, so he won't be back in the office until Friday at the earliest."

"I really do need to contact him today if possible. Do you think I could reach him on his mobile or leave him a message?"

"Of course, he's staying at the Ritz-Carlton, but I haven't got their number I'm afraid, but I think you could get him on his mobile. Give me a ring back if you have any problems."

"Thanks, Emma, you've been a great help, I'll let you know if I can't reach him. Yes, my father's fine, but he's gone fishing on his mate's boat and won't be back for a few days."

She spoke to the hotel and was told Ben wasn't in his room so she rang his mobile with no luck so she put her phone down thinking it was strange he'd had to go to Austria himself; when surely someone else could have sorted the problem out, especially when Ben was in sole charge of the company whilst her father was in Spain. It must have been a real emergency, still slightly odd though. Instead of making her feel better, she felt completely at a loss now. Why had Alex told her specifically not to go to the police? She needed help more than she'd ever done before but there was no one. At that precise moment, Alex's mobile rang. What a relief! The voice on her phone wasn't one she recognised, it certainly wasn't Alex.

"Who is that? Yes, I'm Roslyn. Yes, I'm listening but please, speak more slowly, it's a bad line and your voice is breaking up? That's better, yes. Can he come to the phone himself? Is he all right?" A short pause then she replied. "Oh, thank goodness. Yes, I'm listening."

There was a longer break as she tried to stifle her sudden fear, she could barely understand this man's strong accent but instinctively knew she didn't want to antagonise any person who was holding Alex captive.

"Yes, I've got that. Can I speak to Alex now? No. I haven't contacted anyone else."

A sudden click and the line went dead again, just a soft buzzing sound in the background. She didn't understand. Trying to plead with this man, who was obviously the kidnapper, hadn't worked. Maybe she shouldn't have insisted on speaking to Alex. She prayed inwardly.

'Please God, let him ring back!'

She wasn't sure what to do next, the only thought in her head was for Alex's safety. If he had been kidnapped, it was most likely to be the result of their recent visit to Poland. She looked at his mobile, still clutched in her hand, and couldn't believe he would have left it behind deliberately with his much-loved watch. He never went anywhere without that, it was the only keepsake he treasured from his grandfather. How come she'd never heard a sound if someone had broken into the house during the night and taken him? Maybe he'd heard a noise as he went to the bathroom across the hallway and gone to investigate; that would account for him leaving his phone and watch on the bedside table. Her heart was pounding as she tried to think of something she could do but she felt utterly helpless and alone. Life had gone in a few short hours from being a pleasant leisurely holiday to a total nightmare that she had no control over. Then, thankfully, his mobile rang again.

"This is Alexis, darling. I'm so sorry to frighten you but please, do exactly as he says. He's threatened to kill me if you don't. Please listen carefully, Ros. You must give him the details of that safety deposit box in Krakow."

"Oh, Alex, just tell me you're all right and I'll do whatever you want."

"Yes, I'm okay but you must do as I say. Do you understand, Ros?"

The line went dead again, he'd spoken to her using his full name 'Alexis', something he never did. Maybe he thought she'd understood that he had been trying to warn her not to give him the box's number. But why? Nothing made sense.

CHAPTER TWO

It was all like a bad dream, phoning the police seemed the only sensible thing to do but would she be gambling with Alex's life if she did that? She racked her brain to think of anything else she could do. Then she remembered her father had once used a security company in London when a disgruntled ex-employee had threatened him. He'd said they'd provided an excellent service, both protection and surveillance, no questions asked. Maybe that was just what she needed right now.

She went into her father's office and opened the desk drawer, where he kept his address book, file-o-fax and phone. Under 'S' she found what she was looking for; an email address and phone number, with her father's scribbled '24/7' next to 'Protectu@private.com'. She used her father's mobile which he never took with him on his fishing trips and heard a ringing tone at the other end. She gazed anxiously around the room, waiting and hoping someone would be on duty on Saturday. After what seemed like an eternity, a man's voice, sounding friendly and reassuring, answered.

"You're through to 'Protectu Security', how can I help you?"

"My name is Roslyn Chapell and my father was a client of yours a few years ago. His name is James Chapell and he's the C.E.O. of Cosmocompute."

"Yes, I remember your father well. He still uses our company from time to time. How can I be of service to you, Miss Chapell? My name is Peter Askwith."

Not knowing quite where to start, she decided to give him a potted history of what had happened so far, he listened intently without interrupting. When she'd finished relaying the essential facts, particularly of Alex's insistence that there should be no police involved, she heard a sharp intake of breath at the other end.

"I do understand your predicament, but I must warn you that withholding that information from the police is unwise. But, if he insisted on it, the details you've given me will help me to assign the best person to handle your case. The main thing is for you to keep calm."

She'd mentioned that Alex worked at G.C.H.Q. in Cheltenham and that it was the British government's intelligence headquarters.

"Before we go any further, Miss Chapell, if this is a matter of national security, our company would be obliged to report it to the proper authorities because of the Official Secrets Act."
Roslyn hadn't thought of that aspect before, but it wasn't as if his job involved any confidential issues in this particular case.

"I'm not quite sure but I don't think his kidnapping has anything to do with that. It's a purely personal matter, about a family inheritance. There could be a large sum of money tied up in a family property but I'm afraid I can't be more specific than that. Alex has received some anonymous messages over the past few weeks. He showed me one email he got recently that read, 'You've been warned once. Remember 'Krakow', and another saying, 'Don't forget, we're watching you.' Then, yesterday, he told me someone had phoned wanting to meet him in Puerto Banus but then, for no apparent reason, it was suddenly called off."

"That's enough to suggest a threat of some kind. Has this man mentioned a ransom at all? It can be a very lucrative side-line for crooks in the Costa del Sol."

"I do understand what you're saying but there's been nothing like that so far, only the one short phone message I told you about and then ones from Alex and the other man. Do you think you could trace the calls from this end?"

"I'm pretty certain whoever is holding him will be using throwaway mobiles but don't worry about that. We have other means of tracking down felons. I will set everything in motion immediately, but I must warn you not to use any of your other telephones to contact us again. The first essential is for you to buy a new mobile and get a different sim card for any further communication with our company. That's very important; all your own phones may have been tapped already."

"Oh, my God, I didn't think of that. I can buy a new one as soon as I go into Marbella but what about the instruction to give them the number of the safety deposit box? I have a feeling there was a hidden message in there somewhere, he never calls himself "Alexis.""

"You may be right. If you can, give me the address and phone number of that Krakow Bank, then we can set up a direct link with them. Remember, don't panic. They're only interested in getting their hands on the contents of that security box. I'll ask my team leader, Aidan Spencer, to be your personal contact, his direct line is extension 1325, and call him as soon as you get your new phone."

"Thank you for all that information but should I let them have the deposit box number or not? I still have no idea."

"I think it would be wise for you to speak to Aidan Spencer first, I'll fill him in with all the details then he can advise you. If they ring again, just play for time; say you can't find the bank numbers but you're looking for them. The people holding him want that information and harming him would be counterproductive. So, try to stall them as long as possible but get that new phone a.s.a.p."

When she'd put down the phone, she just hoped her father's mobile hadn't been bugged already. She picked up her bag, forgetting to tell Maria no one would be in for lunch. Her father had a Spanish registered Honda in the garage, so she decided to use that and. drove straight into the centre of Marbella, looking in the mirror to check if anyone was following her. She parked outside one of the city supermarkets, picked up a shopping basket and started looking at various items on the shelves. She threaded her way through several busy aisles ending up behind the furthest one, before leaving by the back door. She looked both ways as she stepped out into a quiet side street, only stopping to check if anyone was behind her but there wasn't a soul in sight. She knew the city centre well enough and remembered the Movistar shop where she could buy a 'pay as you go' mobile and a brand-new sim card with a minimum of fuss.

Pleased with the ease of her purchase, Roslyn decided to stop for a coffee at one of the many places dotted along the main street. She picked up a local paper from the cafe's selection and pretended to read the headlines as she drank her latte. She'd never been in such a mess before and still trembled at the thought of poor Alex, probably at his wits' end, trying to cope with his awful situation. She wished he'd never heard of the family fortune that his great grandmother had hidden so long ago. It had probably been unearthed years ago by an amateur enthusiast with a metal detector. If only Alex hadn't become so fascinated by his Polish ancestry, if only! It was too late to think of that now.

These useless thoughts were not helping, what was done was done. No good crying over spilt milk! She had to think positively and talk to someone who could help her. Alex must be going out of his mind, not knowing what was going on or whether she'd understood his message or not. She had to speak to someone soon, anyone, or she'd go crazy. If only she could have contacted Ben, he would have known what to do

As soon as she'd picked up the car and driven home, she unpacked her new mobile and then went outside to the terrace. With no one about, she called the phone number that would get her through to her new man at 'Protectu Services'. It only took a few seconds.

"This is Aidan Spencer; how can I be of service to you?"

"Hello, Mr. Spencer, I'm Roslyn Chapell. I spoke to Mr. Askwith earlier. He gave me your direct line and insisted I buy a new phone and sim card before I contacted you."

"Of course, Miss Chapell, Mr. Askwith has spoken to me and I have all the details of your difficult situation right here on my desk. Rest assured I will help you all I can."

CHAPTER THREE

Roslyn heaved a sigh of relief, feeling better merely talking to this man, who spoke with such obvious confidence.

"It's so good to hear you speak so reassuringly, I've been nearly going out of my mind, not knowing who to turn to next."

"It's my job and my pleasure to put your mind at rest if I can. Although kidnapping is not an everyday occurrence, we will track down whoever is holding your fiancé. You've already given us the address of the bank in Krakow and we've asked our local agent to put surveillance on their premises, so that anyone making enquiries about this account will be checked and photographed. I will make this matter my first duty."

"That makes me feel much better to know you're on the case so quickly. As you can imagine, I've been frantic with worry."

"I understand completely. You've done exactly the right thing in contacting us so, try to relax and let me assure you Mr. Wilshaw's release is now my most important priority. Remember I'm here for you 24/7 from now on."

"I really appreciate that, just knowing you are only a phone call away is a great comfort."

She was glad to be back in the comfort of the villa once more. She went to her room and changed into a housecoat, she suddenly felt very tired, drained by all the emotional pressure she was under. Maria was nowhere in sight which was not unusual at this time of day, she was most probably taking her siesta, having no food to prepare for an evening meal. Then a phone rang, it was Alex's mobile.

"Oh, Sweetheart, are you all right? I've been so worried, not hearing from you. Please tell me you're okay and no one's hurt you."

There was a slight hesitation at the other end of the line.

"I'm okay but listen, Roslyn, it's really important. Do you remember that man, Bohdan? Well, he's here now, so please, give him the number of the Krakow account and the security box. They won't let me go if you don't get them."

It was 'Roslyn' now, so it must be very serious, he really meant it this time.

"Yes, I understand, Alex. Is he the same man who drove us around in Lwiw?"

She was trying to keep calm.

"Yes, he is. He's going to phone you soon. Use my mobile and take the call somewhere private where no one can hear you." There was a pause then he continued.

"Do you understand, Roslyn? You know where I keep those mixed up bank numbers."

The words 'mixed up numbers' didn't make sense at first then she realised that had to be his way of telling her to change the numbers round but why? They might kill him if they thought he was lying. Then the line went dead again. She guessed he might be playing for time and she was about to go to Alex's bedroom for the private notebook he kept in his bedside drawer when her new phone began to ring. It was Aidan and he didn't seem too surprised to hear Alex had called again.

"Things must be hotting up wherever he's being held. Do you have any idea why Mr. Wilshaw instructed you so specifically to give those false bank details to this man? Is he someone you both know personally?"

"Yes, we did meet a man in the Ukraine and his name was Bohdan, but he was only a driver. I know Alex was a bit suspicious about him even then.

"Mm, well! It's often people like that who work in criminal organisations. Don't tell anyone else he may be involved. Let's keep it between ourselves."

"Well, the only other person I tried to talk to, with my dad being away, was his business partner, but he's away in Austria on business."

"Did you ask where he was staying?"

"Yes, he was at the Ritz-Carlton in Vienna, but I couldn't contact him. That's when I got Alex's frantic call, sounding very frightened, then the phone went dead, and I haven't heard another word since. Do you think they'll do something to Alex? They won't torture him, will they?"

Roslyn's voice faltered at the thought, but Aidan insisted she'd done nothing wrong so far and that no one would kill him before they got what they wanted.

"Do you have any idea what's in the deposit box?"

"I only know there's a very old envelope addressed to Lukasz Wilowski and plans of two manor houses that my fiancé's great grandparents once owned. Alex and I have been trying to discover where their property was buried before his family was imprisoned in 1939."

Aidan paused for a moment, noting this latest piece of information. He didn't really want to cause Roslyn any further anxiety but felt he had to warn her she too could be in danger if there was a considerable amount of money involved.

"From what you've just told me, I strongly advise that you have your own personal security from now on. I can arrange that for you immediately."

"But if I have someone else here with me, they'll know I've contacted the police or someone and they might kill Alex anyway. I can't do that. If anything happened to him because of me, I would never forgive myself."

"Roslyn, listen to me. We have female escorts everywhere You can say she's a friend of yours who's come to stay for a week or so. Your own safety is important but don't tell anyone, not even your father. He will believe you if you say you invited a girlfriend to be with you while Mr. Wilshaw was away."

Roslyn's thoughts were in freefall. How would she explain another woman in the house when her father got back? Easier said than done. When Aidan rang off, she couldn't keep still, so she changed her clothes, put on a jogging outfit and headed for the beach. She held Alex's mobile tightly in her hand. Why, in these idyllic surroundings, did she feel such dark foreboding of the danger ahead? It wasn't Alex's fault; she and her father had encouraged him to follow his dream. It wasn't just about the money, he really needed to find out if all the old stories he'd heard from his grandmother were true. When they'd started to delve more deeply into his family history, only then did he begin to realise the extent of his own loss when the war had changed the Wilowski fortunes forever. No wonder he was so keen to find not only his lost inheritance but also his own place in the family's history. The phone stirred in her hand, its vibration brought her out of her reverie.

"Hello, who's this?"

"Hello, Roslyn. This is Bohdan, remember me?"

Before she could stop herself, she blurted out.

"How could you do this to us, Bohdan? We trusted you and believed you were helping us. Why are you holding Alex hostage? We never did anything wrong to you."

"I know what you think but it's not all my fault. I work for someone else and I have to carry out his orders."

"What do you mean? You're the one keeping him prisoner and he thinks you're going to kill him if you don't get what you want. "

"Look, just give me those bank account numbers and Alex will be freed when we have access to the box. You don't know this other man, killing someone means nothing to him."

Her phone went dead again. Who was this man really? Obviously, he wasn't just a paid driver but who was the boss he was working for? She ran back to the house, stamping the sand from her feet before she opened the door. She knew she shouldn't have spoken so harshly, especially when he was holding all the aces, but it was done now. She couldn't play for any more time. She went straight to Alex's room and looked in his holdall where he kept his private things. She rifled through them and found the envelope that held the Polish bank details. All she could do now was sit and wait. Aidan couldn't advise her, she could only hope Bohdan would call again. The next hour passed very slowly and, with every minute, her heart sank more and more. Maria called her name from downstairs, there was another call on the house phone, so it couldn't be anything to do with the kidnapping.

"I'm coming, Maria." She called as she rushed to the phone.

"Hello, Roslyn, this is Ben, I heard from Emma you wanted to speak to me. Sorry, I couldn't get back to you before now, but I've been extremely busy here in Vienna."

"Oh, Ben, it's wonderful to speak to you. I'm so glad to hear your voice."

"Why? What's the trouble? You sound very upset. Emma said you needed to speak to me urgently."

Roslyn poured out her heart to him, trying not to cry with relief. When she'd finally told him the whole story, she heard a heavy sigh at the other end.

"You must be so worried! I'm very sorry but I just wish you hadn't contacted our security people so soon, I'm not blaming you at all, but it sounds as if Alex's life was already in danger and this could make it worse. Thank God, you didn't tell the police. Now, listen carefully to me, I want you to call Aidan Spencer again and tell him you've spoken to me. Then I'll explain that, as your father's partner, I'm going to deal with the situation and handle everything. I don't want to worry you or James anymore and, if there's a problem, I want him to contact me."

"If you think that's the right thing to do, I'll do as you say."

"I'm always here for you, Roslyn, and you can depend on me, no matter what."

They exchanged a few more words and she thanked him again for his support before she put the phone down. Roslyn felt very lucky to have such a wonderful friend to call on in her hour of need. She went upstairs to her room although she wouldn't be able to relax until Alex was safely back with her. She didn't give a damn about the stupid treasure; it had brought only misery so far. Then her new phone began ringing.

"Roslyn Chapell? My name's Gill Armstrong, and I work for Aidan Spencer at 'Protectu' in London and he's asked me to contact you directly. He wants me to act as your bodyguard until Mr. Wilshaw is home again."

"Yes, Mr. Spencer told me to expect your call, but I think that might be a bit premature at this stage. My father's partner, Mr. Edelman, is going to tell Mr. Spencer that he will deal with the matter himself from now on, so I don't think I will need you to come after all."

"I know it may sound a bit over-the-top, but I have to warn you, you may still be in danger, being on your own isn't wise. Mr. Spencer feels I should come over to stay with you until your fiancé is safely back at home I'm afraid you don't realise the sort of people you're dealing with here. They know where you live and will use you too, if need be."

"I don't want to seem rude, but I don't think I need your protection, Miss Armstrong. As I already said, Mr. Edelman's taking over the whole thing, liaising with the kidnappers and everything so I'm happy to let him do that."

"Well, Miss Chapell, Mr. Spencer is one of the best security specialists in the business and doesn't want to take any chances with your safety. You can't always be sure of who your real friends are in a situation like this. If you'll allow me to act on your behalf as 'an old schoolfriend' and take Mr. Spencer's advice, I know you won't regret it."

Roslyn's brain was working overtime and she couldn't think straight anymore. What should she do for the best, listen to a complete stranger or depend on Ben who knew her so well? Who could she trust?

"All right, Miss. Armstrong, I'll do as you say for the moment until my father comes back. Are you in Marbella now?"

"Yes, I can come to your house later this evening at about 8 and we can decide what you want to do then."

Roslyn put the phone down and just stared into space. If only she could go back to the time she first met Alex when they were students in Cambridge. Her mother had died only a short time before and she was determined to make her father proud of her, so she worked hard and rarely went out socially, but she'd always remember the first night she met him, one night in the Eagle pub, where lots of the undergrads congregated. Alex was telling her all about the discovery of D.N.A. by someone called Crick and some other guys in this very same pub. His mates were more interested in beer drinking than scientific discoveries, but she was really interested in his story and they kept on talking all about the Nobel prize Crick had won in 1962. Yes, Alex had always been a very serious-minded young man.

Then, they'd gone their separate ways until that special night when they met again by chance in London. That had been quite an amazing coincidence. She'd been on the way home from visiting her dad in Spain and had literally bumped into Alex when he was having a drink in a pub near where she lived. She recognised him straightaway, but he couldn't remember her name, much to his embarrassment. They'd shared a table, then chatted non-stop before he had to dash off and catch his train. Their life together really took off from that moment on and had never looked back, until now.

CHAPTER FOUR

ALEX'S STORY

Two years earlier, Alex Wilshaw had become bored with his tedious job at GCHQ headquarters. He shared a house with a fellow worker, Jason, when he came to work in Cheltenham; his job was in crypto-analysis and he'd begun to wonder how he had ended up in such a fruitless occupation. He could understand the need for code-breaking at Bletchley Park during the war but found it hard to justify his existence when the internet revolution had opened the secret world of international communication and terrorism to teenage hackers working from their darkened bedrooms, using shop bought or even homemade personal computers. What was the point of it all now?

He would be thirty on his next birthday and all he'd done since he left university was work for one government department after another until he was recruited to GCHQ two years after the new building was finished in 2003. His social life revolved round his fellow workers and drinking discreetly in the local pubs. He'd had a few short-term flings with various girls and then a longer term one but nothing serious enough to make him want to settle down, much to his grandmother's constant concern. He didn't even remember his parents, they'd died in a motorway accident when he was only two years old, and his only other living relative now was his paternal grandma, Alice, who lived in Yorkshire. She'd brought him up singlehandedly since his grandpa died. He loved listening to her talking about his grandfather's family history, back in the old days in Poland. He could sit for hours, looking at the few faded photographs she still treasured from her life with Lukasz Wilowski, the husband she still cherished so many years after his death.

It was Lukasz who had been living with his father and mother in Poland in 1939 when first the Germans, then the Russians, had marched in and confiscated all the family's properties. He was only a boy of sixteen at the time, it was the beginning of a nightmare that lasted for years after their initial arrests, based purely on their aristocratic background. The suffering that followed was only brought to an abrupt end when Russia decided to change sides during the Second World War and join the allies in the fight against Hitler and Germany. With the meagre facts he had gleaned from his grandmother about his grandfather's early life as the only son of the Count and Countess Wilowski, Alex was mesmerised by the stories of the horrors of his captivity in a gulag. From that time on, he wanted to know more and more about his Polish ancestry and whenever he was in London, he headed for the British Library and researched records of the family's genealogy and read all about the bygone glories of the Wilowski family. The results were fascinating and opened a window into a whole new world that he had been totally unaware of; he was a member and perhaps the sole survivor of an ancient family whose history and titles spanned centuries. He believed instinctively that one day, he'd find his rightful place in that distinguished lineage.

When a bulky envelope dropped through the letter box one day, he recognised the neat handwriting, it was his grandmother's. He opened it with care, he didn't want to tear anything inside. It wasn't his birthday, it couldn't be a present, so he guessed it was something very important. There was a letter with a five-page account with the heading 'Lukasz's Story' and immediately he knew it was the document she had promised to search for when he last saw her in May. He'd heard all her Polish stories many times over the years but had never seen anything so personal in his grandfather's own writing before, his heart was beating faster as he unfolded the enclosed hand-written sheets. He hoped they might shed more light on his early life when, after several years of living in England, he'd decided to change his name to the more anglicised form of 'Luke Wilshaw'. Alex sat down, his hand was trembling as he spread the pages out and started to read. It took him less than an hour to follow the harrowing account of the terrible ordeals he'd suffered and felt overcome by the poignancy of this very personal account of the family's story. That same evening, he phoned his grandmother to thank her for the letter and for the very moving account of her husband's tribulations in Russia.

Next morning, he woke up more eager than ever to break away from his rather humdrum life cycle of too much work and very little play. He realised his routine lacked any element of adventure. What had he ever done besides studying and work? At his age, his grandfather had already experienced more than he could imagine. New input and more excitement were what he needed! He picked up his address book to see if any of his old mates from uni were still around, he soon found one fellow student who might live in London and fortunately, he'd kept his home phone number. He only remembered him as 'Big Mike', he'd been an oarsman and seemed a 'larger than life' character on the occasions they'd met at their local pub. Alex had been too serious by far in those days and so, hadn't made the most of the student social scene in Cambridge; the story of his life but that was about to change.

When a familiar voice answered the phone, Alex was delighted that Mike even remembered him, he must have had made more of an impression than he thought. They chatted for a while and ended up by agreeing to have a night out on the town the following Friday evening. They arranged to meet in the bar at Paddington Station, Alex reckoned he could be there by 7 o'clock so they'd have plenty of time to talk about old times. His last train back was at 11:30 so they could spend a few hours, catching up with news about people and places they both remembered. He was feeling quite elated with his new spontaneity, he thought this could be the beginning of a complete lifestyle make-over.

Looking round the bar after his train got in, he recognised Mike straightaway but, after a few beers and 'do you remember when we used to...?', it became blatantly obvious that they had less than nothing in common any more. Then, making suitable polite excuses after an hour or so, they went their separate ways with vague promises to look each other up when Alex was in London again. What a disappointment that had turned out to be as the start to his new free-and-easy outlook on life!

He walked over to the nearest taxi stand, not quite knowing what to do next, then he remembered a lively pub where he'd once had a great time with some of his old pals in Hampstead. It was called 'The Holly Bush'. He thought any taxi driver worth his salt was bound to know it, so he told the cabbie where he wanted to go and was soon in a busy wine bar-cum-bistro which suited him fine. It was noisy and full of happy smiling people, just what he needed!

He found a table in an alcove, he was very hungry and looked at the menu before ordering a pizza. As the place got even noisier, he decided to move over to the bar and have one for the road before he left. Then, he felt someone tap him on the shoulder. He couldn't have been more surprised when he turned around and recognised a girl he'd known years before. The trouble was he'd completely forgotten her name, but she was obviously pleased to see him. His luck seemed to be changing. She was very good looking, even lovelier than he remembered. After a slight awkward silence, he asked if she'd like a drink and they started chatting about the old days and trying to recall various half-forgotten names and places. Time passed quickly but it seemed to stand still for him when he suddenly realised, he'd miss his last train if he didn't go very soon.

"I'm so sorry but I have to dash, my train leaves Paddington at eleven. I'd completely forgotten the time."

Full of apologies and wishing he was staying longer, they quickly exchanged phone numbers, promising to call each other, then he rushed outside to grab a taxi to take him to the station. His last train was already leaving the platform just as he arrived so there was nothing else for it but to bed down in the station hotel for the night. He didn't care, he didn't have to be back at work until Monday morning and missing that train could mean that the gods were smiling on him at last! Now, remembering her name 'Roslyn', he decided he would phone her first thing in the morning and invite her out for dinner. He hoped he hadn't seemed too eager to catch his train when he'd left her in the wine-bar, but this would prove to be the most momentous choice he'd ever made in his life. Little did he or Roslyn know then just what lay ahead of them!

CHAPTER FIVE

ROSLYN'S STORY

A few days before she'd bumped into Alex in London, Roslyn had been sitting on the terrace of her father's house in Marbella admiring the view. The sun was beating down, it was August after all, so what else could you expect? She'd decided to go out when the shops opened later, after her siesta. She still found it a strange custom to lie down after lunch and her father, James, shook his head and bemoaned the waste of good working hours, lost in sleeping. He would never fully understand why the Spanish insisted on taking a nap during the day. He was English to the core, only his arthritis had forced him to seek a milder winter climate as he grew older although his own personal habits hadn't changed one iota since he bought the villa. He didn't enjoy long haul flights and so, Europe suited him better than the Caribbean or other far-flung retirement spots and the hour time difference between there and London made sure he could always be on hand to deal with any crises that cropped up at his company's headquarters although he'd left it in the very capable hands of his younger partner, Ben Edelman. The previous evening, after dinner, trying to sound a little too casual, he'd asked her.

"Where is our dear Markus at the moment?"

"Probably wining and dining some lady love in the Caribbean somewhere, I can find out if you'd really like to know. I haven't spoken to him for quite a while."

She smiled indulgently thinking of her ne'er-do-well brother, who wasn't exactly a chip off the old block. In fact, he was nearly everything his father despised in a young man, he was indolent, spoilt and, as far as James was concerned, a perpetual drain on the family's finances. Roslyn knew all his weaknesses and loved him despite them. He was only three years younger than she was, but she often felt more like his mother than his sister. That was probably why he took advantage of her affection, particularly when it came to him wheedling something out of her. She was his father's favourite child and Markus knew it. He couldn't help resenting her ability to get whatever she wanted from the old man, whether she needed it or not.

Roslyn feeling slightly guilty, spoke to him the following day. He was hopelessly entangled with his latest girlfriend in Las Vegas, gambling more than he could afford and, as usual, losing. The trouble was, as ever, he needed more money to impress his new paramour, an 'up-and-coming' actress, who expected everyone to dance to her tune, often literally. Already, she wanted to go somewhere new, somewhere more exciting; anywhere would do. Poor besotted Markus knew he couldn't go anywhere until he'd paid off his poker debts so another loan from his father was urgently needed. Roslyn told him she felt sure she could talk her father into digging deeper in his pockets, but she would have to spin him some yarn about where Markus was and that certainly couldn't be at the Bellagio and preferably, not in the State of Nevada at all. Later the next evening she contacted him again to say he would soon be getting the money she'd transferred to his bank earlier.

"You're absolutely amazing! How on earth did you manage that, Ros? I know what a tightwad he can be."

"Please, don't ask me too many details. I did have to tell him I was thinking of buying a new car, which is true, by the way. He said he would give me money if I needed it, so it's now speeding its way into your depleted bank account as we speak."

"You're an angel, my lifesaver, I don't know what I'd do without you."

"I know, I know. You tell me that every time I get you out of a scrape. But this time, I want you promise you'll at least try to live within your allowance for the next six months."

The conversation ended with his reassurances he would. Roslyn heaved a sigh of relief as she put her phone down. What would become of her spendthrift brother if his father suddenly refused to bankroll his lifestyle? Even if he should ever think of working for a living, who would employ him with his miserable school record and lack of any suitable qualifications? His only assets were his good looks and ability to charm the ladies, not exactly a formula for success in the cut and thrust of the business world; even his father's name wouldn't get him out of serious trouble if the money ran out. Roslyn repeatedly worried about him and thought,

'Thank goodness mother isn't still alive to worry about him.'

Markus had been her favourite child by far, that's why he was the way he was, and no matter what he did, she always defended him to the death. Being expelled from his final private school at the age of seventeen was the last straw for his father. He'd put up with his dilatory ways long enough and sadly washed his hands of him when his wife, Celia, died soon afterwards. He gave him a handsome allowance provided he stayed out of the country and out of debt. What else could he do with a son who was so addle-brained? Even she knew he had overstepped the mark this time. If only he had been more like Roslyn, who had beauty and brains and succeeded in everything she did. She certainly had inherited more than her share of intelligence plus a natural sweet nature, a winning combination in her father's eyes. Nothing was too good for his daughter. James Chapell sighed as he thought that life was sometimes unfair in its distribution of blessings and good fortune. He himself had come up the hard way, his education had been sketchy to say the least, but he'd been born with a natural insight and ability to spot a niche in the retail market when no one else did.

His first success had been in seeing the early potential of computers, not only in the workplace, but also in the home. He knew nothing about them technically but had a gut feeling that they were going to be the tools of the future. When he succeeded in that particular field by employing young electronic whizz kids, just out of college, who had the expertise he lacked. He also had the foresight to ally his own company with another young entrepreneur's small outfit whose sole purpose was retailing and servicing mobile phones. The two schemes worked well together and so, they became partners, eventually moving into much larger premises and employing more and more staff as the business grew exponentially. Over the next few years, it succeeded beyond all their expectations until eventually, it was listed on the stock exchange with an annual turnover of several million pounds. His very personable partner, Benjamin Edelman, was half Austrian/half English, a first-class P.R. man whose intelligence and charm radiated sincerity in his many radio and television interviews. Their mutual success was phenomenal. The name of their joint venture 'Cosmocompute' was on everyone's lips.

Known to the family simply as 'Ben', he and James had always hoped there might be some romantic spark between him and Roslyn, unfortunately the age gap proved too much for her. Ben was thirty-seven when she was only twenty-one, nevertheless it would have been a marriage made in heaven, as far as her father was concerned. He was everything that could be desired in a son-in-law; brilliant at his job, responsible, well educated, good natured and, in James' eyes, a great asset to the family business. Roslyn hadn't seen it quite that way, she really admired him and loved his mop of curly black hair but thought of him more as an uncle rather than a prospective husband. Ben was secretly in love with her, of course, but he hadn't the right words to put his feelings for her in a way that was designed to capture her young heart. He had been bowled over by her beauty from their first meeting and loved listening to the sound of her richly plummy voice. He hoped she would warm to the idea of him as a future bridegroom as time went on and, even though as he took every opportunity to be near her, nothing seemed to promote any reciprocal feelings. She was happy to concentrate on her budding career; marriage was the furthest thing from her mind. She loved spending time with them both, but her father annoyed her with his constant references to Ben as a suitable partner for her.

His thoughts were mainly focussed on having grandchildren and he often hinted as much. She was equally adamant that it wouldn't happen and was immersed in her new role as head of a new technological team. Marriage and family didn't fit into that equation. Only time would change her mind and that day came by accident when she met Alex again.

CHAPTER SIX

She had booked her flight from Marbella for the following Friday, giving her enough time to get her laundry done and make her home shipshape again. She remembered she'd left her apartment looking like a second-hand clothes shop after she'd hurriedly packed her trolley-case for the trip. She really ought to be more organised or at least, get someone like Maria to do it for her; she was so good at her job but so hopeless when it came to household management.

She hadn't eaten on the plane and thought she'd stop off at her local pub to grab a quick bite after she'd dropped her bags off at home. There was no milk in the house and she didn't want to go food shopping this late, so smiling at her favourite waiter, Gustav, she sat down at a table next to the window. After she'd given him her order, she looked around and could hardly believe her eyes when she saw a familiar figure standing at the bar. She was sure it was Alex Wilshaw, an acquaintance from their uni days, the last person she'd expected to see in London. He seemed to be alone, so she walked over to him and tapped him on the shoulder. He turned around and looked gobsmacked when he recognised her.

"Wow! What a lovely surprise!"

They exchanged a few pleasantries and then he asked her if she'd like a drink.

"That would be nice but I'm just waiting for my meal to come. Would you like to join me, Alex? That's if you're not meeting someone."

He nodded eagerly, he still hadn't recovered from his surprise at seeing her. She'd been one of the gang at the pub they all frequented in their student days. Funny he remembered the name of the pub, 'The Eagle' in Benet Street, but couldn't remember her name. She hadn't changed a bit. She remembered his name and that he was known as a brain box, even in their elated circle. She'd been studying applied maths and physics. Her friend, Megan, had introduced them once, thinking they might hit it off but he was much too serious-minded for her in those days and spent most of the time studying in his rooms. She still remembered his telling her that Francis Crick, the DNA guy, had publicly announced that they'd found the secret of life in that same pub, something which had stuck in her mind ever after. What an amazing coincidence their meeting again after so many years!

"Have you eaten yet, Alex?"

"Well, yes, I have but I can sit and watch you if you don't mind."

Her food arrived with the glass of wine she'd ordered as she smiled at him and said it would be her pleasure. Alex brought his beer with him from the bar and declined another one when Gustav asked. At first, as she began eating, there was silence and she wondered if it had been a mistake to invite him over. Then, they began chatting and started to relax after the initial shock of seeing each other.

"You can't imagine how glad I am to see you. It's great that we bumped into each other after all this time. I don't even live in London, I was just visiting a friend of mine and waiting to catch the last train back to Cheltenham."

He realised he was gabbling, trying to cover up for not remembering her name.

"Yes, it is a strange coincidence. I only just got back from Spain this evening and popped in here because I hadn't eaten a thing on the plane and had no food in the house."

Afterwards, she thought their meeting was, in fact, a million to one chance. Maybe fate was playing cupid for some reason. Stranger things had happened or was it the gods smiling down on them?

After catching up on what they'd been up to recently, they decided to have another drink. Roslyn was surprised to see how much Alex had changed since his uni days, he was quietly confidant but self-deprecating. When he suddenly looked at his watch, saying he must dash to catch his last train, Roslyn was disappointed that he was leaving so soon. They only had time to exchange phone numbers with a promise to keep in touch before he bent over to kiss her cheek and was gone. She wondered if she'd ever see him again. Probably not.

She sat there for a while, then asked for her bill and exchanged a few words with Gustav before deciding to walk home. A nice end to a lovely day she thought as she unpacked and sorted out her dirty clothes for the laundry. But she couldn't help thinking of Alex and wondered if he really would get in touch with her again. She suddenly felt tired and, even though her unmade bed was rumpled, it still looked inviting. She decided to undress and flop into it, a shower could wait until morning. The three glasses of wine had made her extra drowsy as she drifted off into a sound and carefree sleep, dreaming of warm sunshine and being surrounded by happy people. She had the rest of the weekend to catch up on duty phone calls, she knew her father would be out with his card-playing cronies on Friday night and wouldn't expect to hear from her until the next day. The mid-morning sun was already streaming through the window when she woke, she checked her alarm clock and was shocked to find it was nearly eleven. She rarely slept in but this morning, she stretched out again like a contented cat and snuggled down to daydream for a while. Strangely, her first thoughts were of Alex and she didn't know why. He was a personable guy, not outrageously good looking, but everything about him appealed to her. Their conversation had been easy, unlike being on a first tentative date. They hadn't known each other all that well but there was something that had instantly gelled with them as far as she was concerned, and she hoped he felt the same. London could be a very lonely place unless all you wanted to do was go clubbing and socialising with friends or friends of friends. Yes, there had certainly been that spark of mutual interest between them.

Washing her hair in the shower, she thought she heard her mobile ringing in her bedroom; she was too late to pick it up before it stopped. What an idiot she was not to have taken it into the bathroom with her! She pressed the voicemail button and heard Alex saying he would call again later. She liked the sound of his rather husky voice even more now. Could she be infatuated already or was she so desperate to find a suitable man for her father's sake that she was grasping at straws? No, neither was true, she was merely enjoying the thought of another reunion for old times' sake. Even so, she would wait and let him phone her, as he'd promised; no good reading too much into this one brief encounter.

He did call again exactly fifteen minutes later, having remembered her name at last. He'd missed his last train the previous evening, or so he said, and had decided to book into the station hotel at Paddington. He was staying until Sunday, so he wondered if they could meet for dinner. When she said yes, he promised to pick her up at seven sharp. She gave him her address and her heart did a little somersault as she put the phone down. They were old friends but nevertheless, she must tidy the place up, put a bottle of wine in the fridge and do some food shopping just in case she was wrong, and this was the start of something special.

That thought kept her buzzing all afternoon and, after she'd phoned her dad to say she was home safe and sound, she went out and walked to her favourite local shop, bought flowers, some savoury titbits, a couple of newspapers and magazines to make her flat look more like a home instead of just somewhere she crashed every night after a hard day's work. By six, she'd bundled her dirty laundry into a basket in the second bedroom, plumped up the cushions on her stylish leather sofa and the place looked fine but he probably wouldn't even notice anyway.

She got out a couple of wine glasses and, after a final look around, satisfied that everything was as good as it was going to get, she went into her bedroom. The bed was now pristine with her new duvet over clean sheets, she sat in front of her mirror staring critically at her face. Her reflection was fine, even without make-up; her skin was sun-tanned, her eyes sparkled, and her fair hair was thick and shiny. She put on her mascara and some lip gloss before trying on the dresses she'd bought on holiday in Marbella, one particularly suited her slim figure and matched her blue eyes to perfection. She felt good and turned around to see how the back looked when her doorbell rang, she glanced at her watch. It was only 6:45 but she knew it was him, proving he was as keen to see her as she was him. She popped on her shoes and gave herself a final nod of approval before going to open her front door. The bell rang again, he certainly was eager and there he was, smiling shyly and holding a large bunch of roses.

Their first evening together was an unbounded success; Roslyn loved his quick-witted conversation over dinner and his ability to listen too. She felt instantly at home with him, it was as if she'd known him all her life. Alex was equally enraptured with her, she was delightful company and laughed in all the right places when he told her stories of his childhood and listened intently when he described his job at GCHQ, skirting around the forbidden subjects of the official secrets work he did, but she seemed very interested to get a general picture of his job. He found her fascinating too, even though he hadn't a clue about her main interest in photonics. He had known from their uni days that she was very bright and was really impressed that beauty and brains went well together in her case. Later, she invited him back for a coffee and he accepted without a second thought. They had some of the Spanish brandy she'd brought back from Marbella with their coffee; they both laughed as Alex found it too fiery for his taste and spluttered when he took his first sip.

"I'd forgotten you were never a great drinker even back in our student days."

"I suppose I was a bit of a nerd even then. You must have thought I was a real bore, all work and no play."

"Not really, I was always impressed that you took your studies so seriously, so many of the others were just winging it. It was like some sort of a finishing school for people like Martin and dear Nigel, rich boys from well-healed parents, who could afford to get a poor Third at the end of it and then slide into a cushy job in the city."

"I never realised you were so perceptive. I was just a poor grammar school boy with a meagre scholarship to live on. I thought you were in the 'Rich Daddy' league as well."

"Yes, I suppose I was in a way. I wanted to make my father proud of me as well and it was a treat to see his face when I told him I'd got a First."

He took his cue from her and leaned over to plant a light kiss on her lips, his heart raced as she came closer and returned it with a more passionate one. They kissed each other again and he took her in his arms for the first time. Then, he played down his strong physical urge to make passionate love to her, then and there.

'How could I have ever forgotten your name? Roslyn, you are absolutely wonderful!'

It was a perfect ending to a perfect day.

CHAPTER SEVEN

They spent their next weekend in Cheltenham so that Roslyn could get an idea of the city where Alex lived and worked. Jason, his house-mate had tactfully gone off for a couple of days, giving them some space and privacy. Alex had been waiting anxiously at the Spa station for her train to arrive and was thrilled to see her smiling face again. He had decided to take her to the Lumiere Restaurant, it got rave reviews, so he hoped she'd like it. He'd planned some outings over the weekend and was excited to be showing round his own stomping ground. She'd looked fabulous, getting off the train, carrying a small overnight bag. They kissed as she linked her arm in his and left the platform to get a cab back to his place.

After dumping her case in the hallway, he showed her his rather neat living room; it was a typical bachelor pad, sparse but comfortable. When she saw his study upstairs, she realised this was where he spent most of his waking hours when he wasn't at work. The walls were covered in maps, many of them of Poland and surrounding countries. He had old black and white photographs of palatial country houses and palaces with names she couldn't even hope to pronounce, linked to the maps by arrows and there was a rather grand looking family tree with a coat of arms above it. This was another side of Alex she knew nothing about, she looked at him, dying to query his interest in things Polish but knew now wasn't the time to talk history, as he showed her the way to her bedroom and the bathroom.

"I thought you'd like to freshen up a bit before we go out to eat. Would you like a glass of something first, I've a nice bottle of Sauvignon Blanc in the fridge or would you prefer a gin and tonic?"

"I'll drink whatever you're having, I'll be down in five minutes"

"I hope you'll be comfortable and, if you want anything, just shout."

Her room was at the back of the large terrace house but looked out onto a nicely set out garden, complete with a patio, striped awning and a wrought iron table with matching chairs. With a vase of flowers on the windowsill and a handmade quilt on the bed, it was all very cosy, she could see he had made a special effort for her visit. Her bedroom was very pretty and thoughtfully arranged so he'd obviously learned how to entertain a female guest. She looked in the old dressing table mirror, combed her hair and put on some fresh lipstick before she opened her case and unfolded her night things; she travelled light as she always did with only the essentials. Then she opened the door, turned off the light and went downstairs.

He jumped up when she opened the door, he was still nervous about inviting her to his place; it was so different from her ultra-modern apartment and he must have thought she was used to living in the lap of luxury, which wasn't too far from the truth. Normally, she spent as little time as possible alone in her flat, it wasn't a home for her, only a place to sleep. She usually ate out after work either with friends or alone and then slumped into bed after a few glasses of wine and didn't wake until her alarm went off in the morning. It was mostly work and very little play for Roslyn, except at the weekends when she would let her hair down and accept invitations to parties and drinking sessions that were an intrinsic part of London life. She, like Alex, had had a few romantic flings, never anything more and usually lasting no longer than a few months, if that.

That first weekend was magical. They ate, they talked, they laughed, they walked hand in hand around the city and Alex showed her the highlights of Cheltenham at play. They'd made love in his bed; hers was as pristine when she left as it was when she arrived. Their serious conversations took place sitting on the sofa, wine in hand, before they were drawn once more to his inviting bedroom. His lovemaking was passionate but gentle, he made her feel wanted and needed, she felt the same way. It was difficult to say goodbye when Sunday evening came, and she had to leave him to catch her train back to Paddington.

Each evening after that, they talked endlessly on the phone, their weekend destinations alternating. The next Friday, it was his turn to travel to London. This time she was determined to get him to talk about his Polish connections, she was intrigued by the maps and wall charts she'd seen in his study. She felt, even at this early stage of their affair, that they should share something of each other's family backgrounds. Hers was pretty straightforward; Alex hadn't met her father, James, yet but she'd already told him about his telecommunication business in London in partnership with Benjamin Edelman and his semi-retirement to Marbella for health reasons. She'd also spoken about her mother, Celia, who had died when Roslyn was barely seventeen, she'd had breast cancer which she'd ignored until it was too late for effective treatment. Trying to explain her subsequent more complicated relationship with her brother wasn't easy; how she'd virtually become a surrogate mother to him, but she didn't go into too much detail about his father sending him away from England, mainly because of his gambling habits. She felt she was being disloyal to him; after all she loved him, warts and all.

She got the perfect opportunity to open a discussion with Alex about his own family connections when the Sunday papers included an article about Tsar Nicholas and his family, who were assassinated by the Bolsheviks in Yekaterinburg. The children's only fault being born into a family that was blamed for most of the terrible inequalities in Russia. Alex began by telling her some of the similarities between them and his own Polish great-grandparents and his grandfather. It was a subject that fascinated Roslyn, she remembered the film 'Dr. Zhivago' when Alex described the terrible conditions they'd suffered on the train to Siberia. His family history was so colourful while hers seemed pale by comparison. He showed her, on his various maps, where their confiscated properties had been and was flattered that she found it as fascinating as he did. What he hadn't told her was that he already had plans to try and find their hidden fortune and claim what was rightfully his.

So, the pattern of their weekends became set and it worked well. They both had demanding jobs during the week, so Saturdays and Sundays took on a new meaning; lots of talking, love-making as their lives naturally progressed to a more serious level. Alex suggested one weekend that they go to see his grandmother and she was delighted at the thought. They travelled to Yorkshire in Roslyn's car and spent the journey talking about memories of his early years there. He had always known how loved he was by the most important person in his life. He hadn't known his parents at all, they had died in a motorway accident when he was barely two, but he never felt that he was deprived of family love. He would go back to his grandmother's house each afternoon after school and she would tell him interesting stories including ones about his Polish family's life in Krakow before the war. She showed him the few mementos Luke had left her; the most precious one of all was a faded black and white photograph of his very aristocratic looking great-grandmother, Karolina. She was looking directly into the camera, her hair was carefully marcel-waved and framed her classic face, she was wearing a coat with

41

a huge fox fur collar that added to the stylised formal portrait. Luke had carried that photograph with him throughout the war and treasured it as the only image he had of his beloved mother.

Alice, his grandmother, lived in apartment block specially for the elderly although she hated to think of herself as old; she still felt young at heart, despite her white hair and arthritic knees. She did her own daily shopping and enjoyed a busy social life. She was always occupied with some new activity or other; she loved keeping up with the latest trends, she had a laptop, an iPad, a mobile phone and couldn't understand older friends who refused to accept modern technology. 'Old stick in the muds' she called them. Alice welcomed them warmly into her pristine home, no shabby chic and distressed wood for her, the furniture glowed and had a faint smell of linseed oil and lavender. She hugged her grandson and she kissed Roslyn affectionately on both cheeks.

She'd already prepared a mouth-watering lunch with a variety of salads, sliced meats, smoked salmon and tiger prawns. She'd put out an assortment of cheeses too, not sure if Roslyn was a vegetarian or not. She'd erred on the right side with dishes of hummus, mango guacamole and other pates.

"What a wonderful spread, Grandma. You've certainly done us proud."

"Mm! It all looks wonderful, I love guacamole, one of my favourites."

Alice smiled happily when they tucked into the lovingly-made meal.

"Would you like a sweet, Roslyn? I don't have to ask Alex, I know he loves my home-made Angels' Wings. They were my husband's favourites too."

"They sound gorgeous, thank you."

"We always serve black coffee with them; would you like to try that too? The slight bitterness of the coffee makes the sweetness taste even better."

"I'd love to try both, please."

She put a cafetiere of coffee on a side table, already set out with coffee cups and saucers. She took their plates into the kitchen to wash later and sat down again.

"Luke used to say, 'you never truly value a good meal until you've been starving' and the poor man had certainly known what near starvation had been like when he was in Russia."

"It must have been an unbearably hard experience for him and particularly losing his parents so young. I don't know how he ever recovered from those appalling deprivations."

"He never truly did, I think the ghosts of the past haunted him until his dying day. But I'm sorry, you didn't come all this way to feel miserable. Let's eat up and have our coffee, he would have loved to know we are all here together enjoying his favourite dessert."

Alex had said very little but was happy that his grandmother seemed so relaxed; he had wanted them to like each other and get on well. Roslyn was genuinely interested in the old stories, never having heard them from someone so close to his grandfather.

They spent the rest of the afternoon reminiscing and Alice got out a beautiful wooden box where she kept her mementos and old family photographs. Roslyn was glad to be drawn into Alex's tiny family circle with his delightful grandma. It seemed like a great honour to her and this special time would live in her memory forever. Her own mother, Celia, had died so young, leaving her alone to cope with the family's grief while she was still a teenager. That was the only real suffering she'd ever known, it was nearly impossible to imagine how Luke could have endured the deaths of both his parents plus all the other hardships, year after year, and still survived.

Suddenly, the mood changed as Alice showed her Alex's baby photos and the ones when he was growing up, in his school uniform, all smiles and innocence. What a difference! They all looked so happy. Alex kept asking her not to show the ones when he was a skinny teenager with long hair and scruffy jeans.

"Wait until you see mine." Roslyn laughed. "You haven't had that pleasure yet."

The whole visit went too quickly and soon it was time to say their good-byes, Alice couldn't help crying a little as she hugged them both this time.

"You are a lucky boy, you can't always find such a treasure, look after her well."

Alex kissed her warmly and promised they would come again soon.

"And keep writing those emails, Grandma, you know I love to read all your news."

With final hand-waving from the car window, they set off and drove away slowly, making the moment last. As her small figure disappeared in the distance, Alex turned to Roslyn and said.

"I think that went very well, don't you?"

"I absolutely loved my whole time here, I hadn't realised how much I've missed such warm and genuine kindness. I love your grandma to bits."

That made Alex very happy to know it had meant so much to her. Her father was a delightful and erudite man but much more reserved; he undoubtedly loved his daughter but showing his emotions openly came hard to him. Roslyn needed some warm feminine love in her life and he knew his grandmother felt the same about her too.

They'd only had one other break in their new weekly routine up to now and that was when they decided to take some annual leave and visit James in Marbella. It was a wonderfully relaxing time for them. Alex and her father got on like a house on fire; he saw in him the son-in-law he'd tried to envisage for Roslyn after her refusal to consider Ben for that role. Their mutual love was growing with each day they spent together and when they got back to England, Alex decided he would ask Roslyn to read first-hand his grandfather's memoirs which meant so much to him. Now that she had met his grandmother, it seemed only right that she should read Luke's story herself. She already knew his family's former background and his strong desire to go to Poland to research his origins more thoroughly. He wanted to find out more about their day-to-day lives but, up to now, he'd never fully shared the verbatim account of their sudden demise when the Russians invaded Poland in 1939.

When he met Roslyn as usual at the station in Cheltenham the following weekend, they went for a quick meal in one of their favourite cafes and then back to his place. She instinctively knew that this weekend was going to be different. Alex seemed a bit withdrawn and not his usual self, she hoped he wasn't feeling ill. After she'd unpacked her bag, he asked if she'd like a coffee or a drink.

"I've got something I want to share with you, my darling." Roslyn still wondered what could be so serious as Alex went over to his desk, picked up his grandfather's journal and put it in the middle of the coffee table and, without any further preamble, said.

"This is my grandfather's personal record of what happened to him and my great grandparents when Poland was invaded. He wrote it in 1956 so that my grandmother would know our history and it would be passed on to his successors. Grandma gave it to me a while ago and that's when I decided I had to find out more about their previous lives. Now, I would love you to read it for yourself."

Roslyn stood up and put her arms round him, knowing how much this meant to him.

"I'd love to read it, you know I'm very interested in anything about you or your family. I love you very much and hope to part of it all from now on."

Roslyn spent the next two hours reading and re-reading the harrowing catalogue of his suffering. She was crying as she turned the old pages carefully and read the heart-rending story. She was overcome by the account of the years that he'd spent in Russian captivity and the treatment he'd endured. It amazed her that he'd been able to sit down and write his experiences with such clarity and lack of bitterness after what would have destroyed a lesser man.

Now, at last, she fully understood Alex's need to explore the earlier life of this man, his parents and their forbears in a Poland that no longer existed. That knowledge would never restore him to his family's former glory, but he would have at least have found where he fitted into its history. Only by seeing his ancestral birthplace and their former homes would he be able to fully appreciate the enormity of what they had lost and what he too had been deprived of, being the last remaining survivor of a family, whose history had stretched over several centuries.

Roslyn had no doubt that he would continue his search and she wanted to be with him and share whatever he discovered on the way. What followed was the verbatim story of his grandfather's horrifying journey from a life of privilege and wealth to one of deprivation and heartache for all his family. It was Lukasz's own personal history.

CHAPTER EIGHT

'My name is Lukasz Wilowski; I was born in Lwow in eastern
Poland in 1922 where I lived with my parents and where I went
to day school. My father, Henryk, owned a country estate and
manor house, on the outskirts of the city, which we visited
every weekend. During the week, I had to wear an archaic
uniform and I'll always remember the cap with a tassel which
drew jeers and laughter from the local boys who shouted rude
names which I tried my best to ignore. If I complained to my
father, he would merely say that they were simple peasants
who knew no better; my more autocratic mother, Karolina, was
not so forgiving. My life at the weekends and during school
holidays on our estate was totally different. I spent most of my
time riding the beautiful horses that my father bred mostly for
the army; they were his pride and joy. He never tired of telling
me stories of his great grandfather, Count Alexander Wilowski,
who, in his younger days, had travelled widely across the
Arabian Peninsula and admired the Arab horses so much he
decided to import them to improve the Polish blood stock. In
more recent times strong foals were bred from his purebred
stallions mated with sturdy local mares to produce exactly what
the army needed. Their stock of military horses, the mainstay
of any army in those days, had been decimated in the many
battles fought against would-be invaders and so the demand for
his renowned colts was always assured. I remember quite
clearly the inscription above my father's stable doors written in
old Polish script.
   "A man without a horse is like a body without a soul."

It seemed to me my life was as near perfect as one could imagine, apart from the fact that I had no siblings to share it with; my mother, not blessed with good health, had to be content with an only child. All too soon, my pampered life ended abruptly.

On September 1st, 1939, when I was sixteen, Hitler's troops invaded Poland while the Russians were gathering their troops in the east. We knew all was lost on the day when the Polish radio no longer broadcast Chopin's Nocturne. The Germans started to invade the beautiful city of Krakow and very soon thousands of arrests were made. My father had decided that we should move from our estate in Lwow into the city as he thought it would be safer. My mother, Karolina, practical as ever, had already given instructions that all the family silver, her jewellery and other treasures should be buried in the estate grounds to stop them from falling into enemy hands. Then, on September 17th, the forces of the 6th Red Army of the Ukrainian Front started gathering and on the 19th, the first armoured units reached the outskirts of the city and overnight encircled it. After negotiations with what was left of the Polish army under General Sikorski, it was decided that defence of the city was hopeless and so, on September 22nd, the act of surrender was signed which allowed Polish soldiers to leave the city and officers were told they could leave Poland for any country that would accept them. Not surprisingly, the Russians broke their word and arrested all the officers and many important citizens including my father who were either shot or transported to the infamous Starobielsk Gulag in Russia. That was just days before my mother and I were arrested and taken by truck with the few belongings we could carry to an old disused warehouse on a railway siding. We begged for news of my father because there had been countless executions over the past weeks but learned nothing. We feared the worst and never saw or heard of him again.

The next morning, we were crammed into cattle trucks filled with straw, everyone jostling for a spot to call their own, as near the door as possible. Then slowly the train started moving. People separated from other family members were weeping, many not knowing why they had been arrested. The younger ones tried to comfort their older relatives; only children had been allowed to travel with their mothers or aged grandparents. Maybe because I looked young for my age I was still with my mother, there were no men of working age at all. As the weather grew colder with each passing day, we huddled together for warmth, there were many envious glances at my mother's fur coat which she had insisted on wearing; there was still some semblance of decency and respect remaining, the others could see that my mother was indeed a lady. That courtesy didn't last long. The heavy sliding door was opened for an hour each day when a cauldron of foul tasting broth was dragged to the middle of the truck next to a pile of rough hard bread. There were not enough bowls to go around, so mother and I shared our meal as best we could. Hunger is a great appetiser and, after we'd all scraped the huge pot with our remaining bread, nothing was left.

Each morning, we could relieve ourselves by the side of the track under the watchful eyes of the guards. Our overnight filth was thrown onto the nearby fields by the stronger members of each truck, no fresh straw was ever added. As the days went by, the stench in our carriage became almost unbearable; bugs and lice welcomed the warmth of our bodies, sucking our blood for sustenance. Those of us, who could, tried to wait to empty our bowels on the frost hardened ground each day but as dysentery became prevalent so our living conditions deteriorated rapidly. Then the deaths started, the very young and the elderly died first, their bodies being flung unceremoniously from the train as we travelled further and further north. The intense cold was bone shattering, even any sodden straw, that was left, froze overnight. Some of the more able-bodied women tried to make a run for it as the doors were rolled open; not one escaped, all shot in the back by patrolling soldiers. I heard them laughingly shout "Polish bitches!" I could understand that much Russian.

When it seemed impossible for us to survive any longer, our journey ended. I helped my weakened mother in her now filthy coat down to the ground; she was then lined up with the other female prisoners and taken away. I asked one of the accompanying guards in my broken schoolboy Russian where they were taking them only to be shoved aside with the butt of his rifle and that was the last time I set eyes on my dearest Mother. I often prayed her death was swift, she had suffered enough. The rest of us, a bedraggled mixture of youngsters, were herded like animals into corrugated sheds with no windows and rows of rough wooden tiered partitions, again with only straw for bedding. A boy about my own age climbed up to a top bunk and said in a hoarse whisper.

"My name's Ramborski, what's yours?" When I told him, he looked puzzled. "With a name like that you should have been shot by now."

It was clear my family's reputation would get me killed if it became widely known I belonged to the hated aristocracy, so I decided to adopt the more common name of Litowski from that moment on. I always think his foresight saved my life and we became like brothers, sharing our misery and our bread.

If we thought our lives had been tough on the train, worse was yet to come. Each morning we were marched to the entrance of a dark tunnel and made to climb down an even darker hole about six feet in diameter by way of a metal-runged ladder that was bolted firmly to the wall. As I descended I felt the first heat I'd experienced since I left home and there was a dim glow of light from below. When we were all lined up at the bottom of the mineshaft, we saw more prisoners, all hacking away at the walls with heavy picks. Lumps of grey rock fell to the ground and were thrown into small trucks which trundled down a narrow-gauge railway. I didn't think it was coal they were mining when Ramborski said.

"It's rock salt, that's what it is. We must be in Siberia, that's where they send their own criminals, who are sentenced to hard labour."

I'd heard of the Siberian salt mines at school but never imagined I'd ever be in one myself, working twelve hours a day in the near dark, gouging out hard salt that made our eyes water and blistered our raw skin. The only compensation was the warmth. Our rations at the end of each shift were pitiful but we ate as if our lives depended on it, which they did. We were lucky to get a bowl of thin tasteless porridge and a slice of stale bread, often green mouldy. I saw youngsters like myself visibly weaken and grow thinner with every week that passed. I tried to count the days and the weeks, we never saw daylight for months on end, so time ceased to exist. Work and sleep, such as it was, were endless rounds of misery. One blessing was that the lice and bedbugs hated our salty bodies, so the constant plague of parasites diminished as we worked; the only thing that made our lives slightly more bearable again were the weekly showers, cold of course.

During one shift, I was so desperately hungry, my whole body was aching from the relentless back breaking work, I couldn't stand it anymore, so I picked up an iron pick and stuck it into my leg. I cried out with all the force my lungs could muster, the pain was excruciating, and the blood flowed from the gaping wound, A guard came over to see what the noise was about and sent for help. I was taken to the camp doctor who dressed and stitched the wound, telling the officer in charge I must not work until it healed. So, for a few days, I was left on my rough bed, but it didn't last long. I still carry a deep scar on my calf but, at the time, it seemed worth it.

More new prisoners arrived as long-term workers collapsed and died. The guards couldn't bury the bodies, the ground was frozen solid, so they were piled high outside the camp's fences and occasionally doused with petrol before ending up in a putrid bonfire. The disgusting smell made you physically sick. It was a living hell and lasted much longer than we thought possible. Then one day, everything suddenly changed but we didn't know why; we were taken to a sort of medical centre housed just inside the main gates to be officially deloused, we were given uniforms which hung loosely on our shrunken bodies, then marched out of the gulag and forced to walk for days until we reached our transport, old ramshackle wagons. By this time, my Russian had improved by listening to the snippets of conversation exchanged amongst our gaolers, so I was able to make out that the USSR had changed sides in the war and we were no longer enemies of the state. I found out later, the year was 1942. Three brutal and unrelenting years had passed since we left Poland. A pact had been signed giving amnesty to Polish prisoners in the camps all around Russia. I had been there for so long and thought my troubles were over at last, but I couldn't have been more mistaken.

After being taken off the buses, we were herded into rusty old trains that rattled south through Turkmenskaya. The carriages were louse and disease ridden, food was even more scarce, a loaf of bread was a luxury and I watched dozens die of starvation before we reached the port of Krasnovodsk on the Caspian Sea where equally rusty ships were waiting to take the lucky ones, who'd survived on the epic journey, to Persia, the country now called Iran. We weren't welcome there either but at least, the camps were organised and the food edible. In a matter of weeks, we were transported to our next destination, the Persian Gulf. Ramborski and I had managed to stick together then one day we were informed that all young able-bodied men could enlist in the Free Polish Army and would be shipped to Capetown in South Africa. Our ship was slow and, if we were lucky, we slept on deck, but it was luxury compared to anything we had experienced over the past three years. Our arrival in this new country seemed like a dream come true, it was paradise, a sanctuary, and a land of plenty. Hot showers and a clean bed to sleep on were pure bliss. We slowly began to look like healthy human beings again after six months of good food and medical care. All too soon, we were boarding yet another ship to take us from sunny Capetown to a dull, drizzly Southampton. I often wished I could have stayed in that beautiful city where I had been so happy, but the next part of my war was just beginning.

After careful vetting and being questioned by Polish speaking interpreters, my friend and I were transferred to an aircraft squadron in Lincolnshire, I had no idea it was the epicentre of the many bomber airfields in England. With my strength and vigour now almost restored, I was assigned to an aircrew training section where I undertook an intensive course in English and because my knowledge of maths was still pretty good, I was judged able enough to embark on a navigator's programme. At the end of another six months, I was proud to wear a 'Free Polish Air Force' uniform. I had gained a half wing insignia with a capital 'O' which stood for observer as navigators were then called. I was just in time to be part of the nightly bombing missions over Germany. We were, in the main, oblivious to the many innocent lives we destroyed night after night in those deadly air raids; our sole aim was to annihilate the hated enemy. I could never have imagined when I was a sixteen-year-old boy in Lwow that I could have survived all the horrors of my years of inhumane interment, near starvation and cruel slavery, not to mention the heart-breaking loss of both my parents whose fates I will never know. It was like the worst nightmare I could imagine and only the fickle vagaries of war had changed my circumstances from despair to hope once more.

Suffice it to say, I have never forgotten the traumas in Mother Russia and despite a general amnesty granted to all Polish émigrés, I never wanted to return to a Poland still under the yoke of Russian occupation. I had no known family there and for many years, I feared being repatriated to a country and to a life which no longer existed for me. I hope one day my successors may go back in search of their roots and who knows; they may even recover our long-lost treasures somewhere in the grounds of that old manor house, just where my dear mother had instructed them to be buried. I have only one son, Michael, and I would like him to know something of the history of his family and their illustrious past. Hopefully, his name and the property will then be his, by right of birth.

Signed: Lukasz Wilowski 1.9.56.
{Luke Wilshaw}

(This thin paper is already stained by my grandmother's tears as she often read and re-read her husband's tragic story over the ensuing years and then passed it on to me for safe-keeping. Signed: Alex Wilshaw}

CHAPTER NINE

Alex had already made enquiries about a short holiday in Krakow which was now easily accessible from the U.K. as a short break destination. He asked Roslyn if she'd like to go with him and she was delighted with the idea, she was as enthusiastic as he was to visit the city where his grandfather had lived so happily. Then two weeks later, they set off from Heathrow and very soon were landing at the John Paul 11 airport which was about eleven kilometres west near the village of Balice in southern Poland.

They took a taxi from the airport and found their pre-booked hotel, the Saski, very conveniently close to the huge Market Square. It wasn't very fashionable, typically old style, with a slight feeling of austerity about it. After they'd unpacked, they looked round the mainly cobbled streets and found a traditional restaurant serving wild boar and other local specialities; all tasting delicious, full of flavours that seemed to have been lost in most modern cuisine. Afterwards they sat on the outside terrace with their coffee and Slivovic to watch the world go by, in the warmth of the late evening. As the lights came on, twinkling in the trees, they strolled together, past diners eating al fresco and sightseers walking and laughing together. Alex just wished Lukasz could have seen the city happy once more and not the way he'd left it in 1939.

"What I have in mind for tomorrow morning, if it suits you, is to go to the tourist office and get some ideas of organised tours to Wawel castle. I know from my grandmother, there's a family plaque on a wall leading up to the castle and we can ask them about it. If we're lucky, we might find out more up-to-date information about the family's pre-war connections. I was told in England that another castle, supposedly built by one of my ancestors in 1865, is still somewhere in Krakow but I don't know if it's owned by the government or someone else now."

"That all sounds good to me, we'll be able to pick up some local maps and sightseeing tips. Everyone speaks such excellent English, I'm sure we can bend the guide's ear about the family's history. I bet they teach stuff like that in the local schools."

"Yes, good idea, I can't wait until tomorrow."

He was thrilled with the thought of it all, he bent to kiss her and took her arm in his as they walked slowly back to their hotel. Fortunately, their bedroom was at the back of the building, facing away from the street so their first Polish lovemaking wasn't disturbed by the rowdier holidaymakers who had obviously spent their evening drinking a little too much beer and enjoying the local hospitality.

The next day was even more exciting than they'd dared to hope. They'd been lucky enough to find a freelance guide, recommended by the hotel receptionist, who would give them a personal tour of the city. Her name was Krystyna Zaleska and, when she learned of Alex's family history, she showed them the plaque on the wall of the castle-walkway. It was a very touching moment for Alex; he had never seen his Polish name in such grand surroundings and really began to feel he was coming home. Krystyna was a keen student of local history and eager to help them all she could. She told them she usually finished work at lunchtime but would be more than happy to show them round the older parts of Krakow later. Roslyn suggested to Alex that they invite her for lunch and spend the afternoon, with her help, getting to know the city better. It proved to be a very wise move. Krystyna had studied history at university, but she'd never met anyone before who belonged to the old aristocracy. Alex briefly recounted what he'd learnt from his grandmother and told her some of Lukasz's story. She made some notes and promised to get back to them after she'd looked at some of the World War II archives about the Nazi and Russian occupations still held in the 17th century Renaissance Historical Museum.

It seemed Krystyna was heaven-sent, her knowledge of Krakow's history was astounding; she told them what she knew about the mass executions of the Jewish population and members of Cracovian society, described as the martyrdom of the city. After an interesting tour of the old Jewish quarter and other places of historic significance, they said good-bye, having arranged to meet at their hotel for coffee at ten o'clock the following day. In the interim, she'd managed to unearth more information about what had subsequently happened to the Wilowski houses after they were forced to leave everything behind. Next morning, Krystyna looked radiant as she kissed them on both cheeks, greeting them like old friends.

"I couldn't wait to see you. I've had such an interesting talk with the curator at the museum. He'd heard stories of your family, Alex, and said the contents of their town house here were confiscated by the Nazis but says he may know of someone whose grandparents used to work for the Wilowskis before the war. We may be able to speak to him, I have his address and he still lives quite close to the city centre."

"That's amazing news, Krystyna. If we can talk to anyone who has personal knowledge of my great grandparents it would be such a help, even small details will be invaluable."

They took a taxi to the address the curator had given Krystyna and found an old man sitting outside the house in the mid-morning sun. After introductions, he greeted them warmly and touched his forelock to Alex, as was the custom in the old days when introduced to someone of superior rank. His name was Piotr Rzewuski and he invited them into his simple home.

They all sat down in the small parlour as Krystyna asked him questions about the Wilowski family. He spoke at length turning to smile at them from time to time and at last, came to the end of his long story. Krystyna had taken notes and then translated the relevant points. Most of his family, including his grandparents and his father, had worked for Alex's family on their country estates in Lwow, for decades before the war. Apparently, as an afterthought, he added that the only difficulty was getting to Lwow nowadays, they'd have to cross the border into the Ukraine and go by train on quite a long journey. That part of Poland had been annexed after the war and the city had been renamed Lwiw.

Eventually, after many thanks and warm handshaking, they all said goodbye to the old man. Both Roslyn and Alex realised they would have never learnt so much in such a short time without Krystyna. What a wonderful find she was! But the thought of possibly having to travel to another country was daunting and they knew they couldn't do that alone. Alex wondered if they could ask Krystyna to go with them. Once outside the house, as if reading their minds, she said she had some annual leave due to her and would be more than happy to accompany them if they wanted her to do the translating for them. They jumped at her generous offer and Alex added that he would certainly pay her plus all her expenses.

"I do speak Ukrainian quite well and think I could be of assistance when you get there. I also know someone, who lives near the city, and I'm sure he would be delighted to meet you and perhaps show you round Lwiw."

"That is so kind, but we wouldn't dream of asking him to act as our tour guide."

Alex was impressed with the offer of her help but didn't want his trip to be as a tourist; he had a serious task ahead and only a few days to make full use of Krystyna's expertise. He was hoping to contact anyone who had worked on the family estate and who could provide a clearer link to the possible site of his family's supposed fortune and exactly where it had been buried. He wanted their time in Lwiw to be productive and profitable. He was keen to be there as soon as travel arrangements could be made but realised it depended on when Krystyna could leave.

"Well, what's the next thing to do?" Roslyn was eager to be ready for the next day.

"I suggest we all meet up for dinner this evening to discuss our plan of action if that's all right for you, Krystyna? Does that give you enough time to make your own personal arrangements?"

Krystyna said she'd be more than happy to do that. Then, after driving back to the city centre, they arranged to meet at their hotel at eight. When they were in their room, Roslyn kicked off her shoes and flopped on the bed.

"I don't know about you, but I'm bushed. What a day so far!"

Alex was tired too and sat on the edge of the bed, he needed time to digest everything they'd learnt but his mind was too busy to rest.

"I can't believe we've got so much information in one day, it's fantastic. Fancy meeting someone whose grandparents worked for my family."

"And it's all thanks to Krystyna, she's a true godsend. We're so lucky to have found her."

With that final remark, Roslyn closed her eyes and was soon fast asleep, Alex wished he could turn off like that, but he was too excited by everything he'd learned so far to relax. At six, he woke Roslyn with a peck on the cheek and as she opened her eyes, he said.

"I thought we might order some champagne to celebrate before dinner."

"What a wonderful idea! Come here, you gorgeous man."

He needed no further encouragement as he lay down next to her and started to kiss her lovely face. When they finally came up for air, it was after seven and both had to shower and change for dinner with Krystyna, much as they would have liked to stay in bed. Later, they met in the lobby, genuinely glad to see her again. They ate dinner in a restaurant of her choice that served Bigos, a traditional beef stew, served with dumplings then finished off the meal with Sernik, a beautiful cake made with apples and served with whipped cream. The whole evening was going very well and the conversation flowed easily. They were all excited about the next stage of their adventure. Later over coffee and Polish brandy, Krystyna who, unlike them, had been busy all afternoon, finding out about visas and travel to the Ukraine the next day, said in a very business-like manner.

"I checked at the station and there's a nightly sleeper train that leaves Krakow at 9 p.m. and arrives in Lwiw at about 6 a.m. the following morning. I believe it's quite comfortable. There's passenger sleeping accommodation and food is served on board. I've never been on it myself but it's the best and easiest way of getting to Lwiw."

"That's marvellous and it gives us one more day in Krakow before we go."

So, after Alex had paid the bill, they walked back to the hotel and arranged for Krystyna to pick them up in a taxi to go to the rail station the next evening, outside their hotel at 8 p.m. sharp. Roslyn was delighted it was all going so smoothly and was looking forward to spending another day browsing around Krakow

Their train journey the following night was quite uncomfortable, but it gave Krystyna more time to explain more fully what the old man in Krakow had told her. He'd said he still remembered his grandparents well. They had been a hardworking but happy family who not only respected the

Wilowskis but had always been treated kindly. Many generations of his family, including his great grandparents and their children, had worked on their country estate, some as servants in the manor houses and while others looked after the horses and the stables. He had told Krystyna how those same precious horses had later been sold off or seized by the Russian Army. One of the houses had been requisitioned to be the headquarters of the high-ranking officers based in Lwow. He said his family had continued to look after them, cooking and cleaning, until the handover of the city to the Ukraine by the Germans in June 1941. That was the time when the real ethnic cleansing began. The local Ukrainians had previously been a small depressed minority of the city's population and detested their Polish neighbours. The local militia started rounding up the remaining Poles and Jews who were publicly beaten up, then either shot or transported to concentration camps. Luckily, Piotr's family, because they had served their new Russian masters well, had been forewarned of the imminent dangers and so were able to escape back to Krakow before the atrocities began. Roslyn and Alex were now able to understand the old man's great courtesy to them and the reason he lived in Poland, rather than in the Ukraine. His whole family had escaped almost certain death because the Russian officers saw them merely as oppressed serfs, forced to work under the harsh yoke of the hated aristocrats, the Wilowskis. Piotr was now the only person alive who knew that this was far from the truth.

Alex was exhausted and fell asleep, but the women were still wide awake and chatted for ages about their families and upbringing as the train rattled on. Roslyn told Krystyna stories about her brother, who was a thorn in her father's side, because of his gambling and girlfriend troubles while Krystyna regaled her with memories of her overpowering mother. They talked about the many differences in their lifestyles but found they had a lot in common too. Suddenly, with a deafening screech of the brakes, the train stopped as their passports were checked by two surly guards. When, at last, they pulled into Lwiw station, they collected their belongings and stepped onto Ukrainian soil for the first time. Even at this early hour, porters were busy helping passengers carry their luggage to the taxi rank, as they waited for the next cab.

"I think we should go to straight to our hotel and freshen up before we make plans for anything else. I don't know about you, I didn't sleep well last night."

Alex took charge of the luggage as they climbed into the rather archaic-looking taxi, which had seen better days. Krystyna gave the driver the name of their hotel, the Vintage Boutique, before agreeing that they all needed a rest before lunch.

"Maybe we can have a meal later in the bar then I'll call the tourist office. The hotel staff should be able to help too, they must book lots of tours for people on short holidays."

After they'd checked in, they arranged to meet in the foyer in two hours' time.

"Mm, nice room. I'm glad we asked Krystyna to come, aren't you? I listened to the taxi driver and the reception staff talking and can't make out or even guess one single word."

"I know, it's not like any language I've ever come across before."

Roslyn put her arms round Alex's neck and gave him a long loving kiss.

"What did I do to deserve that?"

"Just for being you, darling, and to wish you success in the next step of our exciting odyssey. I do hope you find what you're looking for at last."

Alex felt they were on the verge of finding out something very important and couldn't wait to get started. In her own room, Krystyna picked up her mobile and keyed in a number, tapping her fingers on the highly polished bedside table as she waited for a reply. Then she heard a click and his unmistakable voice at the other end.

"Yurchenko here."

She held the phone close to her ear, she loved the sound of his unusual accent but tried her best to sound casual, despite her excitement at hearing his voice once more.

"Hi, Yuri, it's Krystyna here. We arrived about an hour ago, I'm meeting them soon in the hotel foyer before we go out, exploring."

She listened carefully as he got down to business straightaway and then replied.

"Of course, I won't forget. They certainly can't understand a word of Ukrainian, so all verbal communication has to go through me."

Another pause as she listened again and noted down a new phone number for future use. Yuri was obviously in a good mood, it was reflected in his endearment to her, he always called her 'little krysia' when he was happy. She smiled at his response but one day she would show him she was no little kitten and could turn into a tiger if he cheated her of what she'd been promised. She knew Yuri of old, he was a complete control freak, so despite her inner misgivings, she kept her voice light and cheery, no need to antagonise him now.

"Yes, I understand. This man, Bohdan, will contact me tonight. Yes, I'll make sure he understands. No English and no Polish either, just in case either of them knows more than we think they do. Don't worry, I'll handle it all, Yuri. I wasn't an actress for nothing, I'll give an Oscar-winning performance for their ears only."

As she put down the phone she couldn't help shaking her head, he hated relying on anyone else, even her. She took a last look in the mirror before opening the door to go downstairs and meet the trusting pair who had been so easy to fool up to now. They both greeted her warmly as she came into the bar, she loved her role in the secret drama that was being played out with this nice, unsuspecting English couple. She was more than happy to be complicit in Yuri's plot to recover Alex's buried treasure. He really needed her now and she knew she must play her part in his plan to perfection; that would make him trust her completely. She'd be able to live in luxury once the Wilowski fortune was in their hands.

She still hoped she and Yuri could come to an amicable agreement, but it would only be on her terms, she was no innocent, no man was going to use her and then drop her if she didn't fit in with his future plans and lifestyle. She had already carved out a successful career in the cut-throat world of the theatre with no help from him and she wasn't about to start begging now. She only had to maintain her cool exterior and keep playing the game until she got what she deserved, a half share and nothing less. No smaller crumbs from his table! Then, greeting Alex with no trace of her duplicity showing in her face, she accepted the drink he offered her.

The hotel bar was decorated in traditional style with simple wooden furniture; and the black and white photographs on the walls gave it an old-world atmosphere.

"It's a very unusual hotel but I hope your room's comfortable."

"It's absolutely fine, thanks."

Roslyn was less interested in their room than what they were going to do after lunch. They were all eager to see Lwiw but wanted something to eat before heading into the city, so Krystyna asked the waitress for 'Deruny' which were small potato pancakes, with a delicious filling and then ordered honey cake to go with her coffee. The menu was indecipherable to Alex and Roslyn, so they followed her lead and ordered the same.

"That was really nice, but I won't be able to eat like this for more than a few days or I'll be like a balloon. Ukrainian food is very rich."

After Alex had paid the bill, they had a look round the foyer for more leaflets then ordered a taxi. Krystyna asked the driver to take them to the centre as they wanted to see some of the city's famous old buildings. He grew eloquent in his description of the ancient glories of Lwiw and was obviously proud of his hometown. The drive was very informative and the driver himself was exceedingly well-versed in the history of the place.

It was obvious he enjoyed talking about its past glories and its history from the old Lemberg days when it had been part of the Austro-Hungarian Empire. It was a totally new experience for his passengers too and so the afternoon was well spent. Even on first sight, it appeared to be a city of beautiful architecture, half Renaissance and half Baroque. It could easily have been mistaken for any other European capital given its name "The little Paris of the Ukraine."

After giving him a generous tip and many thanks for his extensive knowledge of the city, they were dropped off at the tourist information bureau, to gather more travel information for the next day's outing.

CHAPTER TEN

They'd soon accumulated a quantity of local maps but more important, Krystyna had arranged a tour for the next day which included the Pidhortsi Castle that had once been owned by an ancestor of Alex's, whose extravagant spending was followed by bankruptcy, forcing him to sell it two centuries earlier. Early next morning, their journey, this time by bus, was pleasant enough and, although the partially ruined castle was interesting, it gave no clues as to the whereabouts of the supposed family fortune. While Roslyn and Alex walked round its lovely grounds, Krystyna asked the caretaking staff if there were any other former Polish family properties in the area and was told there were several manor houses nearer Lwiw. Two had been occupied by some former aristocrats before the war until they were arrested and deported by the Russians who took over one of them to house their officers in 1940 which matched Piotr's story. It had been deserted for many years and was now in a very dilapidated condition. It had all the hallmarks of the place they were looking for and she knew Yuri would be delighted with this news.

Satisfied with this latest information, she walked down the steps leading to the garden and found the unwitting couple sitting on a bench waiting for her. When she told them about the country houses and their proximity to the city, Alex jumped up and gave her a hug. After the ride back to their hotel, Krystyna said she was tired and would go lie down before dinner and meet them in the dining room at 8. Roslyn and Alex were weary with the long journey but ecstatic at the thought of finally going to see the former manor family houses, and even hoping one of those leads would take them to the right location of the treasure. It was all going so well and was almost too good to be true. Alex ordered a bottle of champagne once again to have with dinner and raised his glass to both ladies as he proposed a toast to their success the following day.

In the meantime, Krystyna had passed on the news to Yuri who was almost as happy as Alex had been that the search was going well. Bohdan, his hired hand, had left a message for her to call him if he was needed the following day. She phoned immediately to say she wanted him to bring a car to the hotel and to meet them in the lobby at 9 a.m. sharp, once again reminding him that he was to speak only in Ukrainian. She said she would introduce him as a friend who couldn't speak English then she rang off and changed quickly before she went down to the dining room.

The next day's outing proved to be much more rewarding, with the help of the local maps, they soon found the first manor house on the outskirts of the city, it was set in a wooded area and must have been a delightful residence in its heyday but all that remained was the outer shell of the building and an old mausoleum, which, though damaged, still stood proudly about a hundred yards from what had once been the main building. The name 'Wilowski', badly defaced and barely visible, was inscribed over the portal. The moss and undergrowth that now enveloped the ruined stonework reassured Alex that this was where his grandfather had once lived happily with his parents before the war. He took lots of photographs of the two remaining buildings from every viewpoint and could imagine his great grandmother, Karolina, carefully considering where to bury their precious treasure trove before disaster struck. He wondered if the old man, Piotr, had also have heard stories about the hiding place from his own parents. He would contact him again when they got back to Krakow. Those trusted and devoted family retainers must surely have promised to keep the secret forever and to take its memory to their graves. Maybe the burial site, over the intervening years, had become the stuff of legend, who knows? Perhaps Piotr had kept his knowledge a secret, making Alex even more determined than ever to uncover the truth of its whereabouts.

Peering at the map, he pinpointed with a red pen the exact location of the remaining ruins of the house. The family vault door had proved to be immovable, no amount of pushing and shoving had forced it to budge even an inch. He realised there was only so much that could be achieved in one visit and he would have to employ plenty of strong men to do the back-breaking work for him. He had to find out if he needed permits from either local or government authorities to allow him to undertake his search of the grounds around the old family home. He thought, with suitable proof of his identity, he could get their permission, or it was possible they wouldn't show much interest in his further explorations; after all the remaining properties had been left to rot and be virtually forgotten for so many years. He only hoped stories of possible treasure had been lost in the mists of time too, except in the memory of Piotr. Of course, Krystyna had heard the old man's story too, but Alex had no reason to question her sincerity in wanting to help him unearth the secret hiding place.

Meanwhile, Roslyn had been busy looking round what remained of the manor and could imagine it had once been a house of some wealth and splendour. The doorways and arches set in the crumbling walls still stood firm and had probably led into many other equally luxurious rooms. The old kitchen was identifiable only by a huge blackened fireplace, with a rusty iron roasting spit, that had survived the rigours of war and decay. Having read Lukasz's story, it was easy to imagine the many happy days he must have spent there in a time of innocence before foreign armies overran and destroyed the family's future dreams. Now Alex was the only one left who really cared about what had happened here and no hoard of riches and once treasured jewels could ever make up for that loss.

Krystyna and Bohdan had been talking to each other, feigning little interest in what Alex was doing but were watching keenly as he was making marks on his map from time to time after taking photographs of the various ruined buildings. Could this be the place? It had certainly aroused his interest seeing the old family name on the crypt and they both knew Yuri would want to be kept informed of everything he'd been doing. After what seemed like ages, Alex walked over to Roslyn and they both inspected the remains of the old place together. Krystyna could see them standing still for quite a while, deep in conversation, probably trying to picture the house in its pre-war glory days.

"Shall we go for lunch before we go to the other place you mentioned, Krystyna?"

Alex's desire to see the second property in the afternoon surprised her a bit; she had felt pretty sure he'd already found what he had been looking for and that meant they could have gone back to Krakow early the following day.

"Okay! That sounds fine to me." Trying to sound more cheerful than she felt.

"We do need to eat something first. I'm sure we'll find a tavern or some other place that serves food en route."

Roslyn and Alex sat in the back of the car while Bohdan drove, Krystyna by his side, and soon she spotted a sign "PECTOPAH" [restaurant] set back from the road in a small lay-by. They all piled out and were greeted warmly by the landlord who showed them into an alcove by the window, their meal was delicious, but the conversation was rather one-sided afterwards because poor Bohdan supposedly couldn't understand a word of what they were talking about. The next possible house was about a half an hour's drive away and, according to the information Krystyna had gleaned from the castle staff the previous day, had been not only a Polish-owned house but had extensive stables as well. Alex, aware of his great grandfather's love of horses and the extensive stables there, was very keen to see the second place, saying it could have been where the family used to spend their summer holidays. If it was the right spot, it had once been where his grandfather's favourite horse was always kept.

Krystyna was delighted to hear that news and prayed this would be the right one, their remaining time in Lwiw was precious if they were to be back to Krakow the day after next. So, when they were paying the bill, she asked the owner if he knew anything about the nearby manor house. He was pleased to tell her what he knew of its history and said he had known the last tenant quite well; he was an old farmer and the Ukrainians allowed him free access to the land and outhouses if he did repair work on the dilapidated buildings in lieu of paying rent. When she repeated the story, Alex was very enthusiastic and eager to see it.

"I have a really good feeling about this next one with the stables, it's bound to have some excellent hiding places and with so much outside space, it could have been kept secret more easily than the other house."

The next two hours were very much like the morning routine with Roslyn looking round the old house, which was in a much better condition than the last one, and Alex exploring the stables with his map and marking out certain areas. The grounds, after the Ukrainians took over Lwiw, had been used as a winter shelter for local farm animals. The house itself had been left empty for many years; the old caretaker, who'd lived there, had died and left no heirs. When Krystyna told Bohdan what they'd learnt from Piotr in Krakow, they both agreed it could possibly have been a relative of his, maybe an uncle, who had been given the place by the Russians as a reward for looking after them so well. It all made sense and could explain why Piotr might know about the hiding place on the Wilowski estate. Krystyna, after her initial disappointment in the morning when Alex seemed to dismiss the first house, was much happier that she now had something more positive to report to Yuri. Things were looking up and all she had to do was let Alex and Roslyn carry on thinking she was their willing assistant and helpful friend who would do all in her power to help them. It was the easiest acting role she'd ever had to play.

Yuri was eagerly waiting for news of the day's events, he could barely concentrate on anything else. If Krystyna was right, it was only a matter of time before he could set the wheels in motion to recover the hoard of silver, gold and other precious jewellery that would change his life forever. There would be no need to rely on the many stories he'd heard of other dubious claimants, searching for their confiscated properties and lost inheritances. Alex's story was not alone, there were scores of imposters who refuted his claim to be the sole heir to the buried Wilowski property, Yuri had listened to many of them. Usually, they produced vague recollections of old maiden aunts or spurious testimonies that were obvious fakes. Sometimes their motives were based on pure greed, sometimes on a wrongly-held belief that they had been born to riches that were their birth right too. Yuri himself had heard stories of a distant cousin, an Englishman, showing great interest in the grounds of the family residences. Unfortunately, no one knew exactly where the burial site was and, so far, no one else had been able to find that answer It was no co-incidence that Yuri was anxiously holding his breath in the hope that Alex was already in possession of that missing piece of the jigsaw. Hopefully, the puzzle would soon be solved and he himself would sole heir to those long-lost millions.

CHAPTER ELEVEN

Ben Edelman's story

Ben Edelman, James's partner, was an Englishman too by birth but his extended family had lived in Vienna, before the Germans annexed it in March 1938. His great grandfather, Julius Keller and wife, had lived in some splendour in their luxurious home with valuable collections of exquisite furniture and many paintings by old masters. Nevertheless, they placed equal store on the appreciation of classical music and opera. Their tastes had always been high-brow and they derived their greatest satisfaction from giving their children the best education on offer. Tutors in the finer arts and music teachers were always on hand to enlighten and coach them from an early age. So, Ben could have expected to enjoy a prosperous lifestyle, steeped in comfort and culture. That was until Hitler's troops had invaded their homeland, usurping his family's assets and fortune without any redress. The Nazis had met with little or no resistance as they were welcomed into Vienna by a crowd of over a hundred thousand people who celebrated not only their triumphant entrance into the city but the union of the Austria with Germany. Overnight, it had spelt disaster for the Keller/Edelman dynasty.

Julius Keller, being such a prominent figure in Viennese society, was one of the first Jews to be arrested and taken to Dachau concentration camp, in one of the initial forced deportations. Consequently, the family's homes, businesses and possessions were confiscated. Confusion and lawlessness were rampant throughout the city. Fortunately for some, amid all the carnage, various international organisations, realising that the senseless desecration of synagogues and the summary executions were just the beginning of the horrors that soon followed, still helped thousands of Jews leave the country. Many refugees had been able to join relatives in the U.S.A. but his great grandmother, Rachel, left alone with her young daughter, Sarah, and without American sponsors, was sent to England, practically penniless, with only the few pieces of jewellery they had manged to rescue and sew into their clothing before their home and other possessions was taken from them.

Landing in England and knowing no one, they were billeted initially with a very welcoming Jewish family in London. They were given financial aid through local welfare agencies, making sure they had adequate funds to live a simple life. English lessons were provided for older people and schools found for the children. It was such a big upheaval that many voluntary organisations sprang up to help them adjust to living in such a different country. The trauma of this big change in their circumstances took its toll on the more elderly, unable to cope with the fact that their lives would never be the same again. Rachel was never able to come to terms with the loss of her husband and her reduced status in the world. They had literally lost everything except their lives. On the other hand, his grandmother, Sarah, was young enough to learn English easily and adapt to her new surroundings. She studied hard and eventually, won a scholarship to Goldsmiths College where she trained as a teacher. She and her mother saved enough money from their meagre incomes to put down a deposit on a small terrace house near the South-East Synagogue where the congregation was mainly Ashkenazi Jews who had themselves been immigrants from Eastern Europe in the 1880s. So, they found a group of like-minded people who were sympathetic to their plight, many of whom became loyal friends.

In the meantime, Sarah had been introduced to a prospective husband, found for her by a matchmaker, as was often the tradition with orthodox Jews. His name was Ishaq Edelman, he was quite a few years older than she was and very much wanted a wife who would be able to look after him and help him in his business. He was a very successful pawnbroker with his own thriving premises just off Norwood Road in the East End. As other mothers told Rachel, he was a very good catch for a daughter without a dowry, so the wedding was arranged and, to Sarah's delight, Ishaq was not only a kind and gentle man but a very good provider. She soon gave up teaching and concentrated on helping her husband take care of his shop. He mainly dealt in jewellery, much of which came from other Jewish refugees who, unlike Rachel, had brought their gold with them or from local people were down on their luck. Often, if they couldn't repay their loans he would purchase their trinkets in lieu of the money they owed. Sarah put her mind to learning all she could about the business, including appraising their growing stock of gold and diamonds. She was a willing pupil and loved her work. When she became pregnant with their only child, she was still able to carry on working as they lived in the flat above the shop. Sarah was contented with her life and Ishaq was delighted that he was to have a child at last. When their son was born, they named him Julius Ishaq, and so, he became the first generation of the Keller family to be half English, half Austrian. The only great sadness for Sarah was the death of mother shortly afterwards before she could really enjoy being a grandmother.

The baby grew up to be everything his parents could have wanted, at school he was always first in his class and became an accomplished violinist which made them very proud. His mother carried on looking after the jewellery side of their commercial dealings and soon they opened a shop in a more affluent and prestigious part of London where their fine collection of diamonds and antique pieces was soon noticed and very much admired by dealers and connoisseurs of fine craftsmanship alike. So, all was going well until Ishaq suffered a serious heart attack and was forced to sell his original pawnbrokers' premises. Sarah was kept extremely busy looking after her husband and supervising the new shop while her son, Julius, was completing his studies at the London College of Music. When the boy suggested he could defer his musical career and help his mother to run the business, she was adamant that he should carry on with his education. She was prepared to sacrifice everything for his career.

Later Julius married a fellow student, Hannah, and her parents couldn't have been happier. Their wedding took place in the same synagogue they'd always attended but, when Ishaq's health took a turn for the worse, Julius insisted that he should go fulltime into the family business, knowing his mother would be unable to manage everything on her own. When Ishaq suffered his final heart attack and died, they decided to move into a much bigger house and all live together. So, their new baby son, Benjamin, was brought up jointly by his doting grandmother, Sarah, and loving parents in a happy home, constantly surrounded by music.

His childhood consisted of visits to concerts and art galleries with his grandmother, ensuring Benjamin's love of all things cultural. She would tell him stories of the family's previous lifestyle in Vienna before the Nazis had robbed them of not only their beautiful houses but their collection of valuable antiques and paintings. When he went to school, he studied modern European history and art for his A levels, but he also had a very practical streak and was interested in the latest electronic technology. So, he decided he would forego university and instead, dedicate himself to learning all about the current craze for mobile phones which were then all teenagers 'must haves'. The whole family was shocked, expecting him to follow an academic career, but he used the inheritance his grandfather had left him to open his own small phone shop in the East End. He had certainly inherited his business acumen from both his grandparents, his enterprise was innovative in offering favourable rental schemes whilst also selling the latest expensive brands which appealed to an increasingly affluent younger generation. So, his business prospered as he opened more shops with eager staff, happy to work on very generous commissions and yearly bonuses. His annual sales figures rocketed.

Eventually, his enthusiasm outgrew his still limited finances and, when he had the chance to become a junior partner in a successful electronics company, owned by James Chapell, he jumped at his golden opportunity; together they made a perfect combination. Of course, the fact that James later developed minor health problems and wanted a quieter life in the sun, made the choice even more fortuitous for Benjamin. It was decided that he should take over the daily running of the London offices as an equal partner. The picture would have been perfect if, as James hoped, his daughter, Roslyn, were to fall in love with his handsome new protégé and marry him, making Benjamin his son-in-law as well. Unhappily, that scenario didn't happen.

Unknown to anyone else, Ben had been conducting investigations into his own genealogy and started pursuing the often-thankless task of trying to find out what had happened to the Keller's houses in Vienna. Their valuable paintings were long gone, often in the possession of unscrupulous collectors who bought ex-Nazi loot from equally disreputable dealers on a 'no questions asked' basis. Fortunes changed hands and very few records were kept. On his many holiday trips to Austria, Ben spent his time searching for the whereabouts of the houses previously owned by his family and trying to locate their long-lost contents, it became an obsession with him. He had already obtained old catalogues from several Austrian art galleries which contained itemised details of the former Keller paintings and antiques stolen in 1938. The Nazis had confiscated everything of value from their homes, which were then commandeered as living quarters for high-ranking S.S. officers until the war ended in 1945. It wasn't easy to follow the later route of those priceless objects, but Ben had contacted various professional trackers who were helping him to trace what had rightfully belonged to his family. He had discovered that two of these valuable paintings had been presented as a gift by a German Gruppenfuhrer to a Russian General who commanded the troops occupying the south-eastern part of Poland in 1939. He, in turn, was billeted with other senior officers in a house once owned by some Polish aristocrats who had either been executed or sent to gulags in Siberia. The paintings had been proudly displayed there until the U.S.S.R. decided to change their allegiance to the Allied Forces in 1942. No further knowledge of their whereabouts had ever surfaced but the two possibilities were that they had been sent back to Russia for safe-keeping or been hidden somewhere in the Ukraine. There the trail ended.

Ben's determination to pursue any thread of evidence that could lead him to finding them never faltered, analysing all the possibilities of their fate. He only had the name of the former general to go on, so it was possible that he had kept them himself. In the chaos that followed, fortunes were gained and lost as people's wealth varied under each new party leader. Ben decided it was easier to concentrate on the scenario that the two pictures had been hidden somewhere in the Ukraine. He used his position in 'Cosmocompute' to emphasise the virtue of expanding the firm's interests into Eastern Europe and thus could enhance his search for his own lost property.

CHAPTER TWELVE

The day after Alex and Roslyn got back from Lwiw, they made an appointment with the Bank of Krakow to see if they needed to open an account there to have a safety deposit box. The manager was very helpful and told them only proof of identity and photographic evidence was necessary. They asked if he knew of a reliable translator they could hire for half a day to complete some business in the city and were directed to the City Hall in the main square where someone would be able to help them. They had left Krystyna after saying their farewells at the train station the previous day. It had been a pleasant and comfortable journey back and Alex had given her not only all her expenses and the agreed amount for the time she'd spent with them in the Ukraine but also a very generous tip for all her help. He knew he could never have found the right places to search and photograph without her assistance.

When they went into the beautiful entrance of the Hall, they asked a receptionist if they could hire an official interpreter for the afternoon and were directed to a small office in a nearby street where a young man was working at his computer. He got up and, in very good English, answered that the rate for the company's services was $35 per hour plus travelling time. When Alex asked if it was possible to get someone that afternoon, the young man seemed delighted.

"I'd be very happy to do that for you personally, when would you like to begin?"

His name was Ludwik and he was happy to be out of the office for the whole afternoon. After lunch, they picked him up and got a taxi in the square to take them to the address where the old man, Piotr, was living. During the ride, Alex explained that they had already met this man but wanted to question him further about his connection with the Wilowski family.

"Are you a Wilowski?" He asked, looking surprised.

"Yes, I am. My great grandparents lived here and in Lwow before the war."

"It's very good to meet you, I've heard of your family, but I've never met a member of the old aristocracy before. It's an honour for me to help you in any way I can."

They'd reached their destination and asked the driver to wait when Roslyn said.

"I do hope Piotr's in; we don't have a phone number for him, so we couldn't call him to let him know we were coming."

Alex knocked on the door and soon heard a key being turned. When the door opened, Piotr looked a little bewildered to see them again but immediately invited them into his home. Alex greeted him and shook his hand, introducing the interpreter in the few Polish words he'd learned. "Dobry dzien, Piotr. To jest Ludwik."

Ludwik then spoke in Polish, obviously explaining why he was with them. Alex hoped he wouldn't be too surprised to see them again and asked the young man to explain that they would like to ask him more questions about the old Wilowski houses they'd seen in Lwow. As Alex asked each question, Ludwik translated it into Polish and then turned to them to explain Piotr's answers while Roslyn made a note of them.

It now seemed he remembered a great deal more than he'd told them before; he said his memory sometimes failed him but two important things he now remembered were that his great uncle, Stanislaw, had remained in Lwow and looked after one of the old manor houses after the rest of the family had returned to Krakow, a job he did until he died. Roslyn prompted Alex to ask if he would know which of the two houses they inspected was the one his uncle had lived in. Here, Piotr had to stop and think for a long time, then he said quite decisively to Ludwik that he now recalled it was the one with the one with stables.

"Just as I thought, I was right the first time."

Alex whispered to Roslyn, who now looked a little baffled, replied quietly.

"But you made us all think the second place, the one with the stables was the right one. You seemed to dismiss the first one and lose all interest in it. I don't understand."

"I'll explain it all later, darling."

She knew there must be a good reason for that but didn't want to question him further in front of Ludwik and the old man. Then Alex asked Ludwik to write a question down on a piece of paper with the words 'YES' or 'NO' in Polish after it, which he did. He told him to give it to the old man and ask him to circle the correct answer to the question. He asked Ludwik if he would mind leaving them for a few minutes while Piotr read and answered the question.

"That's okay. I'll go outside and have a cigarette if you don't mind."

"No. That's perfect." Alex replied.

Roslyn guessed this last question was the most important one and he didn't want anyone else to know the answer.

"Call me when you want me."

"Yes, fine. I'll do that."

When Piotr had finished reading and circled the answer, he handed it back to Alex and got up to go into his bedroom. A few minutes later, he came back again with what appeared to be a very old envelope and he handed it to Alex with a smile on his face. Alex nodded to him to let him know he understood, shook his hand and gave the old man a pat on the shoulder. It was a mystery to Roslyn but obviously, it was what Alex had wanted to know, so it must be very important, and she could barely contain her curiosity. He carefully put the envelope in an inside pocket of his jacket as if it was very precious. Then he pulled out a large wad of Polish 100 zlotys banknotes from another inner pocket and handed them to Piotr, who only sighed deeply as if he'd been relieved of an onerous burden. He kissed Alex's hand. No words were needed from either man.

"Could you ask Ludwik to come back, Roslyn?"

When the interpreter returned, Piotr whispered something to Ludwik who nodded his head then Alex explained to him that everything was fine, he had all the information he needed now and he was very satisfied with the job he'd done. So once again, they said goodbye to the old man with heavy hearts. Alex knew he wouldn't see him again and asked Ludwik to thank him with all his heart and to say he would never forget him. There were tears in both men's eyes as they said their final farewells. The old man stayed by his front door and watched them go. His lifelong promise to his own grandparents was fulfilled at last and he could die in peace knowing his service to the Wilowski family was now complete.

Before they dropped Ludwik off at his office he said he had something to tell them, Piotr had whispered to him

"Don't trust the Polish woman."

"That's strange, I wonder who he meant, it could only be Krystyna."

"Sorry, I don't know, but that's all he said."

After paying him for his three hours' work, Alex was still a little mystified but satisfied with the afternoon's result. He now had the last piece of the treasure puzzle in his pocket which he wouldn't be able to read yet, but which eventually would give him the full picture of what his great grandmother had done to preserve the Wilowski's cherished possessions. Roslyn was equally surprised at the old man's remark and wanted to know what he meant.

"I'll tell you everything once we get back to the hotel, Roslyn. Just be patient for a little while longer, and then no more secrets, I promise."

He inclined his head towards the taxi driver as he spoke which she took it to mean that even the walls have ears, one could never tell who knew whom in this city. She squeezed his hand to let him know she understood then sat quietly, thinking of old Piotr and the sadness of his solitary life. He was all alone in his small house with no one to comfort him; Krystyna had said he was a widower and had never had children, so she hoped they could do something more for him when Alex had sorted out his own financial gain from the family property, if indeed it was ever found.

The cab pulled into the kerb outside their hotel, Alex paid and tipped the driver who said "Dziekuje." (Thank you) in appreciation of his generosity. They walked to the reception desk and took their keys before getting into the lift, both happy that their day had proved so successful. Their time in Krakow was coming to a worthwhile end and had been a rollercoaster of emotions especially for Alex who had felt strong bonds with his unknown Polish ancestors for the very first time. Roslyn walked into their room and kicked off her shoes, she felt a strange longing to be back at home once more, surrounded by her own things and listening to a language she understood. She sat down and waited until Alex was ready to tell her all he had been keeping to himself since Lwow.

"I'm sorry, my darling, I wasn't being exactly truthful with you, please forgive me but I've been trying to sort out so many thoughts buzzing around in my mind. Don't ask me why, but in Lwiw, I felt as if I was being watched just a little too closely by both Krystyna and Bohdan. They seemed to be huddled together too much, taking in everything I wrote down and photographed. You were inside the houses most of the time while I was outside looking for clues to the burial site, wherever it is. As I looked around the grounds, it was as if the back of my neck was tingling and my every movement was being catalogued for future scrutiny. Does that sound crazy?"

"No, it doesn't. I know exactly what you mean. Even I was aware that they seemed to be taking more than a casual interest in your search and I thought their relationship was very strange and distant. I'm certain they weren't friends, Krystyna was very business-like with him, more like an employer. I caught them once in deep conversation and she was showing her irritation because he was obviously disagreeing with something she'd said. Very odd!"

"So, do you think that Krystyna wasn't all she pretended to be?"

"It does sound that way, but she's gone now so it doesn't matter anyway."

He pulled the envelope Piotr had given him out of his pocket and opened it.

"Of course, it's all in Polish but it is a long list of some sort. Nice handwriting but indecipherable. We'll have to wait until we go to the bank tomorrow and have it translated by someone trustworthy. Do you think I'm being paranoid?"

Roslyn thought seriously for a moment, and then smiled sweetly.

"You're going slightly mad but never mind, I love you all the same. But you still haven't told me which house was which. Where did your great grandma eventually bury the heirlooms?"

"I'm not a 100 % certain but I'd put all my money on the first house, the one with the family crypt and the inscription 'Wilowski' above the door."

CHAPTER THIRTEEN

It was exactly as Alex thought, the bank manager suggested a local justice of the peace, who could translate the contents of the envelope and write two certified copies for him to keep. One of the copies plus the original handwritten list were locked away in the safe deposit box with the marked maps he'd used in Lwiw. Both Roslyn and Alex had keys in case either needed to open the box separately; their photographs were taken for future identification and kept for bank reference. When all the necessary forms were signed and the bank charges paid, they left and made their way to the airport by taxi. It was sad in a way for them to leave Poland, apart from being Alex's family home, it had given them answers to so many questions that had been left in limbo for over seventy years. Alex would always remember Piotr and his unswerving loyalty to the Wilowski family. When he had given him the carefully kept envelope with the family crest on it, Alex had felt at last he was truly a part of the old dynasty and his search for whatever his great grandmother, Karolina, had buried would not be in vain.

When they got back to London after a pleasant flight, Roslyn was very tired and wanted to go straight back to her flat, so they took a taxi and were soon in her lovely warm sitting room drinking coffee and reliving some of their holiday's highlights. Alex was weary and decided to stay the night but wanted to catch an early train back to Cheltenham the following morning. Their first foray to Krakow had been a wonderful voyage of discovery with so many added bonuses, meeting Piotr being the best moment of all for Alex. They had found out so much more than they ever expected during their trip to Lwiw and meeting Krystyna had opened more avenues than would have been possible without her. Alex began to think he had been a little unfair doubting her motives, when it was possible she had been not only a brilliant guide but her interest in his search had been an innocent one. What could she possibly have to gain from him now? All the essential information was safely locked away in a secure bank that only he and Roslyn had access to; he would try to dismiss all those misgivings and concentrate on what had to be done next.

When he was back at work the next day, he asked his flatmate, Jason, if he minded Roslyn coming the following weekend.

"Mind! I'd love to see her again and I'd like to introduce you to my new girlfriend. We can all go out for a meal on Friday evening,"

"That's great, I'm sure Roslyn would love to meet her. It can be a double celebration, we're going to make our engagement official this weekend. I only have to find a ring now."

"She's perfect for you and you should grab her before she gets away."

They both laughed and decided to start the festivities that evening with a drink or two after work. Alex couldn't have been more pleased, that they could announce their engagement officially at the weekend.

Every afternoon after work, he looked at so many engagement rings in various jewellers, his mind was in a spin. He very soon decided to take Roslyn to choose for herself, he had no idea which one she would like. So, he went into a small gift shop to buy an outrageously fake ring to give her at the restaurant on Friday evening before taking her to shop for the real thing the day after. He knew she would take it in her stride and enjoy the joke, so he got a gaudy gift box tied with tinsel to present to her. With that done, he spent his intervening evenings, making more permanent records of the notes he'd scribbled hurriedly when he was looking at the two Wilowski sites in Lwiw. He updated his wall-charts and maps, while it was still clear in his mind. If he'd forgotten anything he could always ask Roslyn, who had an amazing memory, he admired her attention to even the smallest details. Their romance had blossomed whilst they were in Poland, and recent events had further cemented their commitment to exploring Alex's ancestral past. It was to have far-reaching consequences that neither of them could have possibly envisaged.

When he presented Roslyn with the artificial engagement ring, they all fell about laughing. Jason was staying at his girlfriend's flat for the weekend, giving Alex and Roslyn plenty of time to discuss his plans for unearthing the hidden treasure trove in Lwiw. He had been researching the channels he would have to pursue for permission to do more work on the site. He'd found out there would be no trouble in employing local labour to do the heavy digging but official permits to carry out other work might prove more troublesome. Roslyn wondered if they could ask Ben for some help, he had quite a lot of important contacts in that part of Europe now and could possibly pull some strings for him.

"It's just a thought, I do remember Dad was saying once how much they've expanded their business into Eastern Europe since Ben joined the company."

"I may need all the help I can get right now so it's definitely worth asking him. Even if he doesn't know anyone, he may have some ideas about dealing with officials there."

It was nearly two in the morning before they finally went to bed, tired but very happy. Roslyn had been daydreaming more and more about getting married and settling down with Alex, she knew that he was the man she wanted and could envisage a happy life with him. He had been thinking the same thing for a while but wanted to ask her formally when he gave her the real engagement ring; he knew she would love to have the wedding ceremony in Marbella and possibly, the reception in her father's villa. It would make it a real family affair if his grandmother could be there as well. Roslyn had been planning that scenario, her only slight worry was whether she should invite her brother, Markus, to come. She would love for him to be there, but she had to consider her father's feelings as well.

With breakfast over, Alex was feeling quite excited as they set off for the city centre and he steered her towards a jeweller's, where he'd seen some beautiful rings on display. They opened the door and the salesman invited them to sit down while he carefully placed a black velvet cloth on the showcase and then he brought out a tray of sparkling rings.

"Is there anything here you like, darling?"

"I like them all."

The young man smiled, obviously used to that reaction, said.

"I have a very lovely aquamarine and diamond one that you might like to see."

"I do love aquamarines, could I look at that one too?"

When he'd gone to get it from the shop window, Roslyn turned to Alex and said.

"If it's too expensive, you will tell me, won't you?"

"You can have any ring you like, you're worth it, my darling."

The ring was gorgeous, a large square-cut aquamarine with two big diamonds on each side set in white gold, exactly what she'd always dreamed of; she tried it on and it fitted perfectly. She lifted her hand as it shone brilliantly under the lights.

"I adore this one, it's exquisite. Do you like it, Alex?"

"I hoped you'd like that one. I saw it in the window this week and thought it was just the one for you. It's as beautiful as you are."

"Oh, sweetheart! You're such an angel, I really love it, thank you"

"Well, that seems to be a sale. This is definitely the one that we want, thank you."

The assistant was delighted and brought out a box which matched the ring. He took Alex over to the other side of the shop to do all the paperwork.

"I have to say, that is one of the most pleasing sales I've ever made. Your fiancée has excellent taste and she certainly had no hesitation in choosing it. Well done!"

Alex was doubly pleased that not only had Roslyn made a good choice of ring but that it was the one he'd hoped she'd prefer. The box was wrapped and given to him as he re-joined Roslyn.

"Now, for lunch, I think. Let's go to the place we went to on our first date. Do you remember?"

"Of course, I'll never forget that evening as long as I live."

So, arm in arm, they walked to The Lumiere Restaurant. Alex had already ordered a bottle of Bollinger and as soon as their glasses were filled, he took her hand and gazed into her eyes.

"My dearest darling Roslyn, will you marry me? I've never loved anyone before I met you and please, say you'll be my wife very soon."

As he put the ring on her finger, she smiled at him and said simply.

"You've made me happier than I ever thought possible. I would love to marry you."

The meal that followed was delicious and the champagne crisply cold. Roslyn looked down at her ring from time to time, admiring its simple beauty.

"I wondered if you thought June would be too soon for us to get married. It wouldn't be too hot in Marbella. We can invite your grandma to fly out, and then we'll be a proper family, don't you think?"

"I'm sure she'll be delighted, and she'll be able to meet your father before the ceremony. By the way, do you want a big wedding or just a simple come-as-you-please do?"

Roslyn laughed, Alex knew that only a very special white dress would do for her wedding day.

When they got back to the flat, they decided to phone both her father and Alice to break the news of their engagement. Roslyn was delighted at their responses and then she asked her dad if they could have the wedding in Marbella in June. James was over the moon with the thought of his beloved Roslyn tying the knot under his own roof and hosting the ceremony and reception that he had always dreamed of for her. He exchanged a few words with Alex and congratulated him on his wise choice of a wife.

"I'm so happy for you both and am delighted to have you as my son-in-law, she is the apple of my eye, as you know, and my only wish that you both have a long and blessed life together."

"Thank you very much for all your good wishes and I'm on cloud nine myself that Roslyn's promised to be my wife. I can only reassure you that I will always love her and will try to make her happy, sir."

"That's all I can ask for and I will be more than pleased to have the pleasure of meeting your grandmother for the first time. I'm sure we'll get along famously. I know Roslyn had only glowing words for her and can't wait to see her again."

Alex hoped this was to be the beginning of a whole new life for all the family and only wished his grandfather could have been here with them to enjoy seeing him get married to his beautiful bride. It was going to be a marriage made in Heaven, of that he was sure!

CHAPTER FOURTEEN

Easter seemed to come very quickly. They'd decided to spend two days at Roslyn's place in London before flying from Heathrow to Malaga. James was there to greet them, beaming from ear to ear as he saw them come into the arrivals lounge. Roslyn rushed up to him and hugged him, quite forgetting Alex was pushing the luggage trolley. He shook hands with James and looked in admiration at the happy reunion of his soon-to-be wife and his future father-in-law. This is when he really missed having a father of his own.

"What wonderful news, my boy! You've made me so happy, I had begun to think I'd never see this day."

"I'm delighted too, James. I was afraid she might say no, she's a very special and determined lady, as you know, and I love her very much."

"Glad to hear that, my boy, and I know she's made an excellent choice."

They arrived at the waiting car, the car was still cool, even in the hot sunshine. They piled all their cases in the spacious boot before James drove to the exit.

"What a lovely welcome, I hoped you'd come to the airport, Daddy."

"Of course, I wanted to see you as soon as possible, my darling girl, and my prospective son-in-law. I wouldn't have missed it for the world, even though I did forego my golf session this morning."

He grinned and patted her arm, lifting her left hand to look at her new ring.

"Now that's what I call an engagement ring, a real bobby-dazzler! You have very good taste, Alex."

"Not really, she chose it herself, but I have to admit I did steer her towards a certain jeweller in Cheltenham and phoned them to put that particular ring in the centre of window before we arrived."

"Really, you didn't tell me that, you old sly-boots!"

It was going to be such a good holiday for everyone, Roslyn was enjoying being with the two men she loved best in the world. Alex was looking forward to becoming part of a new family and, for James, the wedding couldn't come too soon, then hopefully, before long, the patter of tiny feet would naturally follow. Everything was bound to go well or so they all thought.

The journey to the villa took about an hour, Maria had laid out a tray of drinks and bucket of ice under the veranda roof next to the table and chairs set out for a late lunch.

"I thought we'd save the champagne for later but I'm so over the moon, let's not wait!" He called out to Maria. "Traer en la champagne, por favor."

"You ready eat lunch now?" She enquired, somewhat flustered.

"No, No. Champagne solo, por favor; con cuatro copas, una para Tu."

James' Spanish was as limited as her English, but they always seemed to cope. When she brought out the ice-cold bottle and four glasses, Alex offered to open it and managed to do so without spilling a drop, glasses were handed round and James stood up proudly.

"I would like to propose a toast to Roslyn and Alex on their engagement and forthcoming marriage. May all their troubles be little ones!" He raised his glass and saluted them.

"Cheers! Salud!"

They drank to the happy couple, Maria gazed at Roslyn's ring with admiration and tears in her eyes, feeling so honoured, just a simple girl born in the mountains, to be included in this family gathering.

"Me encanta tu anillo, que hermoso!" (I love your ring, how beautiful!)

She responded by kissing Maria on the cheek

"Tu despues, mia cara." (You next, my dear.)

After lunch, Roslyn and Alex went upstairs to unpack and have a siesta, they were tired after an early morning start and the flight. James retired to his study and decided to phone Ben who was still in Austria sorting out a glitch in a system they'd just installed.

"Hi, Ben, James here. Sorry to phone at the weekend but wondered how you got on".

"As a matter of fact, there was more to it than we thought, so I need a guy over here to sort out the issue. I might stay a while longer, all depends on what we find."

"Do you want me to come back to London to keep an eye on things there?"

"No, no, not at all, everything's fine. Max will take charge while I'm away and you know how competent he is. Please, don't worry, I'll keep you in the loop."

"Okay, as long as you're sure. We must discuss a way forward to give you a bigger share in the company when I see you next."

"Look, James, that's not necessary now, I'm happy that you put so much trust in me. To change the subject, how's our lovely Roslyn and her young man?"

"They both arrived a few hours ago and the happy news is that they got engaged after their holiday to Poland. I still haven't spoken to them about what happened there, I do know Alex was delighted to be in the land of his ancestors and

92

wanted to get to know more about his great-grandparents' former property over there."

"I'd love to hear all about it when we get together, sounds a lot like my own family history. It's quite a coincidence that we seem to have so much in common. I'd like to talk to him about it when we next meet."

"You must come over to Marbella soon and you can talk to him yourself."

"Anyway, James, lovely to speak to you. Give them both my very best wishes and hope I get an invitation to the wedding."

"You certainly will, I'll make sure of that. Well, cheers for now and good luck in Vienna. Bye"

As he headed off for a stroll on the beach before the sun set, James thought to himself,

'What a great guy he is, it's a pity Roslyn didn't fall for him.'

The following week was one of great jollity; they lunched and dined out and just enjoyed being together, talking non-stop. They exchanged their news with James who was very keen to learn about Alex's latest discoveries and assured him he would help him financially, if necessary, and back him all the way if need be. The only downside to the week was when anonymous emails started to arrive for Alex, obviously aimed at trying to intimidate him. He couldn't imagine who was sending them. They said he was being watched and that his life was in danger if he ever went back to Poland or Lwiw. It brought back memories of his doubts about Krystyna's true intentions. Was she just an innocent bystander or was she working for someone else undercover?

"They're not going to stop me, Roslyn, just when we're about to find where the money is buried, I can't be frightened off that easily."

Roslyn was beginning to worry but she knew he must do what he had to do, he wasn't a man to be cowed by vague threats. When he got yet another email, repeating the warning, Alex became angry; there was never any return address and he felt he was being played like a fish on a hook. The next message was even more direct; this gave him a time, date and a location in Marbella where he was told to meet the e-mailer adding 'if you know what's good for you'.

He could have laughed at the gangster style language but knew he had to tell Roslyn and her father, who would try to talk him out of the meeting, which, of course, they did in no uncertain terms. They both thought he was taking a huge risk liaising with an unknown crook, especially in a foreign country, but he assured them he would be very careful and make certain they met in a public place with plenty of people around. Then, for no apparent reason, the meeting was cancelled by email again, with no further explanation. It kept annoying Alex, who couldn't figure out why all the cloak and dagger stuff. Was it a setup of some kind or just another way of frightening him? He didn't have long to wait before a new text appeared on his mobile.

"Tell no one. Saturday 7 a.m. sharp at the Old Beach Hut."
He knew the location so no problem there. James was going fishing, so, apart from Maria, he and Roslyn would be alone in the house, so he could slip out of bed and be back in time to waken her for breakfast. He knew she'd been longing for a leisurely lie-in and besides she wouldn't even know he had gone.

During dinner on Friday evening, Alex told them he'd received another email cancelling the previous meeting, which was a great relief. They'd both been against him taking such a dangerous step into the unknown and had asked him to call the local police, but he refused, not wanting to involve them if the emails were only a scare tactic. Roslyn was still very anxious

94

and developed a bad headache, so she excused herself from the table, leaving the men to have a late-night cognac with strong black coffee. James purposely decided not to discuss the contentious subject and instead talked about more cheerful topics like their wedding plans and possible guest list which lightened the mood. He had already insisted on hiring the best wedding organiser in Marbella who would make sure everything went off without a hitch. He asked Alex if they had made any honeymoon plans because he had a few interests outside his normal telecommunications business and, unknown to Roslyn, he now co-owned a small boutique hotel on the beach in Kingstown, St Vincent, managed by one of his former employees who had also taken early retirement. Alex thought it sounded a perfect spot for a relaxing two weeks in the Caribbean sun. Tomorrow, he'd ask Roslyn what she thought of the idea.

Alex wished him a successful fishing trip and hoped to see him soon. James went to his room, a contented man, delighted at his daughter's choice of a future husband, he would make an excellent son-in-law and a good father. Roslyn was already in bed, sleeping soundly, when Alex quietly opened the bedroom door. He put his watch and mobile phone on the bedside table then decided to take a quick shower so as not to waken her in the morning before his early start.

Mixed thoughts were still buzzing round in his mind as the hot water drenched his body. Who could these mysterious persons be who were trying to prevent him from unearthing his fortune? He only wanted what was rightfully his and no one was going to make him change his mind with idle threats. He wished he knew the identity of the man who was so keen to besmirch his family name. The time had come to face whoever wanted to steal his inheritance and more importantly, cheat him of his birth-right and dishonour many generations of his predecessors.

CHAPTER FIFTEEN

Alex had been missing for 24 long hours and Roslyn, after listening to all the advice she'd been offered, still didn't know what she should do. Reading the headlines in one of the Sunday morning newspapers had been like a sudden slap in the face for her, she couldn't believe her eyes and felt the bile rise in her throat as she re-read them.

"The body of a man was discovered floating in a small cove off Nueva Andalucía beach, west of Puerto Banus this morning. The police are anxious for any person with information to contact them immediately."

There had been no further contacts from anyone and she was going crazy with worry. Could the body the police had found be Alex's? It could be anyone, she realised that, maybe some inexperienced swimmer who'd got into difficulties or a drunken tourist taking one risk too many. She was beginning to get paranoid about not hearing from him but calling the police still wasn't an option. She'd tried to phone Ben again but there was no answer and she couldn't contact her father so, she was getting desperate. She'd already had a phone call from Gill Armstrong, who was going to act as her bodyguard, saying she would be arriving in the late afternoon and would be with her as soon as possible. Roslyn had told no one of her arrival, except the maid, Maria, who was busy preparing a room for her, next to Roslyn's. If only Alex's mobile phone would ring, then, at least, she could speak to him again and feel less helpless, but she knew she mustn't panic at this crucial stage of the negotiations to release him. She'd found all the information about the security box, but Bohdan hadn't contacted her and seemed in no hurry to do so, which worried her even more.

At that moment, her new phone rang, it was Gill who'd just arrived in Malaga and was in a taxi heading to the villa while they were speaking. Roslyn could have wept with joy to hear a friendly voice at last.

"I'll be at your place in just over half an hour, any news?"

"Nothing." She replied glumly. "But I've just read the headline in our local paper to say a body has been found in the sea near here and I can't help thinking it might be Alex."

The tone of her voice sounded to Gill as if her new client was struggling to keep a tight rein on her emotions. All she could do was to assure Roslyn that the odds of its being him were thousands to one. She knew in her heart that her reassurances wouldn't calm her down for long and thanked God she'd arrived in the nick of time. The taxi took ages to wind in and out of the flow of traffic from the city, she took out her iPad and began re-reading Aidan Spencer's latest email with 'CONFIDENTIAL' emphasised in the heading. In it he had voiced his concerns about Ben not wanting the company to be involved any further with either the kidnappers or the negotiations. He advised her that Roslyn's safety was now their primary concern and emphasised the need for compete discretion, not even her father must know of Gill's true purpose in staying in Marbella. He felt the fewer people who knew the truth the better, no further reasons were given. She clicked the email off and wondered why Aidan was so adamant about the absolute secrecy of her job. Surely her father and Ben Edelman were above suspicion, but she bowed to whatever her boss ordered. It wasn't for her to question his instructions.

As the taxi drew up to the villa, Roslyn opened the door. The driver lifted her luggage from the boot as Gill greeted her 'old friend' with a kiss on both cheeks. They smiled at each other. Roslyn, feeling a great sense of relief, asked if she'd had a pleasant trip and ushered her into the hallway. As the car drove off, Maria busied herself taking the cases to her newly prepared room which met with Gill's every need. She'd even added a huge bowl of hand-picked flowers from the garden.

"I'll give you a little while to freshen up then show you the rest of the house before dinner. Maria's a wonderful cook and the weather's so balmy, I thought we'd eat alfresco this evening. The view over the fairy-lights of Marbella is lovely from the terrace."

Gill thought this was going to be one of her more pleasant assignments in such luxurious surroundings, but she mustn't be deluded into thinking that her job was going to be easy. Roslyn seemed a delightful person and she knew instinctively that they were going to get on, they were about the same age which gave credence to her being just a college friend. She didn't think Mr. Chapell would be any the wiser and especially seeing she had inwardly digested all the background information Aidan had provided about Roslyn's education and career so far, the only details she needed to get from Roslyn were more recent events in her life so that she had the full picture.

Later, sitting outside with their after-dinner coffee was the ideal time to find out exactly what had been happening since they last spoke. Maria's lack of English was also a blessing, so they could talk openly without her understanding a word. The first rule of Gill's job was to trust no one and always be on her guard against loose talk, Roslyn had been trying to keep her inner turmoil under control until they were alone. Gill suggested a walk on the beach the next morning so that they could speak freely, just in case the villa was bugged which seemed very unlikely but had to be taken into consideration. When the whole series of events leading up to the Alex's disappearance and the later phone calls had been recounted, only then did Roslyn break down and cry. Gill put her arm round her shoulder and whispered.

"Hold on, you're doing fine. We'll find him and I'm sure it won't be long before we have some more news and hear from the kidnappers. Remember, I'm here for you, my first concern is to keep you safe and I won't leave you until Alex is back home again."

This seemed to calm Roslyn down, but it didn't allay her anxiety about the body that had been found. She asked Gill if she would phone the police anonymously to find out if they had identified the drowned man.

"It could be Alex lying there but I must know for sure. With your experience, maybe you can think of some suitable explanation for enquiring about a missing person without making them suspicious.

"Yes, I can do that, I can say I'm calling from England about someone who's on holiday here and that I was concerned when I heard the news. I don't necessarily have to tell them the truth; I could be any one, a concerned relative and give a false name. They will have dozens of people phoning about that headline in the paper. Don't worry about that, it's all part of my job. I'll use my business phone which can be checked if they need to, but I doubt they'll bother."

"Can you make that call soon before I go out of my mind?"

"Yes, sure, before we go for our walk in the morning. Just tell me once again about the phone conversation you had with Bohdan, he seems to be the only tangible link between the kidnappers and your visit to the Ukraine."

Next morning, as they walked back across the beach, Roslyn told Gill about the whole Lwiw saga including Bohdan's business-like relationship with Krystyna, their friendly guide. It all sounded rather implausible to her now, she was amazed that they had both been so gullible and had been taken in by it all.

"Do you think this Krystyna is involved as well?"

"I honestly don't know, but how come she knew Bohdan at all if he's now one of the kidnappers? It sounds a bit fishy to me."

The call to the police had been inconclusive but they were told that a facial photograph of the dead man would be published in the next edition of the newspaper, which did nothing to ease Roslyn's fears. James was due back the following morning and Gill thought he might be the best person to go to the police, particularly if Alex was still missing. He would have to know about the disappearance and possible kidnapping immediately plus the headline in the paper. She realised Roslyn wouldn't be able to keep her worries to herself once her father was home.

The next evening meal was a very strained affair with neither of the women able to summon up an appetite even for Maria's excellent dinner and she was obviously disappointed as she cleared away the dishes. They both decided on an early night, finding small talk difficult under the circumstances, the only thing they did discuss was how to provide a suitable background story of their relationship so that her father wouldn't suspect Gill was anything other than a good friend of Roslyn's. They both lay in bed in their separate rooms, thinking of the day ahead and hoping that they would hear some good news.

The next morning was dull and cloudy, most unusual for the time of year, so they ate breakfast inside and waited for something to happen but there were no phone calls and the only disruption was the sound of a car in the drive way, which made Roslyn jump up, she knew it would be her father. He was busy unloading his catch and saying goodbye to his fishing pals as she ran up to him and threw herself into his arms. He knew something was terribly wrong and held her close.

"What's wrong, my darling girl? Whatever is the matter?"

"Oh, Dad. It's awful, Alex has disappeared."

At that moment, Gill appeared and smiled sadly.

"I'm sorry to have to meet you this way, Mr. Chapell, I'm Gill Armstrong, an old friend of Roslyn's. She asked me to come and stay, I hope you don't mind."

Poor James was completely nonplussed and could only shake her hand as he held on to his daughter, still weeping and not making any sense.

"What do you mean, disappeared? When did this happen? I've only been gone for two days but I was afraid of something like this. We should have taken more notice of those threatening messages."

"All I know is that Alex went missing early on Saturday morning. Roslyn received a voicemail and calls from both him and a man who said he'd be freed when he gave them some details of a safety deposit box in Krakow. That's all I can tell you."

James was stunned, only a few days ago he'd left a happy household full of exciting wedding plans and now this.

"Has anyone called the police yet?"

It was all too much to take in, but his main concern now was for his daughter, she was crying uncontrollably but he was so grateful that Gill had been able to come over to help her.

"I shouldn't have gone fishing, I should have been here for her. What an idiot I am! Why didn't I take my mobile phone with me?! If only I hadn't gone, he might still be here."

James blamed himself for leaving her as she still clung onto him, trying to tell him what had happened, but her words were as confused as her thoughts

"Don't try to talk now, Roslyn. Let's go inside and try to make sense of it all. We'll sit indoors and have a drink."

After she'd calmed down and managed to tell him exactly what had been happening including Alex's insistence that she mustn't contact the police, she told him she'd phoned Aidan Spencer in London because she hadn't known who else to turn to and knew his company had helped her father in the past. He agreed she'd done the right thing. Then, finally, when he learned that a dead man had been found in the sea nearby, it was decided he would go to the police station the following morning to look at the body and, hopefully, put her mind at rest. Gill listened to the conversation, making mental notes of what was said to report back to Aidan later. She could see the two people in front of her shared a very close and warm relationship which would make her job easier, just a shame James didn't know the whole truth about her role, but she supposed it was for the best.

Next morning, the police station was quiet, there had been a serious traffic accident on the motorway just outside Marbella and it left only one senior officer on duty to deal with their unidentified victim. James was taken into a sort of anteroom with a large internal window while the body was brought in on a trolley from the morgue. When the sheet was pulled away from the man's head, he took a close look and, shocking though the sight was, he heaved a big sigh of relief. Thank goodness, it wasn't Alex. It was the face of a stranger.

James sank into a chair and breathed deeply, relief flooded through his body. A young woman, who spoke good English, had been brought into the viewing room to help him if need be. Seeing his ashen face, she feared the worst and offered him a cup of coffee which he politely refused.

"Senor Chapell, I'm sorry you had to go through that ordeal, but I have to ask you this question. Can you identify the body you've just seen?"

"No, it was no one I know, I'm glad to say."

"Thank you, Senor, for your co-operation and your time. What was the reason you came here this morning to identify this man's body?"

"Well, my daughter and her fiancé are here on holiday and he left the house two days ago without leaving a note, so we're worried about him and were afraid the body you found might be his. I'm sure there is a simple explanation for his absence, they probably had a little tiff, I'm sure you understand. You know how young people in love are. I'm sorry to have bothered you, Senora, and thank you for your concern."

Roslyn was over the moon when she heard the good news, but James was still grateful to have Gill here. For her part, she hated the subterfuge but knew she had to obey her orders from Aidan that no one must know her true role in Marbella. She had managed to phone him briefly and keep him up to date with the latest twist in the ongoing saga. As far as Alex was concerned, there had been no ransom demands. When he had been ordered to drop the case by Ben Edelman, saying that he alone was going to act as the go-between in the negotiations for his release, he'd had no alternative but to obey his instructions but still had grave misgivings about the wisdom of the decision.

Since the drowned man's body hadn't been Alex's, he'd set up a meeting to discuss the whole affair with his 'Protectu' partners in London and it was proposed that Aidan should fly out to Marbella to advise Mr. Chapell on his options and possibly act as a go-between with the kidnappers if that was what he wanted. The instructions that Mr Edelman had given them previously could possibly be ignored as they all felt they should give their full co-operation and support to James Chapell as senior partner of the company that had originally employed them. Aidan went over all the information he had and realised he would have to be very diplomatic in his handling of this awkward situation. He phoned their travel agent, booked the next available flight to Malaga then went home to pack his bag. He knew he would have to phone Marbella first because he didn't want to blow Gill's cover so a quick call to James Chapell to say he would be in Spain on business would be all that was necessary, then, hopefully, the whole story would come out. He would then be free to offer the firm's help with no one any the wiser. Then it was for him to decide on Mr. Edelman's role in any future negotiations.

The phone rang for a while before James answered it, sounding very apprehensive, but when he recognised Aidan's friendly voice, he relaxed and, within minutes, had told him what had happened. This gave him the ideal opportunity to offer his help when James quickly added.

"If you haven't booked in anywhere else, we'd be very happy for you to stay here with us. We have a friend of Roslyn's staying but I'm sure we'd all be grateful for any suggestions or help you can give us. My daughter is in a bad state now, she's worried to death as you can imagine. Please, say you can come."

"Of course, I will. I'll do whatever I can to assist you for as long as it takes. The only thing I must do is re-arrange my present schedule and let the office know of my change of plans. They will understand."

Aidan hadn't expected it would be so easy, but he now had the perfect excuse for being closely involved in any further events. He decided he wouldn't disclose the fact that Ben Edelman had taken him off the case. There had to be a plausible reason for his decision, probably wanting to spare Roslyn any further grief and she may not have told her father when she was so distraught. 'Let sleeping dogs lie' was usually the best policy in his experience. He fired off a quick email to Gill to put her in the picture before taking a taxi to the airport. The subsequent flight gave him enough time to decide on a plan of action with various strategies to cover whatever the next few days might throw at him. It was to prove a testing time for everyone concerned.

The next 24 hours were full on; with Roslyn in the care of Gill and James, she was trying to hold herself together, but her fiancé's safety was always uppermost in her mind. Aidan, taking on the role of James' official advisor, wanted to shield him from any future exposure to the kidnappers. His fishing pals, without knowing the truth about the disappearance, kept him busy playing golf during the day and having a few drinks in the evening. These absences gave Gill and Aidan time to discuss their mutual ideas, they had acted out their parts very effectively in front of the family so, it was good for them be able to talk freely when they were alone. Gill was the only person who had heard the full story from Roslyn and so, was able to fill in the blanks Aidan wasn't aware of; neither of them could understand what was in the kidnappers' minds breaking off communications without getting the details of the safety deposit box in Krakow. It just didn't make sense unless their hiding place had been disturbed or there must have been a drastic change of plans since Bohdan spoke to Roslyn last. The mystery deepened.

After a couple of days, Roslyn had regained some of her former resilience and decided she must contact Alex's grandmother in England before any news of his disappearance reached her. Her phone number was in his diary and when the phone was answered, Alice greeted her warmly and was keen to hear all their news, Roslyn tried to break the news of his being missing as gently as she could with assurances that she, her father and various professionals were doing all in their power to find him. She didn't mention kidnapping and his grandma's immediate response was one of total disbelief that Alex was not there. On the other end of the phone, she cried quietly but also had a very steely but genteel quality, despite her immediate grief, and sent her good wishes to her father. Then Roslyn asked if there was anyone she could call on to stay with her, Alice said she just needed to be alone for a while to come to terms with the news, but she had friends who would help if she needed them. Roslyn assured her she would keep her informed as soon as they had some news and phone her every day.

No one was aware that Alex had arranged another meeting with an unknown person on the previous Saturday morning and, as there were no sightings of him after he left the villa, the trail had gone cold. If only he hadn't decided to take the law into his own hands or had told someone what he was planning to do, they might have been able to follow up his rendezvous at the Old Beach Hut and find someone who had seen him there with a stranger. Even the exact time of the encounter was guesswork. Only early morning joggers, swimmers and the beach patrol would have been around so any leads as to what had happened after Alex met his unknown kidnapper remained a mystery.

Now that Aidan was in residence, they talked endlessly, Roslyn was glad to have met him at last and share all she knew with him; the threatening calls and Bohdan's involvement plus the demands that she should give them the safety deposit box details. Then suddenly nothing, no more warnings and just a sudden realisation that something inexplicable seemed to have changed the kidnappers' strategy. It was as confusing for Aidan as it was for her. The discovery of the body in the sea was one of her worst moments when she'd had the sickening feeling that it could be Alex. She already blamed herself for not contacting the police despite their dire warnings, she should have followed Aidan's original advice and not listened to Ben or anyone else, but it was too late now. What had they done to deserve such a terrible blow to their wedding dreams and other aspirations!

The only thing she knew for sure was that it had to do with the discoveries they'd made in Krakow and the Ukraine. Whatever Bohdan had said about his minor part in the whole thing, he was the only person who had been in Lwiw and was now in Spain. He had been lying all the time, but he had neither the brains nor the funds to mastermind such an audacious plan. He'd told her he was just following orders so who was his boss? Racking her brains to find an answer, she still wondered if Krystyna had known more than she admitted. As Gill had said 'you never know who your friends really are in these situations'.

Aidan and James discussed all the possibilities confidentially, not wanting to frighten Roslyn with what might happen to Alex. Her nerves were frayed enough without putting any more stress on the poor girl. James was totally perplexed.

"I wish I could work out what they've gained by kidnapping Alex and then making no further demands for either money or information. It seems inexplicable to me."

"It may be just another ploy to get Roslyn so scared she'll do anything to get him back. They have time on their side and ultimately, they must know that whatever is in that security box is worth a lot of money, probably more than they could earn in a lifetime by demanding a ransom."

Only two other people knew the real identity of the man behind the kidnapping, Krystyna and Bohdan, and it was in their best interests to keep that secret to themselves. As usual, Yuri was safely in the background, sending his orders but keeping himself out of harm's way. But when he realised Bohdan had blown the whistle to Roslyn about someone higher up being the real boss, he knew he had to take charge of the botched situation for once and all.

CHAPTER SIXTEEN

Yuri Yurchenko had already booked a flight to Malaga, it was no good leaving things to Bohdan, he knew he would have to stay until everything was sorted. Then he rented a car for the drive to Ronda, his favourite city, where he kept an old farmhouse up in the hills. It was a property he'd bought years before, in a false name, with a bonus he'd earned for recovering some priceless stolen paintings for a grateful client. He loved the remoteness of the place, far from the bustle of the Costa del Sol. The old house had a useful barn attached to the house with a cold storage room and deep freezer that the previous owner, a farmer, had used for keeping freshly-killed sheep's carcasses before selling them in the local markets. It had provided a perfect hiding place for Alex after Bohdan had drugged him and driven him from Marbella, only 35 miles away. He'd used the old farm truck and been back in an hour with no one seeing any unusual activity. If only the rest of it had gone according to plan, Yuri cursed the man's stupidity as he drove, trying to think of a way to sort out that problem as well.

If Roslyn had given them the bank details when she was asked, Alex might be a free man now and he would have the Krakow safety deposit box in his possession with the secrets it held. That was all he was interested in, he didn't want to harm anyone. Then simple-minded Bohdan had to open is big mouth and disclose the fact that he was working for someone else, that's when it had all started to go wrong. If he'd told her that much already, what other secrets would he reveal in the future?

So far, no one, apart from Krystyna, knew that he was the one who had been involved in the kidnapping idea from the beginning. Sorting out this ensuing mess would now be his greatest headache.

After the unproductive phone calls to Roslyn, he had to think of a new strategy to get the information he needed. At first, they'd relied too much on her being so frightened she would immediately divulge the account details, but he'd been wrong. So, he'd phoned Bohdan and ordered him to rough Alex up a bit, just enough to ensure he would beg Roslyn to give them the details. But, despite that, he'd still tried to pass on coded messages about mixing up the account numbers when he spoke to her later. What sort of an idiot did he think he was dealing with? That's when Yuri found out that Bohdan had spoken to her directly which had been a big mistake. He'd always known that if you wanted a job doing properly, you had to do it yourself; that was the first rule of survival. That's when he had decided to fly to Spain, to sort out the mess once and for all, before Bohdan could implicate him in the whole saga.

He arrived at the farm in the late evening, it was dark when he reached the front gate of the property, now securely padlocked against any intruders. Very few people walked up the pathway, but Bohdan obviously had taken no chances. The unwieldy lock finally gave way as he inserted the key and struggled to turn it. He tugged at the rusty chain and it dropped to the ground, he swung the gate open and propped it firmly with a huge stone. He headed the car towards the barn and parked, leaving his lights trained on the heavy oak front door then fumbled for his house keys and was soon inside the old place, once again cursing Bohdan for his fatal indiscretion. He switched off the car's lights before going back into the hallway, gazing round to see if anything had been disturbed but it all appeared just as it had always been, sparsely furnished with very few personal touches.

Alex's secret hideout was right at the back of the house, secluded and hidden from prying eyes by a big coniferous hedge. Coming through the door, Bohdan greeted Yuri warmly, it was obvious he had been drinking and his speech was slurred. Yuri tried to hide his annoyance, took out a thick wad of Euros from inside his jacket and placed it on the table in front of him.

"That's for you, Bohdan, for a job well done. I knew I could count on you, good man. How's our guest doing? I hope you didn't bruise his face too much."

Bohdan laughed as he picked up the money, he had no idea Yuri was lying to him.

"Thanks, Boss. I did knock him about a bit, he'll remember to do as he's told from now on. He must think I'm an ignorant peasant, trying to make a fool of me."

Yuri only smiled at this remark, he must keep him sweet for the moment. He had just one more important job for him to do before they parted company for the last time and he wanted him to think all was well between them. They'd wasted enough precious time trying to get the information from Alex and Roslyn, he now had to put an end to this charade and pursue another course of action.

"There's been a change of plan, Bohdan, we can't keep Alex here any longer, it's too dangerous. Tonight, I want you to drive him into the hills above Mijas and leave him near the road leading to Alhaurin el Grande, I've marked it on the map for you. He must be blindfolded all the time, do you understand? When you see the signpost, keep the truck lights dimmed and make sure no one sees you drop him there."

Bohdan was puzzled by these latest instructions but knew better than to challenge Yuri.

"Yes, boss, but why can't we just let him go in Marbella?"

"Good question! But if you drop him off near to the spot where you picked him up, someone might recognise both of

110

you and remember your face. Then the police could start looking for you."

"Alex knows what I look like anyway. He knows my name and he'll tell them everything."

"But they won't be looking for you here in Ronda, they'll be searching the remote areas round Mijas, miles away. Then we'll be long gone, back in Kiev drinking vodka! We will have fooled them all."

Bohdan loved that idea, he was sick of being treated as if he was stupid, first by Krystyna, then Roslyn. Who did they think they were? He was as good as them any day. He smiled at the idea of outsmarting those people, Yuri obviously appreciated the job he'd done.

"I want you to drive straight back here, don't stop off anywhere for a drink. Remember, you mustn't be seen anywhere near Marbella. Then we'll clean up this place and head out to the airport and home."

When Alex had been given another Propofol injection to make him sleep, he was blindfolded and put in the back of the truck. Bohdan, though slightly drunk, drove carefully over the rough track until he got to the main motorway then speeded up for the journey to Mijas. There was very little traffic on the road at that time of night and so the trip took just over an hour and a half. The short drive further up in the hills beyond Mijas took another 15 minutes and then he saw a signpost to Alhaurin el Grande. He turned off his lights and parked his wagon on a side road with only two small houses visible in the distance. He looked around and, with no one in sight, opened the back of the truck, lifted the still sleeping Alex out and propped him against a tree. He removed his blindfold and handcuffs, covering him with an old horse blanket before climbing back into the cab. He released the handbrake and quietly rolled the truck down the slight incline of the road, without turning on the engine. Very soon, he was back on the road to Mijas and then home with no problems for the remainder of the journey. He was delighted with his uneventful trip and glad to have seen the last of his prisoner. Daylight was just beginning to glow over the horizon as he drove on the motorway then once again took the old road up to the farmhouse.

Yuri had put his rented car into the outhouse he used as a garage and shut the door. He was already clearing out the house and had lit a fire in the grate to burn all the evidence that could implicate them in Alex's disappearance. Together, they tore open the thin mattress he'd slept on, hid the filling under the straw in the barn and then burnt the outer cover, sheets and blanket on the open fire. Then they washed all the pans, crockery and cutlery they'd used in the house.

"Pack up all your stuff now and put your bag in my car, make sure there's nothing left anywhere inside that can identify you or Alex. When that's done, clean the truck, inside and out, it must be spotless. We'll put it in the barn before we leave so no one can prove it's been used while you've been here. Don't forget to get rid of any unused food and scrub all the surfaces. We mustn't leave any clues or fingerprints for anyone to find. Not a soul must ever find out what went on here, do you understand?"

Bohdan was tired and hungry but listened to Yuri's instructions. He wasn't a fool and didn't need to be told what to do.

When all the incriminating evidence was destroyed and the old truck cleaner than it had ever been, instead of throwing away the booze he'd brought with him, Bohdan took a huge swig from a bottle of vodka; it was a shame to waste it. Better not let Yuri see him though, he didn't want to cross him after he'd been paid him more than he expected. He couldn't wait to be back home amongst his own kind again and relaxing with people who spoke his language. Yuri was still busy burning every scrap of evidence while he carried on drinking from the bottle of liquor. Why not? No more baby-sitting that crazy Englishman!

Yuri, for his part, was mulling over in his mind what to do next, he had quite a few loose ends to tie up before he left Spain. The kidnapping hadn't worked out as planned, he'd have to think up a new game plan. It was Yuri who was taking all the risks and now, he had to make a serious and irreversible decision about what to do next. Roslyn already knew someone else was involved in the kidnapping so, that meant Bohdan couldn't be trusted anymore. He was the weak link in the chain and no longer a reliable asset, he had to go. There were two obvious choices; whether to kill him here and now or fly him home and dispose of him later. Better to get rid of him while they were alone with no curious witnesses.

After doing a final inspection of the property, he went into the kitchen where Bohdan was downing the dregs of his vodka. Seeing the perfect answer to his dilemma, Yuri asked to join him for a final drink. Bohdan grinned and staggered, half drunk, over to a cupboard under the sink, producing his last bottle of extra strong local brandy. After they'd both proposed toasts to everyone in the Ukraine, Yuri watched him finish the rest of it, slumping heavily onto a nearby sofa. The rest was easy; he grabbed a cushion and pressed it down over his now senseless face with all the strength he could muster. At first, Bohdan struggled; his arms flying up in the air, his legs kicking the floor repeatedly until there was no more life left in his body. He went completely limp, he was dead. Yuri dragged him through to the cold storage room and opened the now empty freezer. Then lifting him up, he doubled Bohdan's knees up to his chin and laid him neatly on his side in his cold coffin. By morning, he would be frozen solid, his immediate problem was solved. The rest of his plan wasn't quite as easy, he still had to dispose of a corpse in Spain without raising anyone else's suspicions. He would need help from someone he could trust and only one person came into his mind, Krystyna.

CHAPTER SEVENTEEN

Roslyn woke up suddenly, wishing her nightmare would end, but each morning when Alex was still missing, her hopes for his safe return dwindled. Gill couldn't have been more supportive, but she could see from her father's face that he too was beginning to fear the worst. Aidan was as ever, level-headed and optimistic. She couldn't sit around and do nothing, she couldn't change anything but there had to be a glimmer of hope, amidst all this despair. Then she heard the phone ringing downstairs.

Maria's voice came next, calling her name. She jumped up and put on her housecoat before rushing down the stairs. Aidan opened his door, wondering what was happening. Roslyn took the house phone from the girl and listened.

"Yes, I'm Roslyn Chapell. Oh, thank God, is he all right? Yes, please give me the hospital address and we'll be there as soon as possible, within the hour. Thank you so much."

She put the phone down, her relief was indescribable. She shouted for her dad and he appeared bleary-eyed from his bedroom, not quite sure what all the shouting was about.

"Oh, Dad, he's been found, isn't it wonderful? He's okay. I must get dressed and we should go, he's in the Carlos Haya Hospital in the city. Please, hurry and get ready now."

There was complete pandemonium as everyone hurriedly washed and dressed. Maria, who was in the kitchen, preparing breakfast, came out, saying.

"Que passa? (What's happening?)

"Senor Alex is all right, es bien."

Everyone's smiling face explained it was good news, so she went back to her cooking, thinking all English people were crazy.

In less than half an hour, everyone was ready to go. They all piled into James' car and he drove to the hospital as carefully as he could, which was quite difficult with Roslyn laughing all the way and acting like an excited little girl again. He hadn't seen her like that for years. As soon as he stopped at the hospital's main door, she didn't wait for anyone else, she ran in and asked a receptionist which ward Senor Wilshaw was in but unfortunately, the girl only spoke Spanish. By that time, Gill had joined her and asked.

"Por favor, donde es Senor Wilshaw? Lo admitieron esta manana."

She'd asked where Alex was, telling her he'd been admitted that morning. The girl looked at her computer screen and replied.

"Esta en la habitacion diez. Tome el ascensor hasta el primero piso, es el segundo a la derecha." (He's in room ten. Take the lift to the first floor, it's the second on the right.)

"Muchas gracias." (Many thanks.)

When Gill had spoken Spanish so fluently, Roslyn was amazed, it was another aspect of her supposed 'old friend' she hadn't known. They both headed for the lift and when they reached the door of his room, Gill let her go ahead to see Alex alone.

"Oh, my darling, I was beginning to think I'd never see you again."

He was lying in bed looking very tired and bruised but grinned at her.

"Me too, my love. This is the best moment of my life. Come here and kiss me."

She put her arms around him and kissed him as gently as she could. Their reunion was cut short by a nurse who came in and was surprised to see her patient in such an amorous embrace.

"Que passa, Senor?"

Alex laughed and said to Roslyn.

"This is Sister Valeria, my guardian angel. She speaks English too."

"I'm very pleased to meet you. I'm Roslyn, his fiancée."

"Good morning. I'm sorry I must ask you to leave now, I must give my patient an injection. Senor Wilshaw needs much rest after his bad experience."

"Yes, I understand. I was just so happy to see him again, I couldn't wait."

"I think the doctor would like to speak to you, he wants to keep him in overnight to make sure his injuries are not serious. His bruising could be superficial but we're waiting for the x-ray results before we can allow him to go home."

"I only want what's best for him. I'll see you very soon, my darling."

Roslyn kissed Alex good-bye and told him she'd be waiting outside. Her father and Aidan had joined Gill and they couldn't wait to hear how he was.

"He looks surprisingly well, a bit bruised, but he's amazing after all he's been through. I'm so happy."

Her father hugged her, they were all talking animatedly when a doctor approached them and introduced himself.

"I'm Dr. Garcia and I'm delighted to meet you."

"My name's James Chapell, this my daughter, Roslyn, Senor Wilshaw's fiancée. This is Miss Armstrong and Mr. Spencer, my advisor."

"I'd like to speak to you and your daughter privately, if you don't mind."

They went into Alex's room, but he was sleeping soundly after the nurse had given him another tranquiliser. The doctor said he had been brought to the hospital by the police early in the morning after he'd been seen walking unsteadily on a quiet road just above Mijas and taken to the police station by a local farmer. As he had no identification on him, they decided he needed medical attention before being questioned.

"You speak excellent English, Doctor."

"Thank you, I worked at St. Thomas's in London as part of my training and married one of your lovely nurses over there. We always speak English with our children at home"

"Ah, that explains it."

James was delighted that there would be no language barrier, he always felt he should try to learn Spanish but had never quite got around to it. Dr. Garcia smiled indulgently, he knew so many expats in Marbella who said exactly the same thing.

"When I examined Senor Wilshaw, I was surprised that, despite his bruising and being drugged, he seemed to be in good physical condition after his ordeal. He told us his name and gave us your telephone number. We'd prefer to keep him in for 24 hours to make sure he has no adverse reactions to his medication. It's often the case that a person appears to behave normally in the first hours after suffering a trauma, but a true picture of the mental state only emerges a few days or weeks later."

James said they preferred that the hospital be extra cautious in their diagnosis. Roslyn told the doctor that they were happy to go with whatever he suggested but obviously they would like to have him at home as soon as possible

"I think we need to contact the police too, we'd like to know exactly how and where he was found. We came straight here when we heard the good news."

"Of course, I quite understand. I presume they will want to question Senor Wilshaw too. We will be in touch with you as soon as we have done all the tests and are sure it's safe to send him home. Thank you for coming so promptly. It's been a pleasure to meet you and rest assured we are always here to help if you need any further advice."

James broke in at this point.

"I have a good friend in Marbella, Dr. Delgado. I think you might know him, he was in the orthopaedic department here before he retired. I'm sure he'd be happy to keep an eye on Alex when he's back home."

"Yes, I know him very well. We sometimes have a round of golf when I have the time and he usually beats me." He smiled.

"He is a great golfer, we play at the country club. We must make up a foursome sometime. Thank you so much for your medical advice and I'd like to add that if there are any expenses incurred in Mr. Wilshaw's care, please, don't hesitate to send me the bill, whatever the cost."

After saying good-bye, Roslyn went over to Alex's bed and kissed the sleeping man tenderly before they went out to Gill and Aidan.

"Let's go downstairs to the cafeteria for a drink and discuss our plan of action before we go to see the police."

After a lengthy talk, it was decided that the two men should make the initial enquiry at the station and ascertain the facts before divulging any information to them. Aidan advised that they keep the kidnapping to themselves. Roslyn felt that Alex would want that too. So, the two women took a taxi home while James drove to the local police headquarters in the town centre. It was nearly lunchtime when they walked into the reception and asked for the officer in charge as they would like some information about an incident that occurred earlier near Mijas. They were shown into an inspector's office and asked to wait. James was happy to let Aidan do the talking so when a grey-haired man of about 60 appeared and shook both their hands. Aidan began by giving him the details in his halting Spanish but felt more relaxed when the officer spoke in English.

"Thank you for coming so soon." Looking at his notes, he continued. "The young man had no identification on him, he seemed dazed, so it was decided to take him to the main emergency department in Marbella."

James was amazed yet again that the inspector spoke English so fluently and said.

"We are very grateful for that. Could you give us the name of the man who found him, we'd like to thank him personally?"

"Of course, it was Senor Tomas, he owns a smallholding up in the hills and I can give you his address. But I must ask you why your friend was wandering alone in the countryside so early in the morning?"

Now it was Aidan's turn to give him a brief, if somewhat false, account of Alex's circumstances. They had already discussed the reasons for not disclosing the kidnapping. There could still be some dangerous people around who wished Alex harm, especially now that the police were involved so, James and Roslyn had readily agreed to the necessary lie.

"Senor Wilshaw said that the previous evening on his way home, he'd gone into a bar and ordered a beer. He thought his drink tasted very strange and had been tampered with so, he called the barman, but he just laughed in his face; then some of the locals joined in and an argument started. The next thing he knew, they were throwing punches. He must have passed out at that point with the after-effects of the drugged beer because the next thing he remembered was waking up, bruised and covered in a rough blanket by the roadside. His wallet was gone, and he had no idea where he was. So, he started walking along the road until a man in a truck stopped and gave him a lift. The last thing he recalled was being in the bar, the fight then nothing after that. Later he guessed the motive must have been robbery because they realised he was a tourist."

"Yes, I'm afraid there are still some dangerous places where foreigners are easy targets for thieves and pickpockets. When your friend is fully recovered and out of hospital, we will need a statement from him so that we can follow up our enquiries but I'm not too hopeful of catching the men who robbed him."

James produced his personal card and handed it to the inspector.

"Of course, inspector, I'm sure you're right, he just went into the wrong bar at the wrong time and, unfortunately, paid for his mistake. You've been very helpful, and it's been a pleasure to talk to you. Thank you for your time and your courtesy."

They left the station feeling it had been a job well done with no one aware of the actual circumstances of Alex's release. As soon as they got home, Roslyn phoned Alex's grandmother, who she knew must be worrying herself sick about him.

"Hello, Alice, this is Roslyn. You'll be delighted to know Alex's okay, he was found this morning. He seemed to have lost his memory and was taken to the police station by a local man. Now, they've taken him to a hospital in Marbella for a check-up."

"Oh, Roslyn, I'm so relieved he's not injured. Does he remember anything at all?"

"Just a little, but not much."

Then she began to tell her about him being found on a roadside with no wallet, no identification, nothing,

"Anyway, he started walking down the road and was picked up by a farmer in a truck. When the police took him to the hospital, he gave them his name and this phone number, so we went there straightaway. He seemed tired but very happy to see us. Then, we talked to the doctor who wanted to keep him in overnight for some tests. We only got back about five minutes ago."

"Thank you very much for ringing me so quickly. When you see him, give him my love and tell him to be more careful where he drinks in future."

120

"I'll certainly do that but don't worry any more, he's in good hands now. I'll keep you up to date about everything and I know Alex will phone you as soon as he can, we talk about you a lot and the wonderful time we spent with you in Yorkshire. Look after yourself too."

Roslyn's mind was still in overdrive, but she thanked her lucky stars his ordeal was over. She realised it could have been much worse, he might have died. She just hoped Alex would finally come to terms with everything and decide that all his plans paled into insignificance when his life had been hanging in the balance and it all could have ended so badly. She prayed he would make the right decision for the sake of them both. All he really needed now was some loving care, surrounded with people who loved him.

CHAPTER EIGHTEEN

Alex was recovering well and feeling no major ill effects after his traumatic experience, but he had another major problem ahead of him. He had to decide if he should continue his family search or forget about it altogether. Only he and Roslyn knew everything that had happened in Lwiw, but the situation was completely changed now. Any further explorations in that area, especially with Bohdan and unknown others still in the background was not only dangerous but could be suicidal. James was adamant that Roslyn shouldn't be exposed to any more threats and Aidan, though less emotional in his thinking, could understand why he didn't want his only daughter faced with such emotional turmoil. After the police were satisfied that the main aim of the local muggers was to steal Alex's wallet, they took little further interest in his case, knowing the chances of retrieving it or arresting his assailants were remote. It was an everyday happening in many tourist areas, the increasing use of drugs pointed to more sinister events creeping into their usual round of petty thefts.

Gill, on Aidan's instructions, stayed with Roslyn for a few days more so as not to arouse James' suspicion that their story of being old school friends wasn't true. He went straight back to London, there was little of value he could do in Spain now that he was sure the kidnappers would have flown the coop already. The earlier intervention by Ben hadn't been mentioned so James was no wiser about his involvement and he advised Roslyn to keep that information to herself too. Gill thought she should follow Aidan as soon as was practical, and when Roslyn and Alex decided that they must go back home too, James was left with no further excuses to delay them. The extra time they'd spent in Marbella was blamed on her father being ill, as it seemed easier to suggest the extension of their holiday was due to his having a bad bout of 'flu rather than a case of kidnapping. So, no great harm was done with only a slight deviation from the truth.

On their last evening together with James, they were all happily drinking final glasses of champagne on the terrace, when he stood up and he tapped his glass.

"I would like to make a formal announcement, just to say that, as a wedding present, I intend to give you, Alex and Roslyn, a place of your own so that you can spend as much time as you wish in Marbella without your old man too close for comfort. And, lastly, I've decided to build a guest annex next to the house, especially for your grandmother, Alex, so that she can come over to visit whenever she feels like sitting in the sun and being pampered. Then, I would always be around to take care of her when you're not here."

Roslyn looked at Alex and at her father, her face glowing with delight.

"What a wonderful gift, Dad! I can't believe how very kind you are. I haven't talked to Alex, obviously, but I'm sure we're both over the moon and the villa next to you for Alice to stay in is just the icing on the cake. I'm sure she would love that idea."

Alex shook his future father-in-law's hand and put his arm around his shoulder.

"Well, I'm practically speechless for once in my life! How can we both thank you enough for your generosity, I'm totally overwhelmed."

"My motives are not entirely selfless, you know. I want you both to be near me, as often as you can. So, in fact, I'm thinking of myself too because my dearest wish is for you both to be happy."

There wasn't a dry eye amongst the group as he gave his speech. At last, all his dreams seemed to be coming true, his daughter and her husband close by and hopefully, he'd be sharing his grandchildren in the future.

The next morning, with all their packing done, Gill, Roslyn and Alex took a taxi to the airport even though James had wanted to drive there himself. They knew he'd had a tough time too, trying to keep strong for his daughter's sake when all the furore of the kidnapping was happening. Maria was coming back the following morning, so she would look after him and tend to all his needs. There were sad good-byes but happiness that their next meeting would be for the wedding. When their plane landed at Heathrow in the early evening, they decided to eat in town before they went their separate ways. Gill felt like part of the family already and reminded Roslyn that she was only a phone call away if she ever needed her.

The very next day, Roslyn contacted Ben to reassure him that Alex had recovered well from his terrible ordeal and hadn't suffered any long-term harm from it.

"Thankfully, Ben, you didn't have to deal directly with Alex's kidnappers but your offer to help me was exactly what I needed at that moment. Just knowing you were there for me, trying to safeguard me from dealing with that awful man, helped me more than I can tell you. You stepped in when I was at my wits' end and I'll never forget what you did for me."

"You should know by now, I would do anything for you, and for Alex, of course. I'm just so glad that dreadful experience ended well. You'll never know how much you mean to me, Roslyn. You're very dear to me."

"That's very sweet of you to say so and, apart from my eternal gratitude, the second important reason for my call is to invite you officially to our wedding, I know Dad's mentioned it to you already, but I wanted to ask you myself. We've set the date for Easter Saturday, the 24th, and you could bring someone else if you like. It's only going to be a small gathering with Alex's grandmother on his side and a few friends. Dad wants to push the boat out but, apart from asking my brother, Markus, there's no one else as far as our family is concerned so we're hoping to have the ceremony and the reception here at Dad's place."

"I couldn't be happier for you and I'd be more than delighted to be with you all."

"I'm so glad you can make it for our big day, we both look forward to seeing you. Sorry, I must go now, we're getting ready to go to Cheltenham for the weekend before we start work again. One thing I'd like to ask you, as a great favour to me, is not to tell anyone else about what really happened to Alex when he was kidnapped, we're trying to put it all behind us. No one knows about the threats except you, Dad and my friend, Gill. Would you do that for me, Ben? I'd be truly grateful if you could."

"Of course, I won't say a word to another soul. I'm just glad it's all over. I only wanted to help you, I hope you know that."

"Yes, I do, you have my eternal gratitude for that. Thank you so much."

Roslyn couldn't believe how lucky she was to have such good men in her life. Her only niggling regret was, as usual, the absence of her brother but he might still come to the wedding if James was in a forgiving mood. She decided to phone him later, wherever he was, and ask if he'd like to come. She thought she could persuade her dad that it would make her day if he was invited too.

So much had happened since they were last at Alex's place yet it all looked the same, Jason was happy to see them again. He'd already split up with his new girlfriend and was fancy-free once more. They all went for a drink to sympathise with him, having to tell him a few half truths about what had happened in Marbella. Alex was feeling very tired and Roslyn still worried that he hadn't fully recovered from his ordeal even though he was trying not to show it. The next day, they spent most of the morning adding explanatory footnotes to those they'd made about their Krakow and Lwiw expedition, Alex spread out the photos he'd taken to add to his Polish collection. Looking at the pictures now, he wished he'd never got himself in such a deadly mess, he'd never dreamt that that last meeting with Bohdan would lead to his being held captive and drugged. The memory of the kidnapping still haunted him; he found it hard to forget his fear. He felt betrayed and stupid at the same time. Those nightmares still haunted him, even though he tried to keep them to himself. Thinking clearly at last, he finally decided the search for his dream was too dangerous. That mad Ukrainian could have killed him with no one knowing the truth. There would be no more fantasies about possible riches; it was all over. Roslyn's love and happiness were the only things mattered in his life now.

After much soul-searching, he spoke to her about his decision. She wasn't too surprised, knowing he hadn't taken this step lightly and also, he didn't want to continue working in Cheltenham. He'd been bored with his old job for quite a while, he couldn't see the point of working in analysis and de-coding anymore. He wanted to move to London, firstly to be with Roslyn but also to pursue a new career in electronics. He'd spoken to James about it, he was keen to start something more challenging and was particularly interested in the future of robotics, the next big leap into the field of automation. This was music to James' ears, he'd wanted to pass on his share of the business to his new son-in-law and could see an ideal partnership developing between him and Ben. So, in less than two months' time, all their mutual dreams seemed to be coming true. The discussions were well received by everyone concerned. After resigning his old job and giving Jason his final advice about not forgetting to bring the ring for the wedding, Alex was ready to leave his old life behind for good.

Time passed very quickly and very soon they were again landing at Malaga airport with Grandma Alice enjoying her first trip to Marbella. Excitement filled the air as the house was made ready for the guests and the festivities. The building work had made steady progress and the outline of the new annexe was taking shape. Roslyn was delighted to learn her brother, Markus, was arriving from Miami with his present girlfriend. She was a very sweet twenty-year old, who hung on every word he uttered. James was in his element, surrounded with old and new members of the family. He was overjoyed that Alice was such an interesting woman and had taken a strong liking to Gill Armstrong, his daughter's so-called 'school friend'. The wedding party had grown now to include Ben's new lady, Johanna, an Austrian lady he'd recently met, who owned an art house business in Vienna, a perfect match for him with his love of all things cultural.

The wedding day was perfect, the sky was blue and not too hot. Roslyn looked amazing in her mother's old wedding dress, which brought a few tears to her father's eyes. Jason, the best man, made an excellent speech and there was general laughter about his story of the ostentatious fake engagement ring Alex had presented to Roslyn before the real one arrived. Alice was very proud of her grandson and her only wish was that her husband, Lukasz, could have seen him standing next to his new bride. The most touching moment for everyone was Alex's mention of his grandfather whose predestined life had been completely overturned by the deaths of his parents and loss of the Wilowski's fortune. He finished his speech by expressing his deepest wish that the whole family would now rest in peace. It was a fitting tribute to his Polish ancestry and, at last, a decorous ending to the family's story.

Then they kissed everyone goodbye before flying off on their honeymoon to St. Vincent.

CHAPTER NINETEEN

Meanwhile, poor Krystyna was getting increasingly frustrated waiting for Yuri to contact her again. She began wondering if he was just playing for time and she was becoming increasingly sceptical about his plans for untold riches that were supposedly within their grasp. She'd heard nothing of Bohdan since their last meeting and started to doubt that Yuri was telling her the whole truth. Why was it taking so long to unearth the burial site when the English couple had been so sure of its exact location? It only needed a few strong men to do the heavy work then it wouldn't be too difficult to arrange an unfortunate accident to happen to Alex who would still be excavating all the surrounding areas for his lost fortune. She couldn't believe she had wasted all this precious time, twiddling her thumbs in Krakow. At that moment, her mobile started to ring. She saw the number was a Ukrainian one so, it had to be him. She heaved a huge sigh of relief.

"Hi, Yuri. I'm so glad to hear you voice, I was starting to fear the worst. You should have called me before now, I've been worried sick about you."

"Sorry, I know I should have phoned but I've had so much to do. I had to fly to Spain to see Bohdan but everything's okay now that we're back in Kiev. Don't worry, I have some good news for you and I'd love to meet up with you as soon as possible."

He decided not to tell her at this stage, that the Bohdan situation was still unresolved.

"I want to see you too. Why did you have to see him again? I thought you'd finished using him for good, you said he was a pain in the neck anyway."

'You're nearer the mark than you'll ever know.' Yuri thought to himself.

"It's a long story but we'll catch up with all the news later. Can you to fly to Malaga as soon as possible? We can have a few sunny days by the sea, if you like, then we'll drive to my place near Ronda and stay there for a long romantic holiday. You deserve it after all good work you've done for me, I can't wait to see you again. I'll arrange for you to pick up your plane ticket at the departure desk in Krakow on the 21st. I'll leave it in your name then I'll be waiting for you in the arrivals lounge in Malaga on the 23^{rd,} at about 20:45. I hope you can manage all that, then afterwards, we can fly back to Krakow together and have a wonderful time getting to know each other all over again."

Krystyna was practically speechless with his enthusiasm and was dying to hear his latest news. After such a long separation, her doubts about his intentions had been uppermost in her mind, but at last, her dreams were coming to fruition. The phone went dead as he ended the call, but she was so happy, she didn't care. All she wanted was to see him again and this time, with her share of the money. The trip to Spain was just the beginning and a golden future now loomed on the horizon for her. She looked in her wardrobe and put her clothes in two piles, one for the warm climates she now envisaged. and the other to be given away to the poor. The world would be her oyster from now on and hopefully, they would be together again enjoying their newfound wealth.

Yuri had known for a long time, that there was some sort of family connection with a distant Polish cousin, who had also been a member of his great grandmother's family in Lwow before the war. He had always hoped that he was now the only remaining heir to this supposed family fortune. It was on one of his many fact-finding trips from the Ukraine to Poland, he'd met the very attractive Krystyna Zaleska. Apart from her great sense of humour and good looks, he'd been fascinated by her broad knowledge of Krakow's history. They had spent many weekends and holidays together and had realised they shared many other interests too. She loved the theatre and had been a successful actress before she met Yuri and had been awarded a Silver Globe for her main role in a popular soap opera in Poland. Later, when her acting parts started to dwindle and, rather than watch her star fade as she got older, she took up a lucrative job as an advisory city guide. She specialised in local historical tours and longer forays for connoisseurs who wanted a taste of the splendid pre-war dynasties, now long gone. So, Yuri and Krystyna forged a bond of mutual interests that proved both pleasurable and fruitful, it seemed like an arrangement made in heaven.

He'd already spent several years trying to track down his family's hidden money, until one momentous summer when, by accident, Krystyna met Alex and Roslyn in Krakow on a mission of their own. She was acting as their tour guide and realised Yuri's investigations and theirs were inter-linked. This fateful meeting meant that the two men were, in fact, Yuri Yurchenko and Alex Wilshaw, and so, by a strange co-incidence, distant relatives by birth. A couple of generations before, they had been the only remaining descendants of two long dead sisters, the children of the late Count and Countess Sofia Krakowski of Lwow. The eldest daughter, Alisja, had married Pawel Yurchenko, of old Hapsburg lineage, while her younger sister, Karolina, became the wife of Count Henryk Wilowski of Krakow One of the last things Countess Karolina had arranged before the Russians overtook Lwow was to supervise the burial of the family's portable wealth in the grounds of their country house. This amazing occurrence was only discovered when Alex began to take an interest in his Polish ancestry and went first to Krakow, then over the border to Lwiw to search for his so-called roots. Yuri had taken the greatest interest in Krystyna's journey with them, but she hadn't managed to discover where Alex had subsequently deposited a deed-box containing the all-important bank details. This essential piece of information was the lost key that led to the failed kidnapping attempt in Ronda with his accomplice, Bohdan, and then, everything had started to go wrong. There were still as many questions as answers about their possible inheritance.

His next meeting with Krystyna, after they'd arrived in Malaga, had been planned more carefully. Her plane was on time and their reunion was more passionate than she dared hope for, but for Yuri, the missing clues in this convoluted drama were, as yet, unsolved. He still had two major headaches; how to combine the disposal of Bohdan's frozen body and finding the buried money. For Krystyna, there was nothing remotely like that to spoil her joy, the city was everything she'd dreamed of; his choice of hotel directly on the beach was opulent and the rooms luxurious. The only things they hadn't talked about so far were the sharing of the riches and trying to crack the Krakow bank's security system. The two translated letters Roslyn and Alex had left in their London bank for safekeeping were now unnecessary although Yuri and Krystyna were completely unaware that Alex had decided to forget his past dreams of finding his legacy and settle for a happy family life instead.

At first, all seemed to be going well, it was only en-route to Ronda that the wisdom of her decision to fly to Spain began to cause Krystyna some small nagging doubts. Had she'd been foolish to think he really cared about her when all he wanted was her usefulness? Yuri, busy devising a plan of his own, had had a sudden brainstorm on the way to the farmhouse but needed her unwitting co-operation to carry it out. After, he'd carried her case inside, he tampered with the brakes of the hire car and then pretended it had broken down on the track outside. Because his hands were greasy, he'd asked her to phone the rental agency in Marbella to bring a replacement car immediately and to use her name and details for the transaction, which she foolishly did.

Next morning, before she was awake, he unloaded Bohdan's frozen body into the boot of the new car. He then asked her to drive him down to Marbella again to look for a bank that was open and he pointed out an inviting looking restaurant where he said they'd meet for lunch. But he'd already hatched a plan that he thought would work. He would leave her there and when he failed to show up more than an hour later, she'd be confused at first, not knowing what to do. Much later, tired of waiting for him, she'd eventually give up and then surprisingly, find a semi-frozen unexplained body in the boot of her hire car. By which time, Yuri would have been long gone, first back to Malaga then to Kiev with his return ticket in his wallet. His plan seemed to be fool-proof! Yuri would have successfully left Spain forever.

On the other hand, after waiting for well over an hour for him to meet her in the designated restaurant, poor Krystyna was, at first, furious, but then realised something had gone seriously wrong. She had no idea what to do and trying to contact Yuri was obviously futile. Eventually, she asked her waiter if he could help her and showed him the name of the car rental agency, so he looked it up and found the address. Using his instructions, she managed to drive there and explain her situation to the salesman. He was very solicitous and tried to find the Ronda address where the hire car had been delivered to the previous evening but, because Yuri had used her name in the transaction, there were no other receipts apart from hers. Not knowing what to do next, she decided to return the car to the showroom and then take a taxi to the nearest hotel until she could work out her next move. What a swine he was to leave her stranded, knowing no one!

Her mind was in turmoil as she waited for salesman to search for her details while a mechanic checked her returned vehicle. Nothing could have prepared her for the next bombshell. There, neatly laid out in the boot, was a slowly defrosting corpse. The stunned workman, visibly shaken and white as a sheet, stared disbelievingly at her face. It wasn't every day that a respectable-looking tourist returned a rental car with a dead body in the boot. She didn't know what to do or say but, without a doubt, she was certain that the remains they'd found were those of Bohdan. At that moment, all hell seemed to break loose, someone dialled 112 for emergency help and kept her in the showroom until a local police officer arrived with his blue lights blazing. She could understand a little of what he was saying but communicating in Spanish wasn't easy. He asked her a few more questions; her name and details of where she was staying. She was now in a complete state of shock and all she could do was give him her Polish passport while the sales personnel gave him the details of her rental agreement. He found it difficult to believe she had no idea of her actual address, only that it was somewhere near Ronda. The city police usually dealt with petty crimes on the Costa del Sol, but this was a first time for them and they were completely out of their league. A member of the Guardia Civil was called in and he took over while they placed a security cordon around her car then she was taken to the police station for further interrogation. Fortunately, her rental agreement and Polish documents were in order but now, she was having a bigger problem trying to explain why she had been travelling with a dead man in her car. Krystyna quickly realised she had been used and humiliated into the bargain. Yuri had never had any intention of including her in his scheme to get his hands on the money. She vowed she would never be fooled by him ever again! Her anger was nothing compared with the fury she would vent on him if their paths crossed again.

The furore continued as she was taken to the Ronda farmhouse under arrest, they broke down the door and she gazed around the rooms. Evidence of their stay was spread round and the remains of their last breakfast together laid out on the kitchen table. It was hard to believe he'd already been planning his devious escape only hours before they were still happily driving down to Malaga. After the police carried out a thorough search of every inch of the property, nothing else suspicious was apparent; the storage freezer was now empty with no obvious signs that a body had ever been stored there but a forensic team would be able to examine in minute detail the entire area that Yuri and Bohdan had left behind after Alex's kidnapping.

Krystyna had been accompanied by a policewoman for the journey to Ronda and asked if she could collect her belongings from the farmhouse before she left. After much discussion, it was reluctantly agreed she could keep her suitcase but nothing else could be moved as it was now officially a crime scene. After she tried to explain her situation more fully, she was advised by an interpreter that she could avail herself of an official translator and legal representation if it was necessary. It was getting more serious by the minute, but she realised she had to steel herself for whatever lay ahead. Still, unknown to her was the fact that Yuri had cleaned the whole house thoroughly after he'd left it a few months earlier. It had been left spotless and so nothing incriminating belonging to him was found anywhere; no passport, no official documents, nothing to tie him in with the kidnapping or Bohdan's body. The fact that the property had been originally bought by a foreigner using a false name only complicated the matter further. Sitting all alone in a police-holding cell, the gravity of her situation came into even starker focus and she cried for the first time. That did little to solve her present problem. Imprisoned in a strange country, she felt utterly powerless, for the first time in her life. The truth was that he'd got away with murder and managed to put the entire blame on her. What a complete idiot she'd been, how could she have been so trusting of such man?

Yuri, on the other hand, after planning the disposal of Bohdan's body without implicating himself and his successful return to Kiev, was buoyed up by his success. There was still the important matter of the Alex's deed box, securely locked in the Polish Bank, to be resolved. Yuri had been thinking of other ways of getting his hands on the information he needed; one was by using the old man, Piotr, in Krakow to find out what he knew or by following in Krystyna's footsteps to the two Wilowski country houses in Lwiw. He'd decided to lie low for a while until the whole business died down. He was sure there wouldn't be an international incident about an unknown stranger being found dead in Spain. Interpol had bigger fish to fry but he had to get rid of his now redundant Ronda property, preferably to a shady Russian buyer with no strings attached and no questions asked.

CHAPTER TWENTY

He had heard nothing about Krystyna since leaving her stranded in Spain. He'd been busy getting together a team of local men who were prepared to work hard for the money he offered in return for their loyal service. All he really needed were strong men who could do the spade work and excavate the second site near Lwiw, initially discovered and marked out by Krystyna and the late Bohdan. Further attempts to get more information from the old retainer, Piotr, without her help had proved fruitless. Hiring heavy equipment to do the job was easy and, now that he was a bona fide Ukrainian citizen, various officials were prepared to close a blind eye to the dubious legal paperwork he provided and were no longer interested old pre-war blood feuds.

For Krystyna, sitting in a lonely cell, the situation was very different. She was awaiting the arrival of a consular official from the Polish Embassy in Madrid, anxious to know if and when she could go home. The Spanish authorities were satisfied eventually that Bohdan's corpse had been in the farmhouse for several weeks, if not months; long before she'd arrived in Malaga or Ronda. They also realised she couldn't have manhandled a heavy body from the freezer by herself and placed it in the back of the rental car, so either, she'd had help or not known of its existence. Her repeated story of the complete shock and disbelief when the garage found the corpse and her total ignorance of her surroundings gave the whole thing a ring of truth. It was decided eventually that she should be allowed to leave Spain but be available for further questioning in Krakow, if necessary. The false address Yuri had used to buy his property initially could never be verified. So, her dramatic journey, begun with such high hopes, came to a dire end. His promises to her would never be forgotten or forgiven. Her time for retribution would come one day, and sooner than she expected! Krystyna resumed her career in Krakow and was biding her time until one of two things happened. The first was her fervent wish that Yuri would be struck by a great bolt of lightning with as much flesh burnt from his body as she could possibly imagine. More realistically, she had to find someone who would help her get rid of him so that he would never recover one Ukrainian Hryvnia or Russian Rouble of the hidden money. That would be exactly what he deserved!

The fact that Krystyna had been allowed to live temporarily in Poland, after leaving Spain until her court case was settled, was of little comfort to her. Her life was in tatters, she'd got another job easily enough, but it wasn't what she'd had in mind for her future. Her humiliation was complete when Yuri abandoned her to her fate, without a backward glance. She had to admit, even to herself, that she'd been used and literally taken for a ride.

Vengeance had been her sole aim at first, but there had to be something else she could do if all other avenues were closed to her. She had very little money and certainly not enough to finance the lifestyle she'd always envisaged for herself. She needed someone who had the resources to bankroll the venture she had in mind, someone who would succumb to her charm and good-looks as well. She could cry on someone's shoulder if need be, even if that wasn't her style. She needed a man who already had big ideas and was intrigued by the thought of making easy cash and greedy enough to want lots more.

When she first met Alex and Roslyn, she'd realised they obviously had plenty of money and she'd overheard them talking about her brother living the high life in America and her father being retired in a luxurious villa on the Costa del Sol. So, perhaps she could find out more about this mysterious brother, maybe from Roslyn herself. That thought was beginning to intrigue her. Not having heard from either of them for a long time, Krystyna decided to write a short text, inviting them over for a reunion in Krakow on the pretext that she'd managed to find out more about the whereabouts of Alex's hidden cache in Lwiw. She knew he would be eager to hear more about the mausoleum that had his family name over the door. She could invent a believable story about finding a fellow tour guide who had unearthed new information to suggest the exact location of the treasure trove was definitely in the crypt. It was a ploy that might work, it was certainly worth a try.

With the honeymoon couple back in London, life was returning to some normality for James. The wedding celebrations over, Alice had gone back home to think about what to do with her house after she'd decided to move permanently to Spain. Only, Markus hadn't been too eager to leave his father's home, he still had his old debts to sort out, so he put his new girlfriend back on a plane to America and began to look around the more fruitful watering-holes on the Costas for any opportunities that could prove profitable. James had begun to warm to his son's proximity, thanks to Roslyn's influence, and given him the run of the house while he took a long golfing holiday with his friends in Portugal. It was on the understanding that Markus kept an eye on the building work and extension of the new annex, so he was happily driving his father's Bentley around the city and having interesting luncheon dates with new-found friends in Puerto Banus. He wasn't completely mindless and could see the value of proving himself an asset to his father and, at the same time, finding more fertile outlets for his own talents. He'd already met several young ladies who took his fancy, but he really needed to get involved with influential men who had their fingers on the pulse of what made Marbella tick. He wanted to meet the big fish not the sardines. He wasn't going to waste the next ten years of his life gambling his allowance away and chasing beauty queens, he needed to make a name for himself and let his father realise he could make his own way in the world. He had to do something special to set the ball rolling, he was tired of always being in his big sister's shadow. It was going to be his time soon very soon.

Feeling very much at home in his new surroundings and, after introducing a coterie of useful people into his home, Markus's thoughts began to turn to using the impressive surroundings of his father's villa as the backdrop to a sumptuous caviar and champagne evening around the pool, staffed by a host of glamorous girls and backed by a well-known vocal group. He would pull out all the stops and make it a party remember. He had to impress his new-found friends and show James he was the one who was going to follow in his father's footsteps, not Roslyn, and make him proud of his successful son at last. Markus was in his element again. He was enjoying his new status, with an ever-widening circle of acquaintances, girlfriends and business prospects. Being part of this Costa lifestyle was very much to his taste. The fact that his father was footing the bill for his lavish spending didn't seem to concern him, he would repay him with interest when his plans to make a killing were successful.

James knew nothing of Markus's many so-called meetings with some of the less savoury characters who frequented the many bars and clubs around Marbella. He'd decided to give his son some leeway to establish himself in his new surroundings and trust him to be more circumspect about his friends. Unfortunately, none of his father's business acumen had rubbed off on his only son. Markus was dazzled by the yachts in the harbour and the many luxury cars parked next to the more fashionable eateries in Puerto Banus. His desire to be one of this jet-set blinded him to their boasts of making huge financial killings; their dodgy deals and illegal practices were carefully hidden under the surface of all the apparent glamour. He was a lamb, cheerfully being led to the slaughter!

Meanwhile, Roslyn had been holding her breath but was now absolutely sure they were going to have a baby. It had been over three months since the wedding and her latest news only made Alex even more determined to relinquish his legacy hopes and put his own family first. They'd already moved into a bigger flat, they needed the extra space, and it was more convenient for their jobs. Alex had eagerly accepted James's offer to join the company and had been making new contacts with members of the electronics department about the growing research into robotics. It was an area he was very interested in and had already co-opted his friend, Jason, from Cheltenham to join his team. Alex found Ben very easy to work with and as keen on new high-tech automation as he was, a good start to his new career.

CHAPTER TWENTY-ONE

Ben only rarely thought of the strange kidnapping episode now, but he always remembered his promise to Roslyn that no one should ever know what really happened in Spain last year. When Alex had disappeared, taken hostage against his will and then, suddenly released again, without a ransom ever being paid, had seemed very highly suspicious. Although he'd never talked to James about it, he wondered what the real story behind it all was. Why Alex had been held a prisoner in the first place was a mystery and didn't make any sense to him, but he supposed he'd never know the whole truth. Maybe it had something to do with his Polish ancestry and their trip to Krakow. Thinking of Roslyn, as he often did, he decided to speak to James's Marbella number and picked up his mobile.

"It's Ben here, just wanted a word with you but don't worry, it's not urgent."

The phone had gone to the engaged tone, so he would speak to him later. He'd been thinking of taking some time off anyway, after they'd set up a training programme for Alex. Ben wanted his partner's son-in-law to feel completely au fait with company policy and its ethos but not be overshadowed by all the department heads looking over his shoulder.

"Hi, Ben! James here. I know you've been trying to contact me, so I got back to you a.s.a.p. You said it wasn't urgent, but I thought you might have something else on your mind. I'm still here in Marbella but thinking of taking some time off now that Markus is back in situ and coping with things."

"It's great to hear from you, James. Yes, of course, you're right, I did think I'd put some thoughts your way now that Alex is on board. I'm planning some hands-on tuition for him so that he can hit the ground running and get the feel of the company without me actually being here in London."

"Good idea, Ben. I'm sure he'll soon feel at home and find his feet when he realises the policies are straightforward and, as you say, he'll have very sound backing from your teams. He's very intelligent and I believe he'll be an asset to the firm."

"I'm sure he will, James. Now for the next thing, I'd like to take some time off to follow some private business I need to investigate, I wouldn't ask you if it wasn't important."

"You don't need to ask, take as much time as you need. You've been working hard and put in so much extra time since I took my retirement. I would like to say if I can help you in any way, I will but I think it's a good idea for Alex to find his own way around without feeling he's being watched all the time!"

Ben was more than delighted with James's support and could now go ahead with his own plans without feeling guilty about leaving Alex to cope on his own. It had been too long since he'd pursued his own very personal goals which were never far from his thoughts. He'd set his heart on spending more time in Austria and, at the same time, renewing his quest for the valuable artefacts his family had lost during the war. Looking for those lost paintings and antiques had become a sort of obsession with him over the years and his desire to restore his family's good name was still paramount. Now was the time for him to follow his own dreams.

He'd decided to buy an apartment in Leopoldstadt which was very central but also had parks for walking and would be perfect for all his needs. His girlfriend, Johanna, lived nearby which suited him; he wanted the freedom to come and go as he pleased but valued her input and knowledge of the current antique market. He had also made various contacts, mostly in Eastern Europe, with a view to extending his search area and had a network of dealers, keeping an eye open for buyers who might be short of cash or happy to unload artworks with few questions asked as to their provenance.

When Ben was finally installed in his Austrian penthouse apartment, he began taking energetic walks in the leafy park and drinking mid-morning coffees in one of the many cafes along the Max Winter Strasse. He was very happy and felt his whole being come alive as he took in the wonderful sights and sounds of the city, and knew, in his heart of hearts, Vienna was where he'd always belonged. He'd found there was a vibrant café culture with lots of Kosher eateries dotted around the area, so he didn't miss the authentic food he'd enjoyed in places like Reuben's in London. He could feel his ancestors smiling down on him now, urging him to fulfil his dreams of re-installing their once prized possessions in the family home. He often walked the streets trying to find traces of the prestigious dwellings that had once embraced the old Jewish quarter and been the focus of its ethnic culture pre-1938. It had been nicknamed 'Matzoth Island', its history fascinated him and the suburb of Leopoldstadt was itself famous for its long association with New York.

Johanna had done a lot of ground work, trying to trace the very complicated trail of lost and stolen artefacts from many different sources. As soon as the Germans took over Vienna after the Anschluss, everything was fair game; either goods were stolen by ordinary soldiers looking for instant loot or there was wholesale ransacking of private property. The houses were either completely desecrated or systematically catalogued for later transportation across Europe. Eager collectors, high-ranking army officers and influential members of the S.S. became instant millionaires and connoisseurs of art overnight. There were easy pickings from the disenfranchised Jews who had no redress for their losses which violated all the previous laws of decency that once governed civilised society. When everything of value had been taken, those personal treasures were never seen again, this annihilation of whole generations of people and property was complete.

His friendship with Johanna was itself a strange mixture of mutual admiration and respect, he liked her a lot, but his desire to balance the wrongs that had been inflicted on his own family was always uppermost on his mind. Atoning for their dispossession was what had motivated Ben for most of his life. His other major predicament, as ever, was that he loved someone else; his heart was reserved for only one woman and that was Roslyn; at times, interfering with his common sense. He had begun to think his devotion to her was a lost cause but hope always sprang eternal. In the meantime, life in Vienna was all Ben could have wished for; they listened to concerts in the State Opera House, viewed exhibitions of art in various galleries, wandered round the museum quarter, visited the Schonbrunn Palace with its beautiful gardens, took tram rides around the city and often shopped in the night-market; pleasure combined with more pleasure. He had never expected his leave of absence to be so satisfying and productive at the same time.

He often worked long hours inspecting and cataloguing old registers, listing inventories and records from the 18th century onwards. The second world war had disrupted art collections all over Europe on such a vast scale they were irreplaceable. This wasn't taking into consideration private plundering, wholesale theft and destruction of property with very few valid receipts to account for the multi-millions of pounds of goods which would never re-appear or be recovered. Sometimes, Ben's search seemed far too extensive to have a realistic outcome and, at times, he felt like calling it a day and accepting it was too big a task for an army of researchers, not just one man. What drove him on was his insatiable hunger to succeed and not be beaten. It was like Alex's desire to find his family's inheritance but on a much larger geographical scale.

His first real big breakthrough was an email from a gallery in Paris that had bought a painting, purporting to come from his great grandfather's collection, last seen in 1938. He phoned the salesman immediately and found the name of the last seller, who promised to show him the provenance. Johanna checked the history of the painting and found it had been in a private home in Berlin after the war ended in 1945. It had been on the wall of a senior S.S. officer who had fled when the allied troops overtook Germany. It had then passed on to a French soldier who didn't know one painting from another and sold it to a dealer for the princely sum of 100 francs. Then it was lost for years before a new owner decided it was a copy and worthless.

Elated at this latest piece of news, Ben contacted the Paris gallery and said he would be in touch with them as soon as he could fly out to look at the painting if the provenance was proven. Satisfied that it was all above board, he took the next flight and a taxi to 'Galerie Mont Simon' where the owner, now realising the value of his new find, was re-assessing the painting that was last held in the hands of Ben's great grandfather. The price of the picture had escalated exponentially in the last few hours. Another Klimt masterpiece, a portrait of a young girl, stolen in 1938, then sold again in 1942, was not seen again until an astute collector had spotted it as one of the 200,000 artworks that had gone missing during the war. It was later auctioned for almost $80 million, so who could guess its present-day value.

This new information cast doubt on Ben's ability to negotiate a deal to buy any of his pictures now. They would be priced for the super wealthy only, not for him, so his exhilaration was short-lived. He was beginning to wonder if he may have spent too much of his valuable years on a lost cause.

"I'm afraid it's bad news. I haven't a cat in hell's chance of buying the picture. When I arrived at the gallery, the owner had already done his research and realised the painting was one that had disappeared in 1938, but proving it belonged my great grandfather would have been nearly impossible. It will have been squirreled away in some private collection before I could make any legal attempts to regain it legally."

Johanna could hear from his voice that he was distraught, but she was more philosophical about his disappointment and tried to console him as best she could from so far away. He was gutted she knew, discovering that the family artworks were beyond his means would seem like the end of all his hopes, He was absolutely bereft, and she was worried that he would go back to England to lick his wounds then all their plans would be plunged into limbo and she would have lost a good friend and sponsor. Her own company would survive but her relationship with Ben meant more to her than their business dealings, they enjoyed a full social life and their interests were very much in tune with Viennese culture. She hoped his disappointment wouldn't end their way of life; the thought of losing him saddened her beyond words.

The emotional highlight for Ben was when the wonderful news came that after 60 years, full restitution was to be made for the loss of his family's beautiful home and compensation paid, after many legal arguments about the government's financial and moral obligations. So, at last, the Keller family were to be given the full satisfaction of knowing their total dispossession and many deprivations had not been in vain.

CHAPTER TWENTY-TWO

The news from England was mainly good. Alex was enjoying his new job and feeling happy being part of a young enthusiastic electronics team. Ben, back from his time in Vienna, was delighted about the belated restoration of the old Keller family home in Leopoldstadt. James had taken an even more laidback attitude to the London business, knowing his very able son-in-law was now in situ and that Markus was taking a more pro-active interest to supervising the transition of his father's villa. Alice was more than delighted with her own situation, she'd leased her old apartment, so she'd started selling her old furniture and sorting out her unwanted memorabilia ready for the imminent move to Spain. As for Roslyn, her recent bouts of illness were the only things troubling her, but the joy she felt looking forward to having their baby far outweighed any anxiety she felt over a small matter of morning sickness.

Krystyna had kept in touch with her from time to time since their last meeting in Krakow but now that she was in a state of limbo, suggested another rendezvous sometime very soon. She made no mention of the time she'd recently spent in a Spanish gaol or the terrible ordeal Yuri had put her through in Malaga. Unaware of any ulterior motive in contacting her, Roslyn had replied eagerly, telling her the good news about the baby and offering her a place to stay if she ever wanted to visit London. Re-establishing a connection between them and her brother, Markus, was an idea that had occurred to Krystyna as she'd listened to their earlier conversations on the way to Lwiw.

Roslyn had told her that he was very easily led astray by a pretty face and was also a heavy loser on the gaming tables, so she felt sure he would be intrigued by the idea of getting his hands on a stash of valuables. Her story of the hidden legacy and vast wealth, that could be theirs for the taking, might prove too great a temptation for him and, possibly, her last hope for the luxurious lifestyle she had in mind. It was certainly a gamble worth taking.

Hearing that Roslyn had offered her a place to stay didn't sit very lightly with Alex. He'd never fully accepted Krystyna's version of her relationship with Bohdan, particularly after the kidnapping, even though she'd denied knowing much about his background except that he was a friend, looking for a few extra days' work. Nevertheless, he had to agree that she had done a lot of useful research about his family and found old Piotr's wealth of knowledge and reminiscences invaluable so maybe he was jumping to all the wrong conclusions and being far too critical. Alex had no way of knowing what future Krystyna had in mind for Markus and knew nothing of her previous involvement with Yuri. His own life had taken a completely new direction since he'd married Roslyn and any decisions that might endanger both their relationship and her welfare were a million miles from his thoughts. His search for the Wilowski fortune was only a fading dream now that their new baby was on its way. However, that in no way, interfered with Krystyna's plan to arrange a meeting with Markus as soon as possible. Her past experience had taught her that he would probably be an easy target for her feminine wiles; she only had to worm her way into his affections and then, take advantage of his weakness for women and easy money. Her calculated strategy worked better and sooner than she'd dared hope.

James had phoned to say he was coming to London to work out some details of the new partnership he envisaged with Ben and Alex, he'd decided he would remain the titular head of

'Cosmocompute' with the main shareholders being the three of them. Roslyn had insisted he stay with them in their beautiful new apartment in Kensington and it just happened to be the very time she'd already arranged for Krystyna to visit too. James treated the four of them royally, with dinners at the Ivy and at various small restaurants in the vicinity. Krystyna was her usual charming self with a plethora of interesting stories about her acting career; her father, spellbound by her easy wit and manners, was delighted to share the flow of conversation between them all. The baby news had made him so happy and the joy of being a grandfather at last was the icing on the cake. Alex, relaxed and basking in the warm ambience of the company, once again felt slightly ashamed of his distrust of their former tour-guide. Could he have been so wrong? He decided to give her the benefit of the doubt.

"Your grandmother's coming over next week, Alex, to sort out some of her things before she flies out. Why don't you come over and stay for a few days?"

Without the slightest hesitation, they agreed to accept James's invitation to visit Marbella one last time before the baby arrived. He was eager to show them the newly finished mini villa that was practically ready for Alice's final approval.

"What if we could all come out together and crack open a bottle of champagne to celebrate?"

"That's a wonderful idea, Dad, we can help Alice with the move and toast her new home at the same time. Can you manage a few days away, Alex? We could fly out next Friday, it's a long Bank holiday week-end, so it would be perfect."

Noticing that Krystyna was quietly smiling but not partaking of their conversation, Roslyn touched her hand.

"Why don't you come with us? I'm sure my dad won't mind, the more the merrier, and you can meet Markus. He may be off on his travels again soon, now that the building work's finished, so it would be lovely for us all to get together. You

149

can see for yourself what you make of my dear brother after all the things I told you about him on the long train journey to Lwiw. I'm sure he'd be more than delighted to meet you."

"That's very nice of you to include me and I'd love to meet Markus and Alex's grandma too."

"Have you ever been to Marbella? I think you'll enjoy it."

"I once had a quick trip over there but only stayed a few days, so I didn't see much of the place, it was more of a flying visit."

Krystyna hadn't expected all her plans to be falling into place quite so easily. Her mind went back to the tortured hours she'd spent locked up, by herself. in a dingy prison cell. That thought only made her even more determined than ever to get her own back on that bastard who'd left her high and dry in Spain to face the music all alone. But without a doubt, he would pay dearly for everything he'd done to her, she'd make sure he would suffer the same indignities she'd been through, and more!

"Let's tell Dad the good news, he'll be so happy."

She whispered quietly to Alex, telling him she'd invited Krystyna to stay at her Dad's place, and caught a look in his eye that worried her, he couldn't still have any misgivings about Krystyna surely. That was all in the past now and better forgotten, she didn't want anything to spoil her happiness when all her dreams seemed to be coming true. She had now everything she'd ever wanted, a wonderful husband, good friends and the best of all, a baby who would be loved and cherished until her dying day.

They all hurriedly packed and arranged for a taxi to pick them up the following morning. Alex had phoned Alice to tell her the good news about the baby and hoped she could fly out to meet them all over the weekend. The flight back was short and sweet with Markus picking them up from the airport. He was his usual charming self when he met Krystyna and she definitely liked the look of him as she sat in the back of James's luxurious Bentley. It was a way of living she could easily get used to; the warmth and the sunshine had always appealed, compared to the cold of her normal life in Krakow. When they walked into the villa itself, she knew she had landed on her feet, surrounded, as she was, by tasteful rooms and sumptuous furniture. Even in her theatrical days, she had rarely lived in more delightful places, Yuri's rural retreat was run-down and threadbare compared with this idyllic villa.

Lunch, organised and prepared by Maria and her sister, was set out of the terrace and the champagne flowed. James was beside himself with happiness, the news of his imminent grand-fatherhood had been what he'd longed for since the day Roslyn had decided to marry Alex. His inner worries about Markus's future faded into insignificance with the joy he felt at the moment. It was obvious being surrounded by his family had a soothing effect on him, he couldn't stop smiling and talking about all the things he was going to buy for his new grandchild. Everyone caught his infectious enthusiasm and the lunch was an outstanding success with much backslapping and promises to spend more time with everyone in Marbella. Alice phoned to say she was catching a flight the following day and would be in Malaga by six in the evening, so the family would now be complete. Krystyna couldn't believe her luck to have met such a warm and loving group of people all in one fell swoop. Her life was certainly changing for the better and long may it last, but she could never forget her main aim of getting to know Markus. Hopefully, he would be the one to unearth the hidden honeypot and also get rid of Yuri in the process.

He took an instant shine to their new guest and Krystyna found him very easy to twist around her finger; he had always loved the glamour of the theatrical world, so she played up her role as a past winner of a Silver Globe to impress him even more. He invited her out for lunch in Puerto Banus, where he seemed to be on very friendly terms with many of the well-heeled locals and made sure she chatted with all the ones who owned yachts moored in the adjoining berths. She wasn't taken in by his eagerness to impress her but acted her part to perfection. They were invited to join his friends at one of the liveliest lounges for drinks and spent the next couple of hours enjoying the animated company in the Mojo cocktail bar. They had to say their good-byes hurriedly, just in time to take James, Roslyn and Alex to the airport to meet Alice's flight from Manchester.

There were lots of mutual kisses, lots of 'Oohs' and 'Ahs' when they inspected the new annex with its tinted glass-roofed cupola over her part of the house. She was so glad she'd got rid of all her old furniture when she realised how modern and elegant the new villa would be. It had a frosted glass walkway between the garden and the side entrance, so any sudden shower would keep her dry. Her huge sitting room window, next to the pool. would be mostly overlooking the cool shaded patio and adjacent to the main terrace where outdoor lunches were often served. When it was completed, it would be her little corner of paradise, near to everyone she loved.

The two maids had served a banquet, in keeping with the evening's celebration. Markus and Roslyn were so happy to be part of such a festive reunion; she held his hand hoping that Alice's life was going to be as happy as hers. She smiled as Alex led his grandmother into the dining room for her first taste of Mediterranean living. James offered everyone champagne and Krystyna, smiling, yearned for her share of this opulent lifestyle.

CHAPTER TWENTY-THREE

Alex had to go back to London, but it was decided Roslyn and Krystyna should stay and enjoy a little more time in the sun while Markus kept his eye on the men putting the finishing touches to the villa. James had taken time off from playing golf with his regular cronies to show Alice round the highlights of the town and both enjoyed exploring the many shops and boutiques that had sprung up to cater for the foreign investors who had made their second homes on the Costa de Sol. She had spent years dreaming of such a wonderful retirement and her dearest wish was now within sight.

As for Krystyna, what had begun as a purely cynical business arrangement with Markus, was now developing into a genuine feeling of reciprocal pleasure; they enjoyed an easy rapport and found each other physically attractive. He appreciated her sense of humour and she could see that, beneath his veneer of sophistication, he had some little-boy-lost qualities that she found very appealing. Roslyn adored her brother as only a sister could. She knew his many weaknesses but loved him despite them all and was more than happy that he seemed to be taking on some responsibility for overseeing James's building project. The two siblings got on so well together when their father wasn't around, and she was delighted that her new-found friend had taken a shine to him as well. She hoped she would see beyond his superficial charm. Krystyna herself was beginning to see more and more of Markus's good points and a useful ally as well, in her ploy to get rid of Yuri.

As she spent more time surrounded by rich living, Krystyna started working on two possible game plans that might work if she could get Markus away from Spain for a while and back to Krakow. After initially showing him around some of her old haunts, she'd have to invent another reason for taking him to Lwiw to visit the site of Alex's former houses. A holiday away from the rest of the family would give her an excuse for visiting her own birthplace and then, she could suggest travelling to more exciting destinations in search of adventure which she thought would intrigue him. As she already knew, staying in one place too long bored him and, if she sprinkled the story with promises of sexual pleasure, by the time they'd landed in the Ukraine, he would be totally besotted. So, it seemed like the perfect time to set her scheme in motion.

Roslyn was very eager to go home; she was beginning to feel strong maternal desires and her baby was fast becoming the focus of her life. She also insisted that Krystyna was welcome to stay if she wanted but now was the right time for both of them to leave. James was occupied with his own dreams of making his home the epicentre of an ever-growing family with his new grandchild in mind. So, deciding to broach the subject of her return to Krakow, Markus would be left pretty much on his own and, seeing his obvious disappointment that she planned on leaving too, she suggested to him that he might enjoy taking a trip himself.

"I don't really know where I fancy going, I've been living in the States for years and don't have that many real friends here."

"That's not a problem, I could show you Krakow. It's lovely at this time of year and I have an apartment near the city centre with a spare bedroom. You're more than welcome to stay there with me."

He was over the moon at the very idea and his mind was working overtime. Tired of the same old bars and tedious conversations with his father, he certainly liked the idea of a change of scenery, especially with a new lady in tow.

Krystyna wasted no time in extolling the virtues of Poland and he was hooked on the idea. So, they decided to tell his dad and Roslyn, who thought it was a brilliant idea, and the very next day, he booked his ticket and was already packing his bags. Their business class flight was very enjoyable then, they spent the next few days getting to know each other better and enjoying her hometown. Wandering around the old city, taking in the local atmosphere was a completely new experience for him and he loved it. Their intimacy was growing more intense every day and their love-making more satisfying. Things were working well and so, they decided to hire a car for a week to see her favourite skiing resort, Zakopane, and then take in a leisurely tour in the Tatra Mountains. They talked for hours, sometimes in cosy cafes or in quaint hotels, growing closer as each day passed. By which time, Markus was completely in love and sexually intrigued by Krystyna.

After a few more leisurely days, she suggested he might enjoy a short break in Lwiw to show him the delights of the medieval city as she'd done before with Alex and Roslyn. Dropping the hire car off, they set out from Krakow by train. The comfortable overnight sleeper proved more to her liking than the one she'd previously shared on her first journey. The border control guards, though still surly, were eager to get the formalities over and so the journey seemed to go without a hitch. Their introduction to the Taurus Hotel and spa was a pleasant surprise with its emphasis on good food and equally luxurious rooms. They took a walking tour through the lovely old city and Markus loved it, it was so different from his usual gaming tables. Krystyna asked one of the guides if he could show them something of the nightlife later, so they met outside the beautiful Opera House and were taken through the winding streets to one of the themed eateries where they ate a delicious meal in the candle light and drank coffee in the 'Kopalnia Kavy'. Much later, they drank heady liqueurs in one of the inns in the Old Town. It was an evening they would always remember, not only for the wonderful ambiance of the place but also for their wild passionate love-making afterwards. Any evil thoughts of Yuri no longer tortured her mind.

The next day, they visited the Castle that had, in the past, once belonged to Alex's family, had lunch and then took a taxi to the old Wilowski house. Markus was duly impressed by the size of the estate and could fully appreciate Alex's desire to regain his old property. Krystyna only spoke in glowing terms of their earlier experiences in the city that had once been his grandfather's birthplace. He didn't wonder that Roslyn had felt so involved with the whole family saga and had wanted Alex to pursue his destiny. Krystyna could sense his eagerness to hear more stories of the family's status and previous wealth, which were cleverly designed to arouse his desire for more.

"Did they own all these estates before the Russians took everything?"

"I'm not sure about the extent of their land but I do know his great grandfather supplied highly bred Arabian horses for the Polish army. I did quite a lot of research on Alex's behalf to try and find out the history of their connections here in Lwiw, but the 1939 occupation put an end to all the earlier records."

"Did you manage to find out anything about the family heirlooms Roslyn told me about? She said his grandmother had them buried in the grounds.

Markus was truly hooked on her story of the Wilowski fortune, but she was still wondering if she could trust him completely. She had made that mistake before with Yuri and she wasn't quite ready to take him into her confidence yet. The vague whereabouts of the hidden treasure trove were still a mystery although she still felt she was on the right track.

"Do you think it's worth having someone with a metal-detector to look over the place, what have you got to lose? If you do find it and it's been lying there for ages, no one need ever know you found it."

She could see it in his eyes that he felt he could now be part of this search and his interest was growing by the minute, which is exactly what she'd been hoping for; the thought of getting his hands on a possible fortune was already taking shape in his mind.

"Do you think we should stay a while longer here in Lwiw? It seems a shame to miss out on this golden opportunity, we could have another look round and find out if those stories of lost treasure are true."

"Well, I suppose we could find someone who'd be willing to do a bit of detective work on our behalf. The more we find out, the better! No harm in asking any way."

Krystyna knew he was completely hooked already; his mind was firmly focussed on the main prize as she'd hoped he would be, so reeling him in was going to be easy. She certainly wanted to get to the money before Yuri got his hands on it.

Markus was like a cat on hot bricks and, not understanding a single word they all said was very frustrating so, after spending a boring few hours, he was losing interest.

"Well, that afternoon was a complete waste of time!"
Krystyna knew how short-sighted he was in dismissing it all so easily but then, he had very little patience if things weren't going exactly the way he wanted. After a few more words, he muttered something under his breath. This time it was Krystyna who replied.

"Maybe we should leave it for today and think of something else. It may not be not quite as straightforward as we thought."

"Surely, it can't be that difficult to get some poor out-of-work peasants to dig up the whole area for us, not a soul's set foot in this place for years. Only you and Alex know it exists."

Markus now had the bit firmly between his teeth. He needed to pay off his gambling debts and recovering the hidden stash could possibly be his last chance to get himself out of trouble and his hands on a valuable nest egg. Just before he left Spain, he'd received a threatening call from someone in Las Vegas saying, 'Pay up or else!', that's when he'd finally decided to give Marbella a wide berth and go away with Krystyna instead. He'd been threatened with death or worse before if he didn't pay his I.O.U.s but that latest warning was getting too close to home. Buying them back could solve all his problems, he could then find his own paradise island somewhere in the tropics.

Krystyna's mind was working on almost the same lines. It was obvious Yuri would try to get his hands on the loot but if she played her cards right, she could end up keeping the money for herself and getting Markus into the bargain. She knew his father was very rich and how hard could it be to take Roslyn's place in his affections now that she was so wrapped up in her new motherhood plans. James had enjoyed Krystyna's company while she was in Marbella and she had taken every opportunity to make herself agreeable to him. Men, as she knew already, were easy to manipulate and suckers for a pretty face; they were easily flattered, and she knew exactly what to say and do to make him putty in her hands. A marriage to his son could make her life very comfortable without having to give up her hopes that she might have a share in Alex's inheritance, even if it was to be only by marriage.

CHAPTER TWENTY-FOUR

Then the unbelievable news dropped like a bombshell on the whole family! Everyone was utterly stunned; total shock was their only reaction to the disastrous medical report that stated their beloved Roslyn was dead. No one could believe what they heard, she was so alive, so happy and now, catastrophe! It was impossible, it couldn't be true.

Markus was having coffee in the main square in Krakow, waiting for Krystyna to join him, when his phone rang. The blood drained from his face as he heard his father sobbing on the other end of the line.

"Dad, what's the matter? I can barely hear you."

"My beautiful girl, she's gone."

Then only muffled breathing and crying in the background as someone else spoke, it was Alice.

"Markus, I'm sorry, your father can't even speak; so, I'll have to tell you this unbearable news myself. Roslyn died last night. We didn't know exactly where you were. I'm so sorry to break it to you like this but your father is beside himself with grief."

"Alice? Tell me again, I can't believe it. What's happened?"

In between the sounds of his dad crying, the story began to unfold, Markus listened, his mind in complete turmoil.

"All I can tell you right now is that Alex phoned us early this morning with the awful news. As you can imagine, we're in complete confusion here, it's just so incredible. Your father collapsed and couldn't speak so I took over the phone just after poor Alex broke the terrible news to us. The doctor's been here all morning and he's given James a strong sedative, but I think you should get back here as soon as possible, he needs to be with you."

"I'll get the next available plane from here and I'll call Alex or Ben in London and find out what's happening there. I'm in Poland at the moment but I'll keep in touch with you as soon as I'm on my way. I know it's easy to say but try to keep as calm as possible for everyone's sake, Alex always says you're a very strong woman and we all need you right now. Thank you, Alice, I'm going to leave you and call you as soon as I know something more, look after yourself and give my love to Dad."

Markus just sat there, overwhelmed, his coffee had gone cold and he couldn't believe what was happening. His first thought was for his poor dearest Roslyn, his big sister, his best friend throughout his life; he still couldn't believe the news, it had to be a bad dream. He hoped to wake up and find he'd been having a nightmare. The waiter gave him the bill as he sat there in total bewilderment. He saw Krystyna walking quickly towards him, smiling, but nothing registered with him, he was in a state of profound shock. She knew immediately something bad had just happened, but she couldn't imagine exactly what.

"Are you all right? You look awful."

He couldn't speak, she bent down to touch his hand, it was icy-cold. He looked up, his mouth was moving but no words came, then, he turned his tear-stained face slowly to break the heart-stopping news to her.

"Roslyn's dead."

"No, I can't believe it! How do you know?"

"My dad just phoned me, he's utterly heartbroken."

Krystyna sat down, unable to think straight, there were so many questions swirling around in her mind but nothing that made sense. She remembered the last time they'd seen each other, Roslyn was so cheerful and the very picture of health.

"I've got to get back straight-away, my father needs me."

"Of course, you must go."

On the way to the travel agent, Markus managed to tell her that Roslyn had died the previous night in hospital, he didn't know anything else, but he desperately wanted to fly back to Spain as soon as he could arrange a flight. He was barely making sense as they took his hurriedly packed his bag to go to the airport; she tried to console him as best she could, promising they'd see each other again soon.

Her lonely drive back to the city was mostly a blur and she knew in her heart of hearts that nothing would ever be the same again, not just for them but for everyone. So, once more, Krystyna's dreams of a fortune and a lavish future life were vanishing before her eyes. She needed time to think, time to re-assess her options and, for the very first time, she felt entirely bereft of ideas and completely lost. Even her frightening ordeal in Spain with Yuri hadn't scared her quite as much as the loneliness she felt now. There was no one, not even the impoverished Markus, to pool their resources and fund a lifestyle that she still yearned for, the hollow desperation she felt was like a bottomless pit.

Her contacts were now limited and the only glimmer she saw on the horizon was her only contact in Lwiw, a man she knew who told her he'd met someone called Yurchenko who was interested in the Wilowski family property and realised instinctively that had to be Yuri still looking for the hiding place, he wouldn't have left Kiev otherwise. So, the only thing that sprang readily to mind was to play another clever game to intrigue Yuri yet again

Alex, sitting alone, couldn't believe what was happening to him; his head lying next to hers on the pillow, gazing at her sweet mouth, at the full lips he would never kiss again. He only wanted to stroke her face, still beautiful but frozen in death. The love of his life was gone forever, his lovely Roslyn, longing for the baby son she would never see.

When the specialist had diagnosed pre-eclampsia after the first three-month scan, they knew it could be potentially serious. She had suffered severe head-aches and blurred vision for a while but her high blood pressure and increasing abdominal pain was giving them great cause for alarm. She was admitted to the ante natal wing of the maternity unit. She died holding his hand, a single teardrop ran down her cheek, he'd never forget her last smile as those lovely eyes closed for the last time. Alex's heart was eternally broken.

Ben had rushed to the hospital just after he heard the news, he was completely shattered when the senior nurse phoned to tell him she had died an hour earlier. It had all happened so quickly at the end, there was nothing anyone could do to save her. They showed him into her room, Alex was sitting there like a ghost, his head bent with tears streaming down his face, his anguish and grief was unbearable. Her lifeless form lay there, peacefully, as if she would wake up at any moment and wonder what all the fuss was about.

"Oh my God! Alex, I came as soon as I could."
He didn't know what else to say. Ben had loved Roslyn from the very first moment he met her, his feelings for her had never diminished over the years even though he knew his love wasn't reciprocated. Like Alex, it was a memory he would carry in his heart for the rest of his life.

"She's gone, Ben. I don't know why, she was so happy about the baby, but it killed her in the end."

Ben knew it was only his intense pain speaking, Alex wasn't thinking straight, the despair was clouding his judgement. All he could do was put his arms round his friend, nothing else mattered at that moment. His own mind was in turmoil, poor James must be in a terrible state, not to mention Alice and Markus!

"I'm going to talk to someone in Marbella right now. If I know James, he'll be a total mess, but I'm sure his doctor will have taken charge of his immediate needs and he'll be heavily sedated by now and in good hands."

Alex was practically comatose with misery, Ben couldn't think of any words that might comfort him, his heartache was written all over every inch of his body. Never in his life had he seen such misery and suffering on one person's face! He had to speak to the doctor in the hospital first and find out the whole story, it must have all happened suddenly without anyone realising Roslyn was dying. He called the nurse and asked if he might talk to someone in charge.

"Could I speak to Mr. Muller, the doctor who was treating Mrs. Roslyn Wilshaw, I'm a friend of her husband and I'm here with him at the moment."

The phone went dead but after a short pause, he heard a man's voice.

"Hello, I'm Andrew Muller, Mrs. Wilshaw's consultant."

"I'm a good friend of Alex Wilshaw, whose wife died last night in your ante-natal department and I need to ask you a few questions. I'm the business partner of Mrs. Wilshaw's father who lives in Spain. My name is Ben Edelman."

"Good morning, Mr. Edelman. I don't usually speak about a patient unless it's a family member, I'm sure you understand."

"I realise that, but Mr. Wilshaw is in no fit state to talk coherently right now. So, I'm desperate to get some facts about Mrs. Wilshaw's case before I can speak to either him or her father. Alex Wilshaw is alone here right now, and I think he needs immediate attention. He's practically insensible to everything around him and is crying like a baby."

"I appreciate your concern and I can give you my assurance we are doing everything we can for him. He has refused tranquilisers and only wants to sit beside his wife. The sister in charge is keeping an eye on him and that's about all we can do right now. About poor Mrs. Wilshaw's sudden death, I'm afraid I can't go into too many details. There will have to be a post mortem as she was taken ill so suddenly, and we are at a loss to ascertain the true cause of her death after she'd been making good progress after the initial diagnosis."

"Thank you so much for that information, Mr. Muller. I'm sure that will help me to sort out some of the questions I will need to answer when I speak to her family and his local G.P. As you can imagine, we're all in a state of disbelief at the events of the last 24 hours but I do thank you for being able to speak to me on behalf of the family."

With that, their conversation was at an end with Ben who was still unable to grasp the finality of his dearest Roslyn's demise; her life had been so precious to him and he still couldn't believe he'd never see her sweet face ever again.

Ben's own stoicism was keeping him from going to pieces himself. The only thing he allowed himself to think about was the situation he faced in trying to alleviate Alex's and James's terrible ordeal. Sympathy alone was not enough at the moment, they both needed time to come to terms with the finality of Roslyn's death. His thoughts immediately turned to Johanna in Vienna. He needed to speak to someone whose shoulder he could cry on; his personal loss and despair was too much to bear on his own and she was the only person who knew him well enough to tell him exactly what he needed to do in these dire circumstances.

Krystyna, on the other hand, was alone, stuck in Krakow in a state of limbo with no one to turn to for help or guidance. Markus had gone back to Marbella, but she didn't know for how long, his first priority was to be with his father. He phoned her when he got to Spain and said everything was in complete chaos there. James was still heavily sedated, Alice had taken charge of the household management while he was liaising with Ben to get all the details of the latest happenings in London. A post mortem was being carried out but nothing more had been said about a date for the funeral. Alex was totally out of it; apparently, he was walking around like a zombie, not making any sense. It was decided the best thing to do was just keep in daily touch with everyone and play each day as it came. So, Markus and Ben were holding the fort until such time as something new was heard from the hospital.

The next two weeks passed in slow motion. The hospital released Roslyn's body and so funeral arrangements could be made at last. Ben helped Alex to talk a little about her death as best as he could while James, Alice and Markus flew to London and stayed in a hotel until such time as they could all decide what to do next. The day of the funeral was overcast, and the grief-stricken group of mourners sat silently, deep in thought and heartsick, after the tearful service, waiting for the hearse to take her body to the graveyard. White lilies covered her coffin as she was borne to her final resting place, next to her mother, in the family plot. No one could find any words to comfort each other; each one lost in their own private world of misery. Memories of their lovely Roslyn, taken from them much too soon, filled them all with such pitiful anguish and desolation that no tears could wash away the pain they felt. James, Alex, Ben and Markus would never forget her as long as they lived.

Three months later, when Alex had overcome his initial mourning and heartache, he still didn't want to go to Marbella again for a while, he needed to be as close to his and Roslyn's home as he could. He threw himself into his work, spending early mornings and late evenings with his friend, Jason; both getting more and more dedicated to the world of robotics. They had forged had a strong bond during their student days and still enjoyed working together, Ben encouraged their joint ambition to get more involved in this branch of electronics, so their shared enthusiasm provided yet another direction to take their lucrative business even further. James was still in the throes of deep grief, it was only Alice's presence that made his life bearable. She was always there for him, providing his only consolation when he felt his life was pointless; she wouldn't let him give in to his depression and her comforting kindness made him realise what a wonderful woman she truly was.

The next three months passed slowly in a sort of blur, James hung around the house, still unable to comprehend the complete absence of his beloved Roslyn. Markus tried his best to be a good son to his father, but he still missed Krystyna's company but, even he realised this wasn't the time to introduce her as his new girlfriend. He couldn't help himself being drawn back to his old haunts, the lovely girls and the banter of the barflies who gathered every night to console him and so he began to forget the recent past. He'd spoken to Krystyna several times on the phone but any mention of her coming back to Marbella became irksome for him, he needed immediate gratification, that had been the story of his life so far

When their calls became less frequent and the thrill of finding a supposed hidden fortune began to sound like pie in the sky now, Markus thought he could find other delights nearer home. Much as she didn't want to believe it, Krystyna knew she was on a losing streak yet again but still yearned for the bright lights and glamour of wealth once more. How could she bear the lacklustre life of Poland when she'd just began to see a different world beckoning from sunny Spain?

CHAPTER TWENTY-FIVE

After her many fruitless calls to Markus, she definitely noticed a marked change in his tone and attitude, it was obvious from their conversations that he had already become quite a different person from the man she'd charmed in Krakow and realised that period of her life now seemed to be over. She wondered if she could be blatant and pushy enough to contact Yuri again but, after the way he'd treated her in Spain Then, she thought better of it. He'd obviously used her for the sole purpose of getting to the money and had no further interest in her. So, another chapter of her life had ended too, but she wasn't someone to give in so easily and there were many more fish in the sea!

Markus had become a tower of strength to his father, since Roslyn's death. Nothing had ever touched him as deeply before and he wanted to make amends for his past mistakes by trying to be the dutiful son James had always wanted. Sadly, he could never change his spots entirely. He still kept an eye open for opportunities to promote himself as a successful businessman among his old cronies who continued to feed him stories of the easy money to be made on the Costa del Sol; still known as the 'Costa del crime' by some of its more criminal elements. He enjoyed playing the big shot among this crowd, he liked to boast about his latest exploits and the wonderful woman he'd met who knew the whereabouts of a great fortune that was there for the taking. They smiled knowing his tales of old but still wondered if there might be some truth in his loudmouth bravado. Rumours began to circulate about this cocky

Englishman who was telling all and sundry that a goldmine was there for the taking but unfortunately, it was situated in a hard-to-find location somewhere in the Ukraine.

Alex and Ben had grown much closer over the past few months. They talked endlessly about the growth potential of the robotic industry and all agreed it was a future that was just waiting for entrepreneurial expansion. They all three decided, with James's blessing, to set-up a separate company with four equal shares and call the partnership 'Future World Robotics'. It gave Alex a new slant and direction in his life, his enthusiasm for the project took over all his waking hours and he'd never felt so engrossed in anything since starting his Polish history search. When Alice saw him in London on one of her rare visits, she hardly recognised him as the same grief-stricken grandson she'd seen at Roslyn's funeral. It did her heart good to see him full of energy and thinking of the future once more and it gave her a great boost to know he had at last come to terms with his loss and was beginning to look forward to a new exciting life. It was only what he deserved.

One day, Alex called the Bank in Krakow to inform them officially of his wife's death and ask them to close their accounts, together with all the paperwork, that was to be forwarded to him in London. The many documents, together with old Piotr's letter, he'd placed in a new deposit box for safe-keeping and hadn't looked at them since. They had all been translated in Krakow before he and Roslyn left the city for the last time. So much had happened after that and now was the first time he could sit and digest all the information contained in the English version of that last known letter written by his great-grandmother just before she'd had all their valuables buried in the grounds of their old house. As he looked at the letter, he wondered if all her treasures were still lying there after all those years. It seemed unlikely after such a disastrous world war. The overthrow of the city and its occupation by the Germans before the Russian army took over had been bad enough but the final blow was its annexation by the Ukraine, post 1945. Poland had suffered more than most countries in its turbulent its history; it had changed its borders at least three times in his great- grandfather's life time. Long ago, the present Lwiw was proudly named Lemberg, part of the old Austro-Hungarian Empire, and one of its most beautiful cities. Alex could barely imagine the pain of his family's last hours together when the world was crumbling about them. He shook his head sadly, his heart still grieving for their loss but knowing nothing could have changed the inevitable fate that awaited them in Siberia.

As the days grew longer and the sun began to rise higher in the sky, Ben suggested that he and Alex might like to have a break from all their hard work, leave Jason to take over the running of the business for a while and go on holiday together somewhere in Europe. At first, Alex was slightly dubious but then warmed to the idea of some relaxation where they could unwind and forget the everyday world of commerce. It was decided that Greece might be a good choice, clear blue seas and warm sunshine seemed ideal and so, with tickets booked to Athens, they set off to have some fun, a word that hadn't crossed their minds for ages. Sitting on the beach, soaking up the ambience of Glyfada, they talked for hours about everything and nothing. They hired a boat and sailed to Hydra where the quayside had all that could be desired. One evening, after drinking Ouzo and chatting with two English girls, they took off to Poros, spending a few heady days on the boat, eating and drinking more wine before heading back to Athens. Having dropped the girls off with promises of future meetings, they spent their last night, talking earnestly about the feeling of mutual loss they both felt when Roslyn died and how much they still missed her. It was a cathartic evening in many ways and a fitting ending to a much-needed break.

"Do you ever wonder what our lives would have been like if our families hadn't lost all their material possessions because of the war?"

Ben thought for a moment and then he said in a very serious tone.

"Yes, strangely enough, I do, a lot. When I was in Vienna, I felt complete for the very first time in my life, as if this was my true birth place."

"Me too, I loved Poland immediately and fell in love with Krakow and Lwow. Strange isn't it? We neither of us had ever been to those places before but we both had the same emotion, A sort of second-homecoming!"

"Did I ever tell you the story of about our trip to the Ukraine? I'd already felt I should try and find out about my family's history, even before Roslyn and I went to Krakow. We managed to find out much more about my great grandmother's underground valuables than we thought possible. But, only when a so-called friend of Krystyna's learned that I was trying to find the hidden stuff, did the whole saga of my kidnapping begin. He held me prisoner with all sorts of death threats before letting me go without any other obvious explanation. Poor Roslyn was there on her own and had to deal with all the menacing phone calls, so when I got eventually got back home safely, I decided it was too dangerous for both of us to continue the search and we just gave up on the whole thing."

Of course, Ben had known from Roslyn about the aborted kidnapping, but he decided he wouldn't say anything as he'd promised her that he wouldn't There wasn't any point in going over that painful time all over again, and so he just listened to what Alex had to say. Then started to tell him his own story.

"It is really amazing that you and I have shared such similar histories! My grandfather lost everything when the Germans marched into Austria and commandeered his house, his businesses and everything else because they were Jews. Just

170

like your great grandfather, he was also sent to a concentration camp and the family was left with only the clothes they were wearing. Fortunately, my great grandmother and her only daughter were two of the lucky ones, they escaped to England with nothing but their lives. The only difference is that there were several valuable paintings, stolen from our house and confiscated by the Nazis before being shipped off to Poland and that was the end of the trail. No one knows where they finally ended up."

Alex listened in amazement, he'd never heard that story before and couldn't believe the similarities; two long-lost families with disinherited children with no idea of each other's predicament. Half joking, he said it might be an idea to pool their resources and claim their birth-right. The conversation lasted long into the night with many suggestions and with lots of "What ifs?" and "Why don't we? thrown in, as they each explored and pooled their suggestions. Where to start was the big question, both concluded they had very little to lose so decided to give this latest joint effort one last go before they flew home.

After three months of hard work, getting their business plans in London up and running, they started on some intense planning for the next stage of their mutual enterprise. Ben spent a lot of his time re-examining the last known whereabouts of any long-lost Keller family paintings, as he had done before in Vienna, and scoured all his earlier sources for any newly discovered artworks. Meanwhile, Alex had read in detail all Piotr's information about his old uncle who'd looked after the senior officers stationed there before they were all ordered back to Russia in 1942. He re-read the translations of all the old letters and looked at the pictures of the old mausoleum which must have held some valuable secrets too.

On the other hand, Yuri, now in Kiev, still felt sure that he could still be the true heir to the money. He'd already made plans for extensive excavations near the old stables that had aroused Alex's interest. He used Borys and Kuzma again to carry out the back-breaking work, covering as much ground as they could but, with nothing to show for all their efforts. They'd got tired of doing all the donkey work and complained bitterly about all their hard slog for nothing. Sick of the whole treasure story and thinking it was long gone, probably dug up by a farmer years ago, they asked for their wages and packed the job in, leaving Yuri with yet another dead end. He still believed it was there somewhere but nothing could make them stay so he headed into the city for a good meal and a decent night's sleep before driving the 250 kilometres back home.

Alex, knowing nothing of these recent events, would have been relieved to know that his subterfuge about the location of the burial site had worked and Yuri had given up his search. Only Piotr's most recent letter, left for him in Krakow, together with a detailed map, had made its present whereabouts now a near certainty. Alex's only reason for trying once more to find the family fortune was his way of saying a final farewell to the past, then getting on with his own life once and for all. It took a further few months before he and Ben made definite plans to fly out to Lwiw. Jason had happily taken over the day to day running of the new business and was left holding the fort while they set off on their joint venture. Ben had been in touch with Johanna in Vienna again, but she had no further news of any other paintings being discovered since they last met.

After leaving the Danylo Halysky airport, they hired a car and spent a few nights exploring its wandering alleyways before setting off to look at the ruined Pidhortsi Castle, previously owned by Alex's family. It was now being restored to its former glory and Ben realised for the first time how much of its history must have been lost over the intervening years.

CHAPTER TWENTY-SIX

Krystyna had tried to contact Markus at his father's villa and on his mobile, but he was always unavailable. She couldn't see any light at the end of that particular tunnel and her life had become at best, mediocre. She now saw only had one possible way of improving her lot but that would mean eating humble pie and swallowing her pride, something she wasn't too good at, but needs must. She put on her most alluring voice as she keyed in Yuri's number.

"Yuri, is that you? I've been trying to get in touch with you, it's wonderful to hear your voice again."

Her lies tripped easily off her tongue as she used her greatest acting skills to sound happy to speak to him again. There was a slight hesitation at the other end of the line before he realised it was Krystyna, strange that he had been thinking of her so much recently. He knew she had been incandescent with rage the last time he'd left her to face the music alone in Spain but, if this was what she was prepared to do, it must have taken some guts to phone him again. She had to want something very badly, so he still had the upper with her and that was the way he liked it.

"Yes, long time no see. How's things with you?"

"Good, thanks. I'm doing okay, quite a lot of well-paid jobs in Krakow now." She lied convincingly.

It was like talking to a stranger or a ghost from the past, but she had to do what it took to get onside with him again. She didn't even mention her run in with the Spanish authorities when Bohdan's dead body had been found in their car, it was water under the bridge and she had to make him believe a different story now.

"I wondered if you ever managed to get to Krakow these days and if you fancy getting together again sometime."

"It's been a long time, little krysia, but I've missed you." He lied as well but that old endearment again made her catch her breath, he hadn't called a' little kitten' since the last night they spent together, and she still remembered how she hated it when he used that same phrase as if she was just a plaything, a toy for his amusement. He'd never change but she had to bide her time and keep some ice at the back of her head. She had so much to gain and so little to lose right now.

"What have you been doing? Are you back in Kiev, making more money than ever?"

"Same old, same old! But I have to say life's been dull without you, I know I owe you more than an apology but please, believe me, I've always regretted abandoning you like that."

She knew it was all lies, he was still playing games. He certainly had a very persuasive tongue in his head and he'd always known how to switch on the charm. Now, it was her turn to steer the conversation to her advantage at last.

"I only phoned because I want to ask you a favour and would appreciate your help. My friend, Roslyn, died recently and she left me some money in her will, but I don't know how to transfer it into dollars without letting the government taking a slice of it."

"No problem. Why don't we meet up sometime in Lwiw? I can drive there in a couple of hours and we can meet at the train station. How does that sound?"

It was exactly what she wanted to hear. He was making the first move and maybe she could wrap him round her little finger just once more, she still needed either him or his money.

Markus seemed to have forgotten Krystyna all together and was feeling very relaxed, he was spending more and more time in the company of a delightful French girl who had taken his fancy one night in Mame's Bar, the same busy nightspot he used to frequent, right on the promenade. A favourite drinking place that catered for locals and tourists alike, Markus was on first name terms with the manager, Pepe, and the bar staff who all called him 'El Ingles', a name that he was proud of and felt gave him some gravitas among his fellow compatriots.

He had tried to learn the language but found it easier to speak English, rather than stumble along in his schoolboy Spanish. His newfound girl, Sophie, was very pretty and very young but also worldly-wise beyond her years, she was working as barmaid in the evenings and sunbathing during the day. She had met all his friends who thought he was a lucky man to have found such a gorgeous dolly bird. The fact that his father was rich hadn't gone unnoticed, but such a sweet face deserved a lucky break for a girl who already knew what she wanted out of life and how to get it. He had shortened his name to 'Mark' in keeping with his new lifestyle but would never be able to resist his old ways, he was already totally under Sophie's spell and seemed to have forgotten Krystyna completely.

James had regained some of his former resilience, but Roslyn's death had hit him very hard. Sitting smoking cheroots each evening, as Alice chatted to him on the terrace; he no longer gave two hoots about the business and had begun to drink a little too much wine with his late-night brandies. Their lives had always been companionable but now, they needed each other more than ever to dispel the loneliness they both felt deep inside. They spent more and more time together, reminiscing about old times and wishing life hadn't dealt them such a sad blow when all they both wanted was a quiet retirement. They should have been happily playing with their grandchildren and great grandchildren by now. Alice often felt ungrateful for not being able to count her blessings; she'd had a wonderful husband who'd died too young and a comfortable old age, but she knew James felt very lonely and still missed his wife, Celia. A welcome letter or email from Alex would sometimes lift her spirits a little but the spark seemed to have gone out of her life too when dear Roslyn had died.

Then, one morning, an envelope dropped on her mat, it was addressed to 'Senora A. Wilshaw' with a thick letter inside. At the very same time, another one landed outside James's door for 'Senor. J. Chapell' so he picked it up. It felt quite heavy and the contents were baffling; both were from lawyers saying that they had each inherited a sum of money in the will of Roslyn Wilshaw. When they faced each other across the breakfast table, the wonderment was doubled. Roslyn had left each of them a touching gift, a gold tie pin for him, a piece of jewellery for her plus two cheques but that wasn't the end of it. The main letter was from a lawyer and came as a complete shock to James. He had never known that his late wife, Celia, had inherited a substantial estate from her late father which she had kept a complete secret and then put into a trust fund for her children, especially when she found out that James had packed Markus off to America. It was only the deaths of both Celia and Roslyn that caused the whole legal inheritance mystery to come to light. In the first place, Alex sending Roslyn's death certificate to the various authorities had alerted her late mother's solicitors to her children's trust fund. When the news of their legacy was broken to Markus and to Alex, as her husband, they were amazed that neither of them knew anything about its existence. This new twist meant both these men were very wealthy in their own rights. Roslyn had left all her own savings and her apartment in London to Alex with a proviso that gifts should be given to her father, her brother and Alice.

As he was still in England, getting ready for his trip with Ben, he was able to get some legal friends to throw some light on how international law worked and discussed inheritance by succession with his solicitor. Typically, Markus had gone on a mega spending spree with his new girlfriend and his mates to celebrate his big break, even though he hadn't a clue how much he was now worth. It took another couple of months to iron out all the legalese and jargon that went with foreign lawyers but eventually, after paying the inheritance tax and various international law firms, Markus was left with the best part of £15 million and Alex also became the heir to Roslyn's share of her late grandfather's estate, which amounted to another £15 million. It seemed amazing that both she and Markus had both inherited that fortune from their mother and never knew it.

Mark, as he was now known, couldn't believe his latest streak of luck, he's never been so well off in his whole life, he now had money to burn. He bought Sophie a diamond and emerald ring and himself a new gold Rolex Daytona watch, as they walked round 'Gomez and Molina' in Marbella-Centre.

'It's so beautiful! I love it."

"And that's just for starters."

He laughed, feeling a million dollars in his new Armani linen suit. He looked good and had never felt better with a beautiful girl on his arm and enough money to do exactly what he wanted. His father couldn't tell him what to do any more, he couldn't hide him away in America because he was ashamed of him. He'd show his dad and everyone else what sort of a man he really was before he'd finished.

"Can we go to the Coco-Rico this lunchtime? I want to show Maya my new ring."

"Anywhere you like, Sophie."

Mark felt as if nothing could get any better but how wrong he could be! His luck did change again, this time, for something even better, with a romantic phone call from Krystyna.

But someone else, not too far away, was watching his every move, waiting for a chance to find out where he now kept his money. Mark's boasting hadn't gone unnoticed and this sharp-eyed crook was ready for his first false move which came sooner than expected. A black Mercedes had followed him one night to his father's villa and done a full reconnaissance of the property which had no serious surveillance, the security was minimal, getting in would be a piece of cake. With only two old people living there and a couple of maids during the day, copying Mark's personal papers couldn't have been easier. All he needed was a bank account to get the ball rolling. Mark had barely glanced at his latest statement that showed a few discreet omissions, too insignificant for him to notice.

Carlos Sentosa was beginning to enjoy his job, it was all too easy in many ways, but he knew better than to take anything for granted. He had to keep his eye on the bigger picture; to syphon off 10 grand in smaller amounts was one thing but he hoped for much richer pickings. He'd also gleaned from his various shady sources that Mark 'el Ingles' had come into a multi-million-pound fortune and was thinking of moving with a girlfriend to Rio de Janeiro. Being among the best con men on the Costa del crime, he'd started planning to take some or all of Mark's money from him with the aid of a trusted accomplice, Pedro Lopez, who would be willing, with the added financial incentive of easy money, to aid and abet any scheme his old friend had in mind. Carlos's idea was to fleece the simple-minded Englishman and, along with his friend, Pedro, get a hefty share of the profits.

"It'll be very profitable, but the only things is we'll have to buy are 2 return tickets to Rio first. On the flight out, I'll explain all the details, that you're pretending to be 'Senor Lopez', a rich man from Santiago, who's looking for a luxury home in Rio and that's it, I'll do the rest. You can just sit back and enjoy the trip with a stash of money in your pocket."

CHAPTER TWENTY-SEVEN

Unaware that their lives were about to change yet again in the next few weeks, Ben and Alex were all prepared for their latest exploit, they could now combine their personal ambitions and, hopefully, end the search for their mutually long-lost property. They decided to go directly to Lwiw first and then afterwards, to Vienna. Having arrived at the city airport, they booked into the Nobilis Hotel and later, took a taxi to the City Council Offices, off the main square, to start the serious business of getting as much professional help and governmental information as possible.

"I think the first thing to do is get someone to look at all my papers, they are bound to know someone to help us and translate them for me."

"I agree but I'm sure all the private stuff you've shown me from the Krakow bank about the property in Lwiw should prove you have a serious claim to the Wilowski houses."

"Let's hope so. I don't think we have to worry about the second stable area. I'm fairly certain what we're looking for is somewhere nearer the first house, but I'd love you to see them both before we start on the main digging. The mausoleum should prove very interesting as well, once we've managed to remove the outer door."

It was only a couple of hours before they were sitting in a prestigious City Hall office, talking to a very helpful archivist who promised to put them in touch with various officials re the ownership of Alex's property. He also offered to provide the services of a student from the Ivan Franko University to act as an interpreter while they were staying in the city. It was all going well with an afternoon appointment booked to see a senior advisor in the Records Storage Facility. Later, eating in the hotel restaurant, Alex was feeling very enthusiastic about their first day's achievements, but trying not to feel too ebullient when Ben had to be content with a lesser role in the day's activities. Hopefully, it would be his turn next to have some good news about his own family's lost Austrian possessions.

Meanwhile, in another part of the city, Krystyna was thinking that Lwiw had promised so much for her and Yuri in the past, before all her dreams had started to go awry. Meeting him at the station had been a little strained at first, but she put her arms around him and gave him a long lingering kiss, her heart beating wildly as she held his arm and walked to his waiting car. She wasn't interested in his lies, she only wanted vengeance, but a genuine-looking smile cost her nothing. But she secretly thought

"You'll pay for this, you bastard!"

Now sitting in the foyer of the Astoria Hotel, waiting for Yuri to get their keys, she was wondering how she could bring the subject of Alex's hidden cache into the conversation again. She too was unaware of his latest futile attempt to find the money with those two men doing the excavation for him, but she was still cautious about saying too much. Meeting him again had filled her with mixed emotions, at least she knew all his faults or most of them, they were a well-matched pair. She wanted her share of the spoils, but he wanted the whole Wilowski/ Krakowski fortune for himself alone. Forgiving him for leaving her stranded, trying to explain a dead body in the boot of her car, made her despise him more than ever but it would be her turn now. She would make him pay in spades!

"Sorry to keep you waiting so long, booking us in took ages but we've got a nice view near the park and they say the restaurant's got a good reputation for fine dining."

She smiled, at least he was trying to make all the right moves, so she played along with him.

"What a delightful room! It's perfect, I'm so glad we've made up our differences and we can start all over again."

"Me too, darling, I can't apologise enough for my terrible behaviour. Can you ever forgive me for leaving you in the lurch like that?"

"Well, I was absolutely fuming at first but, if it means that we begin again, I can try to forgive and forget. You've no idea how much I've thought about you."

She didn't tell him the foremost thing on her mind over the past few months was murder, his murder. Instead she kept up her pretence of enjoying their reunion and smiled in all the right places when he tried to manoeuvre her towards the bed; he couldn't believe it was going to be so easy. Later, he reached over to hold her and slowly caressed her body; it was just like old times; making love with her was still one of the best things he remembered about her and she certainly knew how to massage his ego and play all the tricks she'd learned over the years. It was going to be a pleasure to see the surprised look on his face when she finally performed the 'coup de grace', delivered mercilessly with one decisive blow to end his suffering. He would never know what hit him!

Markus, on the other hand, had been over the moon to hear her voice, when she called him while Yuri was taking a shower. The sound of her intriguing Polish accent was music to his ears after listening to that silly whimpering Sophie. As usual, he was already getting tired of her with her constant demands for more presents; it made him more sure than ever that Krystyna was, and always had been, the right woman for him, they were in fact, two of a kind.

"Where are you now, darling? I'm dying to see you. Just tell me when and where we can meet again."

"I can catch a flight from Krakow very soon if you want me to, I can't wait to see you again. I could be in Marbella in about three or four days. I've just got a few loose ends to tie up before I leave. I thought we could head off to somewhere we've never been before and hole up on a tropical beach, just the two of us. Maybe in South America somewhere."

"That sounds wonderful, I can't wait. Just name the day and the hour."

After she put her phone down, she heard Yuri splashing about in the shower, and mentally reviewed the ways of achieving her goal, one was to renew her relationship with Markus and the other was to get rid of Yuri. Both objectives were within her grasp.

Unfortunately for Yuri, the next morning Krystyna asked if they could drive to the Wilowski estate where she still insisted the money was hidden, her only motive was to get him alone and far from the city. He agreed willingly, thinking she knew another site where it might be buried. Walking across an uneven field leading to the stables, she was clutching a large handbag over her shoulder complete with a heavy ten-inch metal bar inside, as he gallantly went in front of her, opening the gate. While he was bending over, trying to unfasten the rusty lock, she quickly pulled the lead weight out from inside her bag and hit him with all her might on the back of his head. Never expecting that sudden blow, he crashed to the ground, his skull, oozing blood and crushed beyond recognition. Seeing him lying there senseless at her feet, she bent down slightly, touching his body with her foot. There was no movement or sound from his lips. She knew, at last, that Yuri, her tormentor, was definitely dead.

It had given her a feeling of satisfaction to see his gaping head wound. Her revenge was complete and was only what he deserved.

'A head for a head and Bohdan's body for his body!'

She carefully wiped the heavy weight and threw it as far as she possibly could over the hedge and into the tall thick grass covering next field, where no one would ever find it. After one last look at his sprawled body, she dug into his pockets, found his car keys and drove back to the city. She parked in a crowded shopping centre, near the hotel. After checking her coat for any possible blood stains and finding none, she quickly walked up to their room, picked up her cases from the bedroom and took the next available flight from Lwiw to Krakow. By the time, someone found his unrecognisable remains several weeks later, she was long gone and already in Spain.

Markus hummed cheerily as he looked over his extensive wardrobe. Should he wear a casual suit or something more formal for their first meeting, Ralph Lauren, Calvin Klein or McQueen? His elation was only matched by his desire to project his new image and dazzle Krystyna with his recent wealth. He was still a child at heart, begging for the approval his father had never been able to give him. With Krystyna by his side, he could end up with everything he'd ever wanted, it only depended on where she wanted to go. She'd had very definite ideas about their travel plans and previously found out in Krakow that there were no extradition laws in Brazil. So, when she arrived in Malaga two days later, Markus had already booked two single first-class flights to Rio de Janeiro.

The first anyone knew of it was a hand-written note, left with Maria, to tell his father that he was flying to South America for an extended holiday. James wasn't even surprised, remembering his son of old and only shook his head sadly. He thought his son would never really change his ways but would probably turn up again one of these days.

CHAPTER TWENTY-EIGHT

Alex and Ben, now armed with official permission, and accompanied by Serge, a student, who was acting as their interpreter, had gone straight to the first manor house and started to mark out the exact spot that Piotr had identified for him in Krakow. They reckoned the burial-site would soon be found with the help of a local metal-detectorist, even though it had lain untouched for over 70 years. It would only need a couple of strong men to locate the secreted hoard and retrieve it from its hiding place. Then they would set about the task of removing the headstone from the family mausoleum, when, hopefully, something of further interest would come to light. What they later found came as a total surprise to them both, an unexpected bonus, a bolt from the blue.

Alex's excitement was mounting as they watched the man carefully move his detector from side to side over the target area, scanning the patch of ground that had been cleared of grass. When the humming sound turned into a clicking noise then changed again, he stopped and waved to indicate he'd found something. Through Serge, he explained he was picking up distinct audio signals and that there were two entirely different sounds from silver and gold rather than the tone that emitted from aluminium junk. He moved his device diagonally, then up and down a few times, trying to determine the exact spot where the signals were strongest. He pointed to an uneven mound and put his thumb up in the air to show he'd found what they were looking for, his face beaming triumphantly.

"I can feel my heart beating like a hammer, I'm getting so excited."

"Me too and it's not even my treasure!" laughed Ben.

The two men hugged each other, Alex was elated. At last, after all these intervening years of waiting, his dream was becoming a reality. Even Serge felt the thrill of the occasion, shook their hands and patted them on the back for good measure. Alex wished he'd brought a bottle of champagne with him but that would have to wait for later so instead he asked Serge to phone the two locals he'd hired to start the dig. They soon brought heavy spades and began digging the turf up first then the soil underneath. About a couple of feet down, one of them felt the hard edge of some sort of container and gave a shout to tell them they'd found something solid in the hole. They made the hole bigger and bigger so that the two of them could climb down and scrape off the encrusted earth around the huge metal box. Loosening the soil from the sides around it, they both bent down feeling two big handles on each side. The older man said something to Serge and made a few gestures making it obvious that it was too heavy for them to lift by themselves, then Serge had a word with Alex and told him they would need extra men to get it out of the ground and put on a suitable base. He looked down into the hole and he realised it was a much bigger job than they had anticipated at first but, after a few words, with the workmen, it was decided that a hoist was going to be needed plus a vehicle to move the container to another location before it could be ready for opening.

It took two days and further negotiations to transfer the newly cleaned box on to a large heavy-duty table in a strong-room in the National Bank. The room was specially set aside for them so that they could examine its contents at their leisure and closely compare the items with Piotr's list. Alex couldn't stop thinking about Roslyn and how excited she would have been to see his family's prized possessions put out on display at last. Each precious piece had been carefully wrapped in soft cotton then in velvet bags and her personal jewellery in chammy leather wallets. There were two magnificent tiaras, both with diamonds, one with emeralds and the other with sapphires; ropes of heavy translucent pearls, diamond and gold bracelets and necklaces, rings, watches, with earrings of every style and colour. Then there were bags full of single gem stones, it was a galaxy of finery to gladden the eyes of any discerning jeweller. When all those pieces were set out on the table, they saw there was another tray underneath, Alex lifted one corner, a heavy satin sheet covered what lay beneath, so he picked up the cloth and a full array of silverware was soon exposed. The table wasn't large enough to hold the all the silver candelabras, a wealth of silver dishes, plates and cutlery; all laid out exactly as they had been on the day his great-grandmother ordered them to be buried.

Alex had expected to discover an extraordinary stash but even he and Ben were staggered at the size and worth of their find. The one stipulation that Lwiw Council had made was that that their experts should be allowed to make a valuation of the items before they were either transported abroad or sold. It seemed like a reasonable request, so Alex readily agreed to have armed security guards on duty until he could organise for their export and appraisal in London. Government officials were eager to help when Alex promised to pay all the expenses for 24-hour police protection to put the display of the treasure trove on show in the main entrance hall of the Opera House for one week. He felt it was the least he could do in return for all the help he'd received from them during his stay in the city.

Ben phoned James in Marbella to tell him and Alice the wonderful news and they were both delighted. Meanwhile, Jason, still holding the fort in London, told Ben not to worry if they had to stay longer, he was enjoying overseeing all the extra time he was spending on their robotics enterprise. So, it seemed that they had all their options covered and it made sense to carry on working on the next phase of their operation until they could open the mausoleum and finally discover the secrets of the Wilowski tomb.

It took the best part of the next week to organise the preparations in the Opera House with lots of high powered guests wanting to see the beautifully laid-out exhibition of the late Count and Countess's regalia and jewellery, dating back to the glorious Lemberg days and the old aristocracy. Alex was treated royally by all the city officials when he presented two fine candelabras to the city's chief councillor, who thanked him for bringing back some of their history for the citizens of Lwiw to see. It was a gratifying moment for him, thinking how proud his grandfather would have been with such an appreciative audience.

Ben was as eager as Alex to get on with the next stage of the work; the men, who had previously dug up the box, were more than delighted to be back at work once again. They no longer needed to use a metal-detector, but they did need extra manpower with lifting and moving equipment to dislodge that heavy stone. Serge arranged this for them the next day and when the gear arrived, there were many scraping and grinding noises as it began to shift, a little at a time. Slowly the gap widened revealing only inky darkness at first but as the daylight began to penetrate the gloom and, with the aid of powerful torches, the crypt was, at last, revealed. It held several tombs containing the remains of Alex's ancestors with dates going back to the 17th century. He stood silent for a while, taking in the moment, and told Serge that he didn't want anything inside moved until the stone was replaced.

"I don't want to disturb their last resting places but would like some time to investigate the interior properly."

When Serge was paying the four workmen their wages up to date, arranging for them to come back in a couple of days, Alex interjected, saying if they guarded the mausoleum on a twenty-four basis, he would give them double pay and a food allowance. So happily nodding, they were more than delighted to say yes. Ben agreed that was the best solution for everyone.

"I think that's the right thing to do, Alex. I'm sure a good night's sleep is what's needed before you make any long-term decisions."

"I know it sounds strange but I'm finding it hard to take it all in right now. Opening the tomb has had quite an effect on me and I feel as if we're going to find at least some solutions to all our research at long last."

Ben realised that what had happened over the last few hours would take time to sink in with Alex. He seemed to be in daze and overwhelmed at the same time.

"It might be hard for you to understand but for me, it's been like going back in time and seeing ghosts of my ancestors all in one place. I've never had a feeling quite like that before ever, Really weird!"

Seeing the glazed look in his eyes, Ben said.

"Now that we have someone watching the place 24/7, I think we should take a break, find a place where the three of us can have something to eat and then drive back to the city."

After a very eventful day and a good meal, they dropped Serge off at home and had a drink in the hotel bar before heading to the lifts.

"Good night and thanks for everything, Ben"

"No worries! It was an exciting day for me too but quite not as dramatic as yours. I'm going to phone home now so is there anything you want to pass on to Jason at the moment?"

"No, I don't think so, I'll phone my grandmother in Marbella tomorrow to tell her the latest news, she'll be eager to know what's happening here."

"Well then, have a good night's sleep and I'll see you in the morning about 8'ish."

After Ben went into his room, he had a quick shower, towelled himself dry then lay on the bed and picked up his phone to speak to Johanna.

"Good to hear your voice again. I've been wondering how things are going."

"Lovely to speak to you, Jo. Well, it's been an exciting day, particularly for Alex. They managed to get the mausoleum open at last, after a lot of shoving and pushing, if you could have seen his face when it was finally done, he was like a man in a trance. There are at least eight separate tombs, two with effigies on the top; a bit like those you see in very old churches. So, we're going back tomorrow to buy some stronger lamps to lighten the place up and then get cracking with an inspection of everything inside."

"Sounds as if you're enjoying it anyway. I do have some news for you too. Do you recall the old lady who remembered seeing some paintings hanging in your grandfather's house when she was a girl? She's been in touch with me again because she's found an old photograph her elder brother took when he was in the same house and it showed two pictures on the wall in the family dining room. She's given it to me and is absolutely certain they were taken in your old home."

"Wow! That's brilliant. It's the nearest we've been to hearing good news for ages."

"I'll fax you a copy to your hotel and you can see them for yourself, I knew you'd be delighted after so many false alarms and disappointments."

They had a few more words after telling her how much he missed her. So, with his curiosity aroused, he went to bed with something to think about other than grave stones and burial chambers. He dreamt of his Austrian grandmother for the first time in ages and took it as a good omen that his luck was changing; maybe it was his turn to find something of value.

CHAPTER TWENTY-NINE

Sitting on a lounger by the pool, Mark felt as contented as any man could be. He gazed at Krys's sun-tanned face and touched her hand lovingly, she responded with a warm smile and squeezed his hand in return. They had both decided to use the names Mark and Krys for their new life in Brazil

"I never thought my life was meant to be happy, but now we've found each other at last, I'm the happiest person alive."

"Me too!" She turned to look at him and was glad she had seen that 'little boy lost look' in his eyes when they'd met in Marbella. Much as his mother had loved him, he had always lived in Roslyn's shadow, never being able to win his father's approval and be the son he'd always wanted. That was all over, and their lives were now cast in a new mould.

"I do love you, Krys, I hope you know that. I have never loved any one like I love you, from the very bottom of my heart. It was only you I thought of in my dreams"

"My, darling Mark, I love you too and our decision to move here was the best choice we could have made. For me, this is paradise on earth."

In her heart, she knew she would have to tell him the truth about Yuri's death sometime, but she wasn't going to spoil this idyll with something as sordid as that, not when their new romance was just blossoming. She still had no regrets about killing him, he got exactly what he deserved! It was her time now with no ghosts around to haunt her new-found happiness.

The next weeks passed in a glorious haze, they swam in the sea, walked on the beach, ate fresh lobster in the restaurant, and had a wonderful time making love in each other's arms every night. It was absolutely perfect, and it seemed nothing was going to mar their new happiness. Only one man could muddy the water for them and it was a man neither of them had met. His name was Carlos Sentosa and he was the same con man who'd burgled James's house on the Costa del Col. He'd heard Mark boasting in the past to his so-called friends about his sudden inheritance and knew that he was loaded from all accounts. That's when he'd broken into the villa and photocopied his bank statements, also paying a local pick-pocket to steal his credit card. So, the stage was set for the next step of his double-cross. He booked a return trip to Rio with his co-conspirator, paid for with Mark's forged Platinum card, and traced their flight details through a naïve travel agent who gave him the name of the hotel where the two lovebirds were staying. Then it was easy for him to book himself a suite in the same hotel. The rest was a piece of cake for a professional smooth-talker like Carlos when he met them next morning by the pool and introduced himself as Felipe Juarez, from Santiago.

"Call me Phil, it's easier." He smiled as they shook hands. They chatted a while until he said he had a business meeting in the city about some real estate he was interested in buying so perhaps they could meet for a drink later.

"Nice chap!"

Krys had to agree but he was then forgotten until they saw him again, having a drink on his own in the bar.

"Would you like to join us, Phil? I did get your name right, didn't I?"

"Si, Senor, and you are Krys, I believe" He kissed her hand and bowed his head. "I'd like a rum and Coke."

Mark beckoned a waiter, and all said 'Santé' as they drank, raising their glasses for a toast.

"Did you have a successful day with your property dealings?" Mark asked.

"Amazingly, yes! I was looking to buy a block of apartments in a very up-and-coming area near the beach, not too far from the main shopping centre. It was an auction and there were a lot of other buyers with the same idea, but I managed to put in the highest bid, luckily for me." He laughed, lying easily.

"Sounds interesting? We think we may buy a place ourselves near the beach when we decide on the right area."

"Well, I'll keep you in mind if I see anything else on my travels, I'll be staying for a week or so maybe we can catch up for lunch sometime."

"Great, we'd like that."

Then he offered them another drink and said he had a date later, tapping the side of his nose twice with a smile and a knowing wink.

Later, they had a meal in the 'Roof Terrace' restaurant and Mark asked if she would like to go to the casino later.

"I'm feeling a bit tired tonight. Do you mind if I go to bed early, darling?"

"No, not at all but I may try my luck for a while."

He always enjoyed playing baccarat, he fancied his chances, if only for the thrill of it. He sat at the gaming table, looked around to see if he recognised anyone and was surprised when he spied Phil talking in earnest to a very flash-looking individual who seemed to be totally engrossed in their conversation. He was nodding his head in agreement and gesticulating, using both hands to show his approval. Mark thought it strange to see him there but perhaps he'd taken his 'knowing wink' in entirely the wrong way, he'd presumed he was meeting a woman rather than a man.

Then he decided to concentrate on the game in hand and bet $1000 on the dealer to win which he did so, content with his bet, he doubled it and won again, he was obviously on a winning streak. If he was sensible, he knew he should go to bed with the money, but he doubled his bet again and won again. What a roll he was on! He was now seven thousand in front and could see one or two people watching his chips pile up, so he pushed all his chips on to the table and said 'Banco' and lost the lot in one hand. Who cared? He had as much money as he could ever need and a lovely woman in his bed, so life couldn't be better than that. Then that old gnawing feeling in his gut started to take over his reckless streak, he asked for more chips, 20 thousand Real, which was okayed by the floor manager. After an hour, he was in the red to the tune of fifty thousand, then suddenly, it was as if a cloud lifted from his brain. He knew if he went on like this, he would lose everything he held dear, including the woman who was waiting for him in their room. He was doing exactly what he'd done so many times before in Las Vegas and the time had come for him to stop making a fool of himself again. He got up and left the gaming table, vowing it was for the last time. It was his eureka moment.

He decided to pay for all the chips he'd lost with one of his credit cards and when the casino teller put it into the cash machine, he scowled and then called over a supervisor, who spoke to Mark.

"I'm afraid your card is no longer valid, senor. Do you have another card?"

"Yes, I do but that's very strange, I was sure it was in credit."

He handed another card to the teller and this time it was accepted immediately. Mark couldn't understand but realised that using his new name had caused the mistake. He concluded that he must have spent more at the casino than he thought and then quickly forgot all about it. His mind was on the lovely woman waiting for him back in his room.

Krys opened her eyes sleepily as his warm body snuggled up to hers, then kissed him. He returned her kiss passionately and ran his hands over her sleeping form, until she was fully awake and enjoying his caresses. They made love until they were both exhausted then turned over and smiled at each other. What had started as a mere flirtation, when they first met in Marbella, was growing day by day and getting more intense. It seemed that they had at last met their alter egos. They had both gone through so many heartaches and disappointments in their love-lives, it was a wonderful feeling have met someone who wanted to be with you forever.

They decided to go to the beach bar for breakfast and enjoy another day reading and lazing by the gently rolling sea. At that moment, a giant shadow fell over their lounge-chairs and, squinting up to see who was sitting so close, Phil appeared above them. He was dressed casually and asked them if they would like to take a drive with him later.

"I might have something interesting to show you. Maybe we could have lunch somewhere first then I can drive you to see my wonderful find."

"Sounds interesting. Is it far?"

"No, but I don't want to spoil the surprise. I'll meet you at one in the lobby, is that okay?"

They both looked at each other and agreed it sounded great.

"Lunch is on me, by the way."

"That suits us, Phil. One o'clock at the check-in desk."

Then they spent all morning wondering what he was going to show them so mysteriously.

"Bet it's a house or something."

"You could be right, but we'll have to wait and see. I feel like a swim before lunch any way and we'll have to shower afterwards."

"Last in the water is a sissy."

Laughing, they chased each other into the sea and then dived in under the water.

"I didn't know you were such a good swimmer." She spluttered as he came up beside her, grinning.

"Plenty of things you don't know about me. You still have a lot to learn yet."

After their shower, they met Phil and set off in his rather expensive looking hire car, unwittingly paid for with Markus's old credit card again. He drove them to a beautiful detached bungalow with a 'FOR SALE' outside, it was in a tree-lined garden with a swimming pool to the side.

"Well, what do you think so far? It's on the market for R$500:000."

They both answered at once to say it was very nice but not exactly what they were thinking of, at the moment. He looked slightly downcast, he had hoped for a more appreciative response but carried on regardless.

"I do have another to show you which might be more your style, it's on the marina, overlooking Copacabana. It's one I've got my eye on myself but it's more expensive."

Mark was going to say money was no problem but held it back, he didn't want Phil to think he was an easy target. The other man wasn't fooled by his hesitation, he had seen his bank account and knew already that money was no object.

"I think that sounds more to our liking."

Krys was keen to put her roots down in this lovely city, she knew the Mark of old had itchy feet and wanted him to be in a place that ticked all the boxes. So, a luxurious pad in the right setting was what she had in mind for them both. The next stop was outside a high-rise apartment block, right on the beach in Copacabana, with superb views down to Ipanema and it literally took her breath away. Phil parked at the back of the building out of the sun and walked them into the imposing white marble lobby where the concierge greeted them while

Phil explained they had come to view the penthouse apartment and showed them to one of the lifts taking them up to the 14th floor.

It was more spectacular than either of them expected, it had a pool with 2 huge balconies, an enormous glass-fronted sitting room, four bedrooms with en-suite bathrooms and a space age kitchen. The views alone were worth a fortune and much as she had admired James's villa, it looked small by comparison. Of course, Mark was blown away by its size and splendour; the whole place was luxury personified to the last detail and it had the effect Phil had hoped for this time.

"Wow! It's absolutely gorgeous, even better than I thought it would be!"

"I'm glad you like it, I knew you would."

They went from room to room spellbound and couldn't find a single fault with the décor and the furnishings.

"The furniture and all the fittings can stay in situ if you like them. Take your time, look around and then I'll take you back to the hotel. I'm sorry I'll have to leave you there, but I have another client to see before dinner."

After a second viewing, they finally left the building, both totally in love with what they'd seen and eager to talk to each other. After dropping them at the entrance, Phil waved and invited them for dinner in the evening to make up for losing out on their promised lunch.

"My apologies but I have to speak to another gentleman who was very keen to see the property I just showed you. So, see you both later."

With that he was gone, leaving Krys and Markus to think about their 'mystery' outing and to wonder who the other purchaser might be. The answer came sooner than they expected.

"Strange he didn't mention the other buyer before, maybe he'll be more forthcoming at dinner."

After a very relaxing siesta, they dressed, drank an aperitif at the bar and started discussing the penthouse and the appeal of the beach being so close. At that same moment, Phil walked toward them with big grin on his face.

"Great news, I've sold that apartment. My client loved it."

Mark was quite crestfallen but Krys found it difficult to believe the other guy had made such a snap decision, it seemed too much of a coincidence. Everything had fallen into place a tad too quickly for her liking and alarm bells began ringing in her head. Was it all too good to be true?

With their friend in such an ebullient mood, it was churlish to bring a note of circumspection into the conversation but Krys knew Mark was very disappointed that the apartment was no longer on the market. He'd fallen in love with it at first sight, something he'd done so often before in his life, so she tried to keep her suspicions to herself. They went by taxi to the Copacabana Palace Hotel and had a drink in the palm-lined bar before dinner.

"Here's to more days like this!"

Phil raised his glass and grinned, quite oblivious to Mark's more sombre mood, and then ordered 2 very expensive bottles of champagne and Beluga caviar to start the evening off with a flourish. The meal that followed was superb and they had one of the best steaks that Brazil had to offer. The two men drank even more champagne followed by cognacs and, as the evening wore on, they were getting steadily inebriated.

CHAPTER THIRTY

Even Krys was feeling slightly tipsy when, at that moment, another gentleman walked over to their table and greeted Phil like a long-lost brother.

"Senor Felipe, how wonderful to see you again so soon. I didn't know you were staying here."

He looked up at him and smiled broadly, slurring his words slightly

"Senor Pedro, this is an honour. Will you join us?"

"Well, just for a while, I'm waiting for a lady to arrive."

He tapped his finger to his nose twice, just as Phil had done on the first night they'd met him.

"These are two of my best friends, let me introduce you to Krys and Mark."

"Delighted to meet you!"

Bowing, he kissed her hand and then shook his.

"Would you excuse me, please? I do apologise but I would like to speak to you for a minute, Senor Felipe?"

"Of course! Perdon! Un momento, por favor."

He stood up as the two men began speaking to each other in Spanish while Krys tried to understand some of the conversation but could only manage a few scraps, including 'apartment', 'for sale' and then, she could hardly believe her ears when she distinctly heard the word 'Marbella' They were obviously talking about the place they'd viewed earlier but why was Mark's hometown mentioned too? When he'd gone, the other two carried on drinking until both men were decidedly the worse for wear. Krys, who wanted to keep a clear head, refused more alcohol and drank only bottled water until, eventually, their host asked for the bill just before midnight. By the time the head waiter had given it to him, he was as drunk as a lord and, while trying to decipher the account, he dropped his credit card on the floor next to Krys's chair.

Knowing he was completely bleary-eyed by that time, she quickly bent down to pick it up for him and was horrified to see "Markus's" name on the card. In a flash, it all started to make sense to her. So, that was his game! Somehow, he had managed to get hold of a copy of his card and was using it to pay his own checks. Her mind, quick as a flash, knew exactly what to do, so she handed it back to Phil without saying another word. After they'd taken another taxi back to their hotel, they all said goodnight and promised to see each other later. Only Krys was clear-headed enough to know exactly what had happened.

She put Mark to bed and decided to wait until next morning before broaching the subject to him. She was still wide-awake in bed, with him gently snoring beside her. She was in her element, planning how to play this new game of 'Guess who Phil is'! It was now patently obvious he was an imposter and not the man he was pretending to be, but it didn't explain how he had managed to get hold of "Markus's" old credit card.

"How are you feeling this morning, darling?"
She whispered his name gently in his ear.
"Absolutely awful! Why did I drink so much?"
"Well, you did over do the champagne and brandy a bit."
"A bit'! That is the understatement of the year! I feel as if I drank a whole vineyard."

She laughed and suggested they should have a hearty breakfast as Mark shuddered at the mere thought of food.

"I'll order room-service and some strong black coffee might make you feel better. I'd like scrambled egg on toast and then let's see how that looks to you."

While she ate, he watched as she had her breakfast; the only things he could manage were two cups of strong coffee and a thin piece of toast.

"I have something to ask you, it's about our friend, Phil. Have you ever met him before or did you know him in Marbella?"

"No, why do you ask? I did meet a lot of new people over there and dozens of 'hangers-on' but I don't think I've met him before, why?"

"He's a conman, Mark. I can't break this news to you any other way, I'm afraid."

"How do you know that, he seems okay to me?"

"Well, last night, which you probably don't remember, when he asked for the bill in the restaurant, he was quite drunk and dropped a credit card on the floor, so I picked it up for him and I couldn't believe my eyes when I saw it had your old name on it."

"My name? How come? What on earth did you do?"

"I just gave it straight back to him and didn't say a word. He was too far gone by that time to know what he was doing. He could barely speak."

"My God! The bastard, what's do you think he's playing at?"

"I'm not quite sure yet but I do know 'our dear Phil' isn't the man we thought he was. Somehow, he's got his hands on your old credit card and is obviously using it. The only good thing is, he probably hasn't used it here in this hotel because he'd think you probably had the same card with your old name on it, so he must have other ones as well."

"I wonder why he wanted us to see that apartment and then suddenly told us it had been sold to someone else?"

"Maybe it was a sprat to catch a mackerel, as they say. He probably is in league with someone else and is trying to con us into buying an even more expensive place."

"You are a very clever girl, but how does he know we can afford such a luxury apartment or how much money I have?"

"That's easy, if he knew you before, maybe even in Marbella, and found out you had suddenly come into a lot of money, he could have done his homework and put two and two together."

"I suppose that could be it; I did give a big celebration party at my father's house when I found out about my inheritance, I don't even remember all the people I invited. The house was full of strangers and probably some gate-crashers too."

"He must have known one of your many friends would have been happy to invite him to the party. Then, he could have slipped easily into various rooms at the villa, including yours, to search for any bank statements and credit cards he could find. Remember he's an expert conman, he knew exactly where to look and all he had to do after that was watch you to find out all about you. Then he could have found out that you intended to fly to South America, so he decided to follow us here with you paying the bill. Not a bad scam really and by that time, he could've had forged copies of your other credit cards, made by one of his criminal pals, and has been using your old one ever since."

"If you're half right and I believe you are, I still can't believe the audacity of the man! Pretending to be so friendly and trying to sell us an apartment that he doesn't own anyway. It's just too much to take in right now, my head's still spinning but I do remember seeing him talking to another man that night I went to the casino alone, that night you were tired and stayed in our room. That man could have been his friend, Senor Pedro, the same man he introduced us to last night. When I think about that night, the casino teller did refuse my first card because he said there was insufficient credit in it. I should have known better, idiot me!"

"Well, I think we should pay him back in Spades, but we must carry on letting him think we know nothing and then we can play him at his own game."

"But how will we do that?"

They continued talking about what to do next despite Mark's sore head. Krys thought they should involve the local police but he didn't like that idea, he wanted to keep it quiet until a more appropriate time. The ideal opportunity fell into their laps a few days later.

"We'll set a trap for him with so much temptation, he won't be able to resist the bait."

Krys had seen the covetous way he looked at her jewellery when he'd admired her huge diamond and sapphire ring that Mark had bought her, and he couldn't take his eyes off the other expensive pieces she wore every night. So, she already knew that he had a weakness for gemstones and, after confiding her scheme to Mark, he was delighted and wholeheartedly agreed to play his part in outsmarting Phil.

The next day, when he mentioned in passing that Senor Pedro had withdrawn his offer to purchase the penthouse they'd fallen in love with, he had the cheek to ask them if they were still interested in buying it.

"Maybe, it's a possibility but we'll have to give it some serious thought and let you know later."

When they'd first arrived in Rio, Mark had visited Sterns, the best jeweller in the city, and asked them to make some special pieces as gifts for his new fiancé and so, he became a familiar and valued customer there and was always invited into a private room to view their latest selections. Later, Krys also became a customer and it was her bright idea to have copies made of her favourite jewels. This was after they had been warned it wasn't safe to wear them in public places where thieves often targeted both unwary tourists and wealthy clients alike. Shortly after receiving this sound advice, they both chose their most valuable trinkets, and, within three weeks, the replicas were ready for their inspection and it was practically impossible for an untrained eye to tell them apart. Then they were hand delivered to the hotel and placed in their own special deposit box within the strong room. The manager was pleased to be able to offer this service for such highly regarded residents. Unknown to anyone else, both sets of jewels were safely locked away.

Later when Phil arrived and booked into their hotel, he started playing the part of an amiable acquaintance. Initially, Mark and Krys had been completely taken in by his pretence of being a mere fellow guest. He then quickly wormed his way into their confidence, becoming a regular sunbather by the pool and congenial fellow guest. They knew he would be leaving soon, he'd said he was only there to look over some properties, so his stay would be short and sweet. At first, Krys had taken quite a shine to him, he wasn't a professional conman for nothing. Such a shame he had to get drunk one night and let his guard down; otherwise everything might have ended with a lot of angst for everyone.

One evening, when they'd started to meet regularly, Phil asked them.

"Fancy another drink before dinner?"

"That would be great, thanks."

But, by this time, both Mark and Krys were aware of his credit card scam and had set in motion a very enticing trap for their false friend. As previously arranged, Krys appeared practically draped in all her best finery with her real sparklers flashing with more scintillation than a Christmas tree. She knew she looked stunning, if a little over the top, but the effect made Phil catch his breath with the anticipation that soon this prize could also be his.

"I was just offering Mark a drink; can I do the same for you?"

"I'd be delighted, thought you'd never ask!"

They sat at the bar and Phil was trying his best to keep his mind on the business of trying to sell them another apartment, something grander and more expensive.

"Such a pity you didn't go for that penthouse, the price was right, and Senor Pedro was a fool to let it go but I have to go next week, I've promised to see a new development up in Recife before I head off home."

"We'll be sorry to lose you and will miss you very much. Perhaps you'll be able to come and see us again, remember you've promised to find us another apartment."

"I certainly won't forget that! It's been such a pleasure for me to meet you and Mark and I'll always think about our short acquaintance with much satisfaction."

Mark came over to join them, as planned beforehand, grasped Phil's hand with a grin on his face and put his arm round his shoulder.

"We have a little surprise for you. We would like to invite you to special celebratory dinner before you leave, to show you our appreciation of your friendship."

"But that's not necessary, your company and amusing conversations have kept me from spending many lonely hours on my own here."

"We insist, we want you to have a night to remind you of the happy times we've spent together so, please let's have a wonderful evening together tomorrow. We'll put on all our best finery for the occasion, I have reserved a private dining room in the hotel so that we can eat, drink and be merry without anyone watching how much champagne we drink!

CHAPTER THIRTY-ONE

Senor Rodrigues, the executive hotel manager, having known them for several months as wealthy and exemplary residents, readily agreed for Krys and Mark to witness the depositing of the two jewel cases from Sterns, the jewellers, in the strong room. He, jokingly, added he hoped they wouldn't sue him if the boxes got mixed up. They all laughed, but he was assured that such a thing would be impossible as they would be able to tell the difference immediately and showed him that the originals had a capital "K" on top while the fakes had an engraved "M" underneath for added security. As an afterthought, he said if ever they were mixed up for whatever reason, there was a signed letter left with the manager as an added guarantee that the whole thing was above-board. Then the real ones were put back in the safe and locked up for safe keeping once more.

Phil was unaware that all the gems Krys now wore were only counterfeit; he had seen the real ones several times when she'd deliberately showed them off for his benefit in the bar or in the restaurant when they had dinner together. So, the trap was set, and the genuine jewels were the bait. He picked up his mobile phone and heard his friend, Pedro, speaking.

"Buenos dias, Pedro."

After they'd exchanged greetings, he carefully explained how he now intended to steal the unsuspecting couples' gems and he offered him 25% of their worth if he would take part in the simplest heist he'd ever done. Pedro was more than delighted to help his 'old friend' and knew from past jobs they'd done together that his share of the loot would keep him in funds until they were able to fly back to Spain. Brazil and Rio were fine for a short while, but he really missed his lifestyle in Marbella. There wasn't much time left before they had to leave so the job had to be done quickly, then home and away; leaving a very surprised pair to find their jewels gone, without any means of getting them back, like lambs to the slaughter!

"They're going to take me out for a farewell dinner tomorrow evening, so you'll have plenty of time to break into their room and get the silver jewel case with all its contents. Just beforehand, I'll tell them not to wear their best glitz because someone in the hotel was mugged last night and the thieves grabbed all their jewellery while they were out with some friends."

"Sounds good to me, I'll be in and out in a flash with no one the wiser until they get back, no fingerprints and no clues!"
The next evening went like a dream. Phil recounted his scare story just before they came into the bar. Krys, who was wearing her finest and most previous jewels for the occasion looked at Mark apprehensively and she decided to go back to their room and put on a simple gold chain instead.

"I'm sure it will be safe there, it's not as if I'm flaunting my stuff outside."

"Don't worry, darling, it'll be fine, we can't be opening the safe again at this time of night. Everything will be okay."

Then they asked the concierge to call them a taxi and, as she was getting in next to Markus, she squeezed his hand to let him know everything was going to their plan. In a very short time, they arrived at the 'Aprazivel', a beautiful outdoor place located on a hillside in Santa Teresa with views over the city to downtown Rio' The champagne flowed freely, and the food was magnificent. They talked volubly about their love of the whole city with its beautiful beaches and the vibrant nightlife that made everyone feel young no matter how old they were. It was truly a night to remember before they had to say their good-byes to each other.

"I'm afraid I may not see you both in the morning, my plane leaves for Recife at 7:30 so I'll have to say farewell tonight and thank you both for all the wonderful memories you've given me. I shall never forget you and I promise I will find you the best apartment in Rio when we meet again."

Krys would have felt quite tearful with his protestations of seeing them again, if she hadn't known that he was a complete fraud and was only out to steal their precious treasures, without a backward glance or slight hesitation. He was an out and out scoundrel but also a charmer which briefly reminded her of Yuri who would have done the very same thing. She still smarted at the memory of the shame she'd suffered at his hands when he'd deserted her but no longer felt any remorse for his death, he had never intended to keep his promises to her anyway. But she'd had the last laugh, after all; Yuri was dead, she was still very much alive and living the life she'd always envisaged for herself.

The theft was a great success, Pedro was an expert and the stolen case with the engraved 'M' underneath was in his hands shortly after the happy threesome left the hotel, it was an excellent result. After Phil and Senor Pedro were on their way to the airport next morning, they decided to revert to their real names of Carlos Sentosa and Pedro Lopez for the journey. They then split the spoils of their ill-gotten gains between them in case an official questioned why they were carrying so much jewellery, although it was well hidden in their dirty underwear. They sat separately on the first flight, one in business class and one in economy, and only came together when they changed planes in Recife for Malaga. After a long and uneventful trip, they both decided to get some sleep before meeting later for the final tally of their joint property.

Next morning, Mark informed Mr. Rodriguez of the theft of the jewels from their room but quickly assured him that only the copies had been stolen, not the real gems, which were still in the strong room. The manager heaved a big sigh of relief to hear that and when he called the police to tell them of the robbery, both Krys and Mark had to be interviewed to verify that the thief had taken nothing of any great value, much to their satisfaction and the jewellers too. So, it was another evening of celebration for everyone except the two main players, already well on their way to Marbella. It wasn't long after landing that Carlos realised he'd been duped by the oldest con-trick in the world; their last-minute swop of the real stuff for the fakes. It took a thief to catch a thief!

Life soon got back to something like normality when all the counterfeit jewels were replaced for the second time and another silver box made with the 'M' underneath. The package was sent by special messenger back to their hotel.

"I would love to have seen Phil's face when he discovered that he was the one who had been tricked and poor Pedro would no longer get his share of the proceeds. He can never again lay claim to being the best con-man on the Costa del Sol, not after we fooled him"

"It serves them both right, I just wish we'd been able to get the police to believe they had stolen the real stuff instead of the fakes, then they really would have been in serious trouble, with 20 years in gaol as well. They've come off lightly."

"Well, it's certainly taught me one thing for sure, never to wear the genuine article to show off in front of anyone."

"I wonder if we'll ever forget this experience. Perhaps, we should take more care when choosing our so-called friends from now on, I used to think in the old days, I'd learnt my lesson but obviously not. Can you imagine if he'd got away with it and stolen everything? It was only your instant reactions and intuition that saved the day."

"Well, let's not think about it too much, we've still got each other and that's the best thing we could ever have. Perhaps, it's all been for the best."

They kissed and realised more and more how much they needed each other. They'd reached a new deeper understanding that would stand them in good stead for their lives together, whatever the future might hold. Krys felt deep down that she had at last met the man she wanted to spend the rest of her life with and knew how lucky she was that he loved her just as much as she loved him.

They soon began looking for a place of their own to call home. He wanted to invite his father to visit and show him he had at last become the son his dad had always dreamed of and it wasn't too late for him to be a grandfather after all, it was all in the lap of the gods!

CHAPTER THIRTY-TWO

The discoveries Alex made when the family vault had been opened were much more interesting than he could have hoped. With the proper lighting in place and an expert from the city archives on loan to them, both he and Ben started the search in earnest with the two workmen carrying out various heavy boxes to be noted and transferred to a special room set aside for them in City Hall. The exhibition of the old Wilowski treasures had been very well received by the city fathers and had earned them a lot of kudos in official circles. They put all manner of helpful people at their disposal including young Serge who was now part of their team on a semi-permanent basis.

The archivist was engrossed in taking down every last detail as he took endless photographs of all the coffins before they were carefully replaced. Only then would the vault be finally sealed, and the old Hapsburg family would once again be allowed to rest in peace. At the back of the burial chamber, Alex had reached up to an elevated alcove which he surmised once held another much smaller coffin, now lying on the ground. He brought in a stronger torch that could light up the furthest corners of the recess and brought out several rolled-up pieces of cloth or canvas which had obviously been hidden away when the tomb was moved. They were inches thick with years of dirt and cobwebs, so he pulled them out to look at later then decided to have the coffin replaced on its original shelf, it could possibly have held the body of a child at some time.

Ben had been waiting for him to explore the rest of the crypt, the air was dank with the smell of old bones and musty with age. He was dying to get out of there but knew this time was set aside for Alex alone, to be there as long as he wished with the long-forgotten remains of his ancestors. This was all that was left of his family and he may never see them again in his lifetime, so it was important for him to be able to say his final good-byes to them in the hope that, maybe in the future, some children, yet to be born, might make this trip to be reacquainted with the last of the Wilowskis.

When the last large stone was in place in front of the vault and the last of the workmen paid off, Alex brushed the rolls of canvas free of dust and put them in the back of their car until he had driven Serge home.

"Shall we have a look at those rolled up papers and see if they are of any use before they get thrown away? I don't fancy taking them into the hotel, They're filthy."

"Okay, if you drive into the hotel carpark and open the boot, we can take them out there. Our clothes are pretty grubby already, so we can take a quick look and then get rid of them if you don't want them."

What happened next was a total surprise to them both. The cloth holding them was so old, it crumbled in Alex's hands, but underneath were two thick rolls of canvas, very dirty but still pliable. He unfolded and rolled each one flat, they were quite small, about 25 x 40 inches, Ben was the first one to show any sign of recognition and he gasped in amazement this time! There were the very same pictures Johanna had recently faxed and sent to him.

"I've seen them before, I can't believe it. It's absolutely incredible!"

"Why? What are they?"

"I think they're two of the paintings that used to hang in my family home in Vienna."

"What do you mean? How could she have sent them? They're here and they've been rolled up in that burial chamber for years."

"I know, but she sent me a fax showing these paintings when I spoke to her the other night. An old lady came to see her a few days ago and said her dead brother had taken a photo of them when they were in my family's house many years ago."

"That's crazy, it can't be, it's impossible. They can't be in the same place at once."

Ben, by this time was nearly speechless; he picked up one of them and held it up to the light. "It is, this is the original of the one she sent me, unless it's a complete fake!"

They both looked at one another as Alex unrolled the other one and peered at it more closely.

"It's certainly very old but the colours are still clear, and the canvas isn't damaged, just a bit frayed at the ends. How amazing!"

"You won't believe it but I'm telling you these pictures look exactly the same as the fax she sent me two days ago."

They looked at each other and then, Alex started laughing.

"It's you, isn't it? You're playing a trick on me."

"No, I swear I'm not, these are the very same pictures Johanna sent me. I wouldn't joke about something like that, I assure you."

Ben's face was ashen as he gazed at each one in turn.

"But where did they come from? I only pulled them off that shelf two hours ago."

"I don't know but when we get upstairs, I'll show you if you don't believe me."

"I do believe you, but it's too weird a coincidence, that's what I find hard to fathom. What I do remember when Roslyn and I first went to Cracow, we met this old man, Piotr, who told us that Russian officers were billeted in our old house in

Lwow after my grandfather and his mother were taken away to Siberia. I've probably told you that story before. He told us quite clearly that, apart from the valuables buried in the garden, one of the officers had some old paintings put up the walls. When they were eventually forced to leave them behind when the Allied troops took over, and they had no time to get rid of all their ill-gotten gains, so they were hidden somewhere in the grounds. I know it sounds a bit far-fetched, but they could be the same paintings. Maybe the officers found some way of opening the tomb and managed to hide the pictures behind that small coffin in the top shelf."

Ben had to agree and said that was the only way they could have ended up there. It was still an incredible co-incidence, but truth could sometimes be stranger than fiction! They were now wrapped carefully in an old coat he'd been wearing earlier to carry them upstairs. He put a sheet on his bed and put them carefully on the bedspread, his fingers trembling as he unrolled the first painting.

"That's it, it's the only explanation for them being there, exactly like the photocopy Johanna sent me. Do you believe me now?"

"I always believed you, but I'm only flabbergasted that both you and I got what we've been looking for all along. I've travelled all over Poland and now, we're here together in Lviv, only to find your long-lost paintings on my own great grandfather's property, hundreds of miles away from their original home in Vienna. What are the chances of that?"

Ben opened a drawer in his bedside table, took out the two faxes he'd received only two days before and passed them over to Alex who said.

"It's still amazing! What are the odds of finding them here? It's got to be millions to one?"

"All we have to do is take them back to London and get a valuation at Christies or Sotheby's before we can be sure the paintings are genuine."

"And what's with the 'us', Ben? They're yours alone. I don't think 'finders keepers' applies here. Remember, we've still got a lot of research to do before we can establish what everything is worth and then we have to make sure that we can legitimately lay claim to our newly acquired possessions."

"I'm sure you're right but, for tonight at least, let's shower, change and have a slap-up meal downstairs. I feel a magnum of champagne is what's needed."

"What a brilliant idea! See you in about half an hour in white tie and tails!"

The rest of the evening passed in a haze of pleasure after they'd remembered to put the two paintings carefully in the hotel vault for safe-keeping until they could arrange for their transfer to London by special courier service.

"If only our lovely Roslyn could have been here with us to share our happiness and success, she was the one person who could be relied on to give me her honest opinion and the courage to carry out my sometimes over-the top ideas. How I still miss her!"

"Me too. I think you always knew I was in love with her. From the first minute I met her, even though she only had eyes for you, I would have given my right arm to steal her away from you. And it's not the champagne talking either, you lucky sod."

"Yes, if only she was here right now, I think we might have had to fight a duel over her but instead, let's drink a toast to the sweetest woman in the world, to Roslyn!"

With that sobering thought, they decided it was time for bed and drank the last of the bottle before heading for the lift and a good night's sleep. They both felt they'd earned it but were still looking forward to another exciting day ahead.

When the Wilowski family valuables had finally been itemised and repacked for shipment to England, Alex had received the good news that it wasn't declared to be 'Treasure Trove' by the authorities in either the Ukraine or the U.K. It now meant it all became Alex's property legally and he could now ask Sotheby's to value the whole lot with all restoration work and cleaning of any damaged pieces of jewellery to be carried out in their workrooms.

Ben had also been busy having his two pictures insured, restored, expertly cleaned and suitably framed in readiness for their return journey to Vienna and he had left all the remaining details in Johanna's capable hands. He asked if Alex would like to go with him to Austria sometime to meet her again and to see his great grandfather's paintings which, hopefully, would one day be hanging in their true place, in the family home which had been returned to the Keller and Edelman heirs under the government's Jewish re-instatement policy. Ben had little interest in their actual monetary value until they were found to be early Rembrandts, then he was ecstatic to know that his long quest had not been in vain.

Their return home was greeted with great enthusiasm, first of all, Jason was delighted to have them both back. He'd managed very well in their absence but heaved a sigh of relief when he relinquished his role as first and second in command at the company headquarters. They insisted that he take a well-earned restful holiday after his stint of being in sole charge. Ben had gone to Vienna to take an extra week off to help Johanna sort out the finer points of importing his now precious works of art and displaying them in his apartment, which had, in some part, been purchased from his own inheritance.

Alex decided to keep things ticking over for a while and, at the same time, plan for the return of the heirlooms which would have to be kept in very secure premises until all the appraisals had been carried out. Then, he would have to think about buying a suitable house that could not only be a comfortable home but also a place to display his treasures to advantage. So, he began delving into the idea of moving out of town and, since he had only himself to please now, considered the idea of a place in the country. He used one of the top London agencies to explore all the possibilities and found it a pleasure to view a selection of desirable houses in the most idyllic settings. He discussed his plans with James and his grandmother who thought it an excellent idea as long as he'd spend long holidays with them.

The only thing missing from his life was, as ever, Roslyn, but that would never change. His great comfort was to know all his other dreams had come true and he felt, as last, he was finally a crucial part of his illustrious Polish family and that he'd been able to give them their well-earned place in such a long and famous aristocratic ancestry. That was the most he could have hoped for all his family's sake and no amount of treasure could ever replace that.

CHAPTER THIRTY-THREE

Alex picked up his phone, thinking it might be another agent wanting him to look at a new property.

"Hi, Alex, you might not remember me, but my name's Aidan Spencer and I once did some work for your father-in-law, James Chapell. This is only a social call to see how you're getting along, I was so sorry to hear about Roslyn, she was such a lovely girl."

Alex was taken aback to hear Roslyn being mentioned but his name still didn't ring a bell.

"I'm sorry, I'm afraid I don't recall your name."

"Of course, you probably don't remember me because most of my dealings were done through Roslyn several years ago in Marbella when you'd been kidnapped. The poor girl was beside herself with worry and asked for my help and I've also spoken in the past with Ben Edelman who worked for James in London."

"Of course, yes. I remember now but I don't think we ever met."

"Yes, we did briefly, once when you were in hospital, I helped James sort out a few matters with the police, then, when everything was okayed, and everyone was satisfied that you hadn't suffered any serious ill effects after your terrible experience, I flew back to London."

"It's all coming back to me now, sorry I sounded so vague but it's a time I'd rather forget but I do know Roslyn spoke very highly of you and valued your assistance."

"I was glad I could help her in some small way, she was a lady of the first order. We also employed one of our team, Gill Armstrong, to help her when she needed moral support."

"Yes, I remember her well, she came to our wedding."

"Well, that's the main reason I'm phoning you. Gill still works for my company and has asked me if she could contact you sometime, she had a very good rapport with Roslyn and wanted to discuss something personal with you. She wanted to go through the correct channels and didn't feel it was appropriate to speak to you directly."

"Of course, that would be fine. You have my number, so she can call me anytime, I'd be delighted to talk to her. I know Roslyn liked her a lot, I think she kept in touch with her from time to time."

"I'm pleased to have spoken to you again, Alex, and if you need anything in the future, don't hesitate to call me."

A few days later, the phone rang in his office, it was Gill.

"Is this a good time? I don't want to disturb you, but Aidan said it would be all right if I called you."

"Oh, yes, Gill, Aidan did mention you'd like to speak to me. Can I help you with anything?"

"Well, I don't want to dwell on the past too much but after Roslyn and I had spent that terrible time together when you were kidnapped, she did talk about you a lot and we formed a strong bond between us. I felt I'd known her all my life and was so happy to go to your wedding, it was such a wonderful time and then we sort of went our separate ways. I can't tell you how shocked I was to hear that she'd died, I did go to the funeral but then I thought it was best to leave you all alone to grieve in private."

Alex listened and warmed to her as she expressed her inner thoughts so openly and it was obvious there was something more she wanted to say.

"I'm very grateful for your concern, Gill, I know she valued your help and friendship when she was at her lowest ebb, so if there's anything you want to say, I'm happy to talk about Roslyn. She was the love of my life and losing her has been the hardest thing I've ever had to bear. I often talk to her sometimes as if she's still here."

"It's so kind of you to speak to me and I realise how much you must miss her, so I won't take up a lot more of your time, but I do have a favour to ask you."

She seemed to hesitate for a moment as if trying to find the right words.

"The thing is I received a letter from her a short time before she died, and I wanted to tell you because it was so personal but thought I'd wait for the best time to talk to you."

"All right, and anything you say to me is confidential, so don't worry about that."

Gill then began to read the letter, it was quite short and very heartfelt. It read simply,

'Dearest Gill,

You may think this is odd, but I can't think of anyone but you that I can tell this to. I have been having very strange dreams for a while now, since I knew I was going to have a baby. I keep having these premonitions that I am going to die, and I wake up crying every night. I know it must seem very stupid of me, I can't tell Alex, he will think it's just because I'm pregnant, but it's not. So, it may be a passing phase, and I don't want to worry him but, if anything should happen to me; please give him this enclosed letter and tell him how much I loved him. If everything goes according to plan, just tear this letter up and forget it.

Your good friend,
Roslyn.'

Alex was too stunned to speak at first. The news was so upsetting, his heart sank, and he felt the tears welling up in his eyes. Gill waited until he spoke again.

"Thank you so much for having the courage to do this, it can't have been easy to keep her secret."

"Well, I didn't know exactly what to do but I had to wait until I felt you could bear to hear about this letter. I have it here, just as she left it. I haven't spoken to anyone else and hope I've done the right thing."

"Of course, you have. It was such a shock I couldn't take it in at first but I'm so glad you did what she asked. How can I get the letter? I don't want it to go in the post in case it gets lost."

"I thought of that too. I could bring it to you or to your office if that's all right with you."

"What about if we meet somewhere in town? We can talk and then maybe, have lunch or something, if that suits you, Gill."

"If you're sure that's okay for you, I could meet you outside Marble Arch tube station on Oxford Street and we could have a coffee. I'm pretty much my own boss so we can meet each other whenever it's convenient for you."

"Tomorrow, twelve thirty!" His voice was very decisive. "Then we can pop into the Cumberland for a drink, it will be nice to see you again after such a long time. I hope you'll still recognise me."

"I'm sure I will, so until tomorrow then. Thank you for your understanding, I just hoped you wouldn't be too upset in the circumstances."

He put down the phone, he could hardly believe that Roslyn had been in such turmoil. She'd never mentioned how she felt deep down and only seemed happy that they were going to have the baby so soon. He just wished he'd known how she felt, then maybe he could have done something to reassure her.

After a very restless night, he told Jason he'd some business to attend to and would be out of the office until late afternoon. He left Ben a quick email and promised to be in touch later. He decided to take the tube to Marble Arch, a car was a waste of time in London. When he got off the train, he walked up the stairs and, at the entrance, looked around. He remembered Gill being a nice-looking woman with dark auburn hair, so he thought he'd certainly notice her. She must have been waiting for him too because he felt a tap on his arm as she smiled up at him, she was slimmer and shorter than remembered. He bent down to give her a peck on her cheek and took hold of her hand.

"Let's get out of this crowd and then we can pop into the Cumberland bar."

She too had forgotten how tall he was but had always liked the look of him, he had an air of authority about him and was obviously in charge of this present situation. He'd probably spent a sleepless night thinking about the letter and wanted to get it over and done with before reading it himself. As he gently took her arm, he walked into the lobby and they both made their way to the bar which was already quite crowded with lunchtime drinkers,

"It's so nice to see you again, Gill. You were very brave meeting me in the circumstances, I suppose you might not have known my reaction to hearing about the letter Roslyn sent."

"Yes, I did keep wondering how you would take the news, it must have been a shock to you."

"What would like to drink, a coffee or something a bit stronger?"

"I would love a Martini Bianco with soda water, if I may/"

"Well, I think I'll have a Campari and soda too."

Alex nodded to the barman and then took the drinks to a quieter corner with two comfortable seats.

"Is this all right for you?"

"Absolutely fine!"

She sat down and, without any preamble, took the letter out of her handbag and handed it to him with a subdued look, still hoping she'd done the right thing. He put the drink in front of her and took the precious letter, also hoping he wouldn't break down when he opened it. His hand shook slightly but he managed to look at Roslyn's handwriting and tried to think of how she felt as she wrote it. It must have been a struggle for her to confide her inner emotions when she was obviously so worried about the baby. He sat down and tore the envelope open and started to read the contents. His eyes did fill with tears, he wiped them away with his handkerchief and re-read the letter before putting it back in his pocket. Gill felt at a loss about what to say next so put her hand on his while she waited for his response.

"Thank you so much for bringing her letter to me. I can't tell you how moved I am by your thoughtfulness and glad you waited to tell me the contents. I don't think I could have borne to read it too soon after she died, I would have been a wreck There were so many things I wish I could have said to comfort her."

"I realise how much you adored each other but I wasn't sure how you would react to a mere stranger taking it upon herself to write to you. I only did it because I promised I would give you her last wishes, in case something unforeseen happened."

"I'm so glad you did and it's lovely to see you again after such a long time."

They chatted for a while and then said good-bye, promising to keep in touch, but knew she probably wouldn't see him again; a pity really, he seemed such a lonely guy.

CHAPTER THIRTY-FOUR

When the three letters arrived within minutes of each other, Alice was amazed. She walked over to James's villa and found him sitting on the terrace in the morning sun reading his paper, his usual morning ritual.

"Morning, James! Did you get the letters?"

"No, what letters?"

He stared at her, surprised at her question and that she had interrupted his routine. She was usually so correct and never intruded without giving him a quick call on the phone before popping in, so it must be something important.

"Not just one but three at practically the same time and by the same post. I haven't opened them, I thought I'd tell you first."

The new maid brought her a pot of tea after he rang the bell which again was a first for her, Maria usually gave them coffee on the patio at about eleven thirty, not tea at ten.

"Well, aren't you going to open them?

"Yes, of course I am but it's strange, don't you think?"

"I would if I knew what it's all about. Open at least one!"

Alice did as she was told, gazing at the first one when she recognised the hand writing, it was from Alex and he was inviting her to his engagement party. She gasped and passed it over to James without another word.

"Did you know about this?"

"No, it's as much a shock to me as it is to you."

They both stared at each other, completely dumb-founded. Alex, back in London, had taken the bull by the horns after his last visit to see his grandmother and James in Marbella. That was the first time he'd introduced another woman to them since Roslyn died nearly three years ago and he knew they'd both been slightly taken aback when his new lady turned out to be Gill Armstrong, an old friend of his late wife. It was not that they expected him to live without a girlfriend forever, but it was so soon, and they were rather astounded to know he had chosen Gill. She was a very nice person but completely different from Roslyn in every way, in looks and in character, they were like chalk and cheese.

"Well, I can't say I'm over the moon about his choice, I just hope he wasn't on the rebound and found Gill waiting in the wings!"

"I did notice that she hung on every word he said."

Alice smiled ruefully and tried to find some adequate words to express her innermost thoughts without sounding too much like a possessive grandmother.

"I suppose he's old enough to know what he's doing but I do wish he'd have waited a bit longer before taking such a big step. Roslyn will be a very hard act to follow."

James's words exactly, everyone could see how much in love he had been with Roslyn, he adored her, and even now, it seemed impossible that he was contemplating marriage again after such a relatively short time.

"Please open the next letter, Alice. I don't know if I can stand any more surprises this early in the day."

She slit open the envelope and found a beautifully embossed card inside. It read

'Frau Hilde Bauer is pleased to invite Mrs. Alice Wilshaw to the wedding of her daughter, Johanna, to Herr Benjamin Jakob Edelman. The ceremony will be held at the Stadttempel Jewish Neighbourhood Synagogue: Seitenstettengasse 4, on Tuesday, September 27th at 4 p.m. This will be followed by a reception at the Grand Hotel Wien'.

In addition, there was a short note written by Ben to say how happy they would be to see her and James if they were able to make the journey to Vienna.'

"Isn't that charming? What a thoughtful gesture of Ben to invite us to his wedding!"

James agreed, even though he thought to himself he'd heard enough marriage news for one day.

"Very thoughtful indeed! Do you think we should go? I'm very fond of Ben, as you know, but do you think the flight would be comfortable enough for you?"

"I'd love to be there. I'm sure Alex and Gill will have been invited too so I think I could manage. We will be looked after very well, and it is only a short flight. Do you know that I've never been to Vienna? I'd love to see some of the sights there, as well as going to the wedding."

"That's decided then, we'll fly to London first and ask Alex to get us tickets for the rest of the journey. I'm pretty sure he'd like that, it will give us another chance to get to know Gill better."

"What a wonderful idea! That settles it, we'll reply as soon as we've spoken to both of the boys and ask Alex's advice about us flying together and spending sometime sightseeing after the reception."

"Yes, that's a perfect reason to see each other after Ben's big day and I'm sure you'll be able to suss out everything you want to find out about your grandson's future wife."

"You read my very thoughts. It's a good way of not appearing too nosy but finding out much more about Gill at the same time. You're a wily old fox, James. Now for that last letter. I wonder who this is from? I can't make out the country it's from, it's covered in so many official black postmarks."

"For goodness sake, Alice, get a move on, I'm dying to know who it's from, but I need a cup of coffee before you read it."

Maria appeared as if by magic when the word coffee was mentioned. Alice chuckled to herself knowing that the maid was always there at regular intervals throughout the morning to make sure 'el senor' got everything he needed. She was a treasure and devoted to James; in fact, they were both lucky to have her and her sister working for them. Ten minutes later, after they'd each eaten a soft homemade almond biscuit and finished the coffee, James was nearly champing at the bit for her to open that last message.

"Please, open it, Alice, I can't stand the suspense anymore." He laughed as she slowly tore the envelope open but then it was her turn to stop and stare at the contents.

"I think this must have been meant for you. I told you I couldn't read the postmark."

James took the letter from her hand, it certainly looked like his son's handwriting, so he began reading the folded sheet of paper in front of him.

'Dear Dad,

So sorry I haven't been in touch for ages, but my life has been very hectic here, first settling into our exciting new life in Rio, then looking for place to call our own.

Krystyna and I had been living together for quite a while, so we finally decided to buy a house and put some roots down at last. We both love it here and, thanks to my mother's generous inheritance to me, we managed to find the house of our dreams near the beach.

I'm going to keep this letter short except to say we got married nine months ago. So, we both want to ask for your belated blessing and want you to know how happy we are.

Probably, the best news of all is that we are now adopting a little girl, who was born just six months ago, and we have named her 'Celia Roslyn' after both my mother and my beautiful sister. I hope you will be able to think of her as your

granddaughter, Dad, and will forgive me for all the hurt I've caused you in the past
You are often in my thoughts,
Your loving son,
Markus.'

James was as white as a sheet as he passed it over to Alice for her to read.

"He always did run true to form so I can't say this news comes as a shock and all I wish is they'll be very happy. It just seems ironic that the grandchild that I always wanted is not going to be Roslyn's, she's going to be a complete stranger to me."

Alice could understand his mixed feelings but tried to put a positive slant on it for his sake.

"I know Markus was a big disappointment to you, but I do think he loves you and is trying to heal those old wounds by telling you he's made a whole new life for himself. For years, he was a little boy lost but now he's trying to make it up to you."

"Yes, I know you're right, Alice. I still find it hard to forget the past, but I will try. Thank you once again for your wise words. What would I do without you?"

Alice smiled and gently touched James's hand, hoping she too could learn to accept Gill and love her as much as she'd loved Roslyn.

When the engagement replies had been answered, Alice phoned Alex to say they were delighted with the news and then asked if they would all be flying together to Ben's wedding.

"I do hope so, Grandma, I'm so glad you are happy with our news and it will be great for you to get to know Gill before and after Ben and Johanna's wedding. We are dying to see both you and James again. How did he take our news? I was a bit worried that he would think it was all a bit too soon."

Alice tried her best to sound convincing that all was well when she knew in her heart of hearts James had been upset to think Alex had decided to get married again. To keep things more upbeat, she told him about Markus and Krystyna's marriage in South America and that they had adopted a baby girl into the bargain.

Their reunion in London after the flight from Spain was very jovial and Gill proved to be a delight, but poor James couldn't help thinking she could never take the place of his lovely Roslyn. On the second evening, after dinner, Alex presented Alice with a beautiful box which he gave to her with his love. When she opened it her eyes lit up, it was a exquisite gold bracelet that he explained had been his great grandmother's and was with the other treasures hidden in the garden in Lwow.

"I hope you like it, I think it had belonged to my Great-grandmother, Karolina. I know both she and my grandfather would have wanted you to have a family memento from the Wilowskis."

"It's a wonderful present and so thoughtful of you! I love it. Thank you so much."

The next day, after talking to Ben about their travel arrangements, they all flew into the Vienna's international airport and then went by taxi to the Imperial Hotel for their stay in Austria. A pre-wedding dinner had been arranged for them and presents given to the new couple the next evening, everyone seemed to relax in the convivial surroundings of the fine restaurant and they all enjoyed meeting the bride's mother before their big day.

Everyone agreed it had been a wonderful idea to have this get-together and get to know each other a little beforehand. Frau Bauer spoke English well and so they all conversed easily and retired later to one of the other lounges that displayed a vast array of after-dinner drinks, impeccably served, when James stood up and tapped his brandy glass.

"I would like to thank our hostess for her hospitality and would ask you all to drink a toast to the future bride and groom and also to our newly engaged couple Gill and Alex!"

Alice was proud of him, including everyone in the toast as she thought of her dear Lukasz.

The wedding itself was a lovely affair and the party afterwards went on until the early hours.

It was only a year after that wedding in Vienna and the letter from Rio, when a third invitation arrived, Alex and Gill had decided to get married, much to the great joy of Alice. She had grown very attached to her new granddaughter-in-law, and now liked her nearly as much as she'd loved Roslyn.

Ben, with his wife by his side, was happy to come over to London for Alex's wedding but had no desire to live there again, he had grown to love and appreciate his native city more with each day that passed, Vienna had become his true home. The company's expansion into the East European market meant that opening another branch in Vienna was a sensible option with Ben at the helm. A new robotics department, now in the capable hands of Alex and Jason, was established and managed equally by both men to encompass their growing interest in the field of artificial intelligence. So, it seemed that the business side of 'Cosmocompute' was changing and moving away from its tele-communications roots towards the age of automation.

James was delighted with their new proposals but felt the time was now right to put his own house in order; he no longer wanted to attend dull board meetings in London and listen to enthusiastic younger men discussing subjects that seemed to him like something out of science fiction. He was happy with his quiet life in Marbella, and still enjoyed rounds of golf with his pals, who spoke the same language as he did. His companionship with Alice and their mutual living arrangements suited them both well. A life in the sun with pleasant company was all he wanted so he finally retired, passing the reins of power over to Ben and Alex.

He looked forward to seeing the many photos that Markus sent him regularly of his sweet little daughter, Celia, who had a cheeky smile that warmed James's heart and when they saw videos of the family with a contented-looking Krystyna nursing her, both he and Alice remarked that it was nice to see such a happy family even if they were so far away.

Their world seemed to have come full circle for everyone at last. For both James and Alice, from the days of his having his own two children and then a lovely grandchild who lived in a foreign country with his only son and his wife. Strange that one never knew what life held in store! It had been filled with such early promise and then with much heart-ache on the way but it was wonderful to know there could be so many happy endings amidst all the twists and turns of life's rich pattern.

CHAPTER THIRTY-FIVE

As for the "Wilowski" collection, as it was now known in major historical circles, Alex had agreed with several reputable museums to keep the most celebrated pieces, either on display or securely stored away. Then, he let a well-known auction house deal with the rest of the antique silver candelabra, cutlery and other personal effects which were sold off separately, after the staggering valuations he'd negotiated with several fine art experts. In the end, he decided that the most expensive remnants of jewellery should be kept in a bank vault for safe-keeping or maybe, for future family use.

After he and Gill married, they carried on living a happy life in a country retreat south of Hazelmere where they kept a few horses in honour of his Polish great grandfather and Gill threw herself into raising pedigree rare breeds of goats and Jacob sheep. He was usually in town for most part of the week but enjoyed being a country gentleman at the weekends.

Still, in his darkest moments, Alex remembered often the nightmare of his imprisonment at the hands of Yuri Yurchenko and found it hard to believe that they could have been distant cousins in the old Hapsburg days. He tried not to dwell on the nightmare of his kidnapping too much but could never forget the treatment that Bohdan had meted out to him during those grim beatings. Being held hostage by him and Yuri, with all the ensuing heartache for both Roslyn and himself, had left an indelible impression on his life. He would always remember the fear he experienced, bound and gagged for days, not knowing how it would all end. Then he thought how insignificant his own suffering had been compared with that of his long dead Polish relatives; starved, beaten and cruelly massacred for merely being members of the aristocracy. After his great grandmother had tried to hide the family's treasure in the grounds of their country home, little did she know what grief and sorrow was to follow when she and her only son were deported to Siberia, never knowing what had happened to her husband who had been dragged away to imprisonment or worse in the middle of the night.

Alex, who thought his life was over when his beloved Roslyn and their baby son had died and felt that he could never suffer such heartbreak ever again, now realised that the treasure he had once searched and yearned for so many years ago in Poland, had cost not only him but his long-lost family much more pain than his new-found wealth would ever be worth. To Alex, it would always be a stark reminder that, for all his worldly possessions, it had become, in the end, his own poisoned legacy.

EPILOGUE

This is a work of part fact and part fiction. The personal names have been changed and a further storyline added but it is based on the true story of a real Polish family, who endured that terrible journey to Siberia and the hardships that followed until the war ended. Only one member of that aristocratic family survived, and he joined the Free Polish Air Force, eventually moving to South Africa, the country that had given him warmth and hope after all the traumas he'd suffered. The treasure, as far as I know, still lies buried in a country estate, where his mother had ordered it hidden for safe-keeping, waiting to be unearthed by some later member of that old aristocratic family whose lives were shattered through no fault of their own.

L - #0124 - 100619 - C0 - 210/148/13 - PB - DID2537832